Connelly's Flame

ALIYAH BURKE

Connelly's Flame

Aliyah Burke

Connelly's Flame

Editor and Formatter: Savannah Frierson

Cover Artist: MMJ Designs

ISBN: 978-0-557-05876-1

To the families of those serving their country.

We haven't forgotten your sacrifice.

Acknowledgments

Any mistakes in this are mine and not to be blamed on the ones who do this for a living. Thanks to Jack for helping me with the vehicles— I know, I know…I owe you.

To my editor and my cover artist. Y'all are the best!

Thank you!

Prologue

So this is what it feels like to be at the end of your life.

The car careened out of control, spilling hot coffee all over the dark-haired man behind the wheel, burning his leg. The burn soon faded from memory as the vehicle crashed through the guardrail along the isolated highway to flip down the snow-covered embankment. The relatively short life of its driver flashed before steel-gray eyes.

Ross Murdock Connelly wished he could see the love of his life one more time. He knew he had been driving too fast along the slick roads, but his desire to see her, to hold her in his arms one more time, had overcome his normal sense. So he had taken this supposed short-cut, an idea that seemed pointless as he grew dizzy from the revolutions the car made.

Tossed from the vehicle, Ross struggled to maintain conscious-nesses as he lay in the snow. Moments later, he felt rather than saw the incinerating blast that engulfed the totaled vehicle. The swirling winds covered the sound of the explosion as the metal ripped apart and flew into the night sky.

"Charmane," his injured voice muttered as his eyes closed again, submitting to the pain-free world of oblivion where a beautiful face with sparkling doe eyes beckoned him.

*O**ne***

"Where the hell is that smoke coming from?" the scratchy voice asked the interior of the vehicle. "I'm the only one who lives up this way. For that matter, who the hell is traveling on this road this time of the year?"

The old Land Rover was moving about five miles an hour. Even at night, the smoke was obvious, billowing across the beams the headlights made as they cut through the snow and wind. As the dented vehicle passed the broken guardrail, the driver knew.

"Damn it," she swore and stopped as carefully as she could, the vehicle still sliding from side to side on the snow-covered ice. Setting the brake, she turned the heat to high and began to shove her body into the thick coat and other winter accessories that had been eagerly discarded the second her body had been warm enough in the car.

Fighting the wind and snow, whose chill cut right through the thick layers of clothing she wore, Dezarae Phoenix Kerry began to yell into the night. "Hello? Hello! Is anyone down here?"

Struggling to slip only a minimal amount, she gazed through slitted eyes and approached the wreckage. "Jesus, Mary, and Joseph." Gathering the thick coat tighter against her body, she realized if there had been people in the car, they were dead now. Still, she looked around.

By some stroke of luck, Dezarae found her eyes drawn to what looked like a human lying face first in the snow, illuminated by the burning glow of the car. Eyes watering from the stinging force of snow pellets, she struggled to get to him.

"Are you okay?" she screamed, only to have her words whipped away into the night. No response. Kneeling beside the body, she touched the shoulder and asked again. Nothing.

The person lying there was a large man wearing only a long-sleeved shirt and pants, no jacket or anything. "How the hell am I going to get you up the hill?" she muttered as she cleared away the snow from his face so he could breathe. Then she checked for a pulse; he had one.

A groan barely reached her ears, but she took it as a good sign. "Hey! Hey, Mister. You okay?" Dezarae noticed his body shivering and, without a second thought, took off her heavy wool coat and put it over his body.

"Mister. Come on, wake up!" she yelled down by his ear. Even through the layers of clothes she wore, she immediately felt winter's bite down to her bones. "Can you move?" Dezarae knew the dangers of disturbing an accident victim, but he would die out here if he didn't move. Her teeth began to chatter.

"I'm here," a gravelly voice said.

Thank the good Lord. "Can you move? Do you think you can help me get you up? Or does it feel like you have a neck injury?"

"I can move," he rasped.

"Okay, slowly now. I will help you."

Inch by tortuous inch, the man moved. Dezarae felt her eyes grow wide as she looked at his body. *Dear Lord, he is fine and big.* As he managed to get to his hands and knees, she helped him slip the coat on. It barely seemed to fit him while it engulfed her.

Dropping into the snow, Dezarae slipped an arm under his shoulder to help support him. *He smells like leather and spices.* Shaking her head, she waited for him to drop more of his weight on her. *Come on, man, I'm freezing here.* "I can help you. Let's go."

Almost reluctantly it seemed, he let her have some more of his weight. As he got unsteadily to his feet, they began the climb up the hill. The farther up they got, the more she supported his weight.

"Good thing I am not a weakling here, man," she mumbled under her breath. "You weigh a lot more than it looks like you would."

Dezarae had never been so happy to see her car. Opening the door, she helped him into the back and just kind of pushed him in. He toppled over to the side and, after making sure his feet were in, she shut the door to move to the other side and drag him across the seat so he was almost stretched out. Then it was back to the tailgate to grab another blanket to cover him.

Climbing into the driver's seat, she allowed the warmth to seep into her body. Taking a drink of her now-lukewarm coffee she pulled off her gloves, wiped her eyes, and began to drive home. She glanced back frequently at the man in her backseat. He had apparently drifted back into unconsciousness.

Pulling into her garage, she turned off her vehicle and got out. "Good work today, Old Man," she said as she patted the green door affectionately. Dezarae moved to the back and opened the door.

The man lying there had a cut on his head, his dark hair cut short. A face that was beginning to show the signs of a shadow seemed sad. Thick black lashes rested against his cheeks.

Cocking her head to the side, Dezarae smiled as she looked at him. He was very handsome...and in danger of getting pneumonia if she didn't get to work. "I don't know who you are, Mister, but you have to wake up again."

"I'm awake," that deep voice rasped although the eyes never opened.

"Sit up and we will get you inside where it is warm. Come on," she insisted.

Like before, he moved slowly. But this time, there was no wind, snow, or hill to fight. So it didn't take long before she was helping him into her bed dressed in only his boxers. *Great, I find a man and he has a damn rebel flag tat on his chest as a backdrop for an anchor. Damn, he is fine, even with that tat; I hope he doesn't get frostbite.*

She gazed over his limbs and didn't see any signs of it, but time would tell. It was important now to get him warm. Dezarae covered him in her blankets and thick comforter before she left to change into dry clothes herself and make him something warm to drink.

Finally warm, dry, and comfortable, Dezarae slipped back into her bedroom to check on her "guest." He had drunk the cup of broth she had made for him but she wanted to wake him up every now and then. His head injury was cleaned and bandaged and, as she looked at him, she saw he was sleeping comfortably.

Gathering up his wet clothes, she searched for any kind of identification and couldn't find a single thing. No wallet, nothing.

"Well," she whispered as she took his clothes out of the room and put them in the washer. "I sure hope you aren't a serial killer." After the load was set, she returned to her room.

"Wake up," she said softly. Nothing. Fearing the worst, Dezarae reached down to pat him on the cheek. "Hey," she spoke in a normal tone. "Wake up."

The second her hand landed on his stubbled face, her wrist was caught in an ironclad grasp. Panicked, she flashed her eyes to his and found herself looking into the steeliest gunmetal eyes she had ever seen. They were alert and they scared her.

Ross had an instinctive reaction when her hand touched his face. Without conscious thought, he grabbed her wrist in his hand. She gave a frightened gasp as her eyes moved up to meet his.

Chocolate. Sinfully dark chocolates were what her eyes reminded him of.

She was pretty, if he wanted to think about it. A thick green sweatshirt and a pair of black sweatpants concealed most of her figure from him, but he would guess she was very curvaceous. A large pair of fuzzy red slippers was on her feet, as if she had killed Elmo or Animal to make them. Her skin was brown, nut-brown, and he would put her height at about five-five. Her hair was thick and curly, hanging down past her shoulders, framing her face gently. Her lips were full and lush.

But it was her eyes that got him. They were dark and stared directly at him with concern and a little bit of fear.

He wished he knew who she was.

A pink tongue snuck out and licked full dusky lips. "Can you let me go please? I am not going to hurt you. I just had to wake you up." Dezarae could feel the intense pounding of her heart. "Please, you're hurting me."

Those eyes never left hers as he dropped her wrist as if it burned him. He remained silent as she stood straight and rubbed her sore wrist. "Sorry I frightened you but I was worried that you had fallen unconscious again," she muttered, still absently rubbing the area.

Those smoky eyes moved down her body slowly and back up again, making Dezarae feel as if she stood before him totally naked. When that intense gaze reached her eyes again, she felt flushed.

Damn it. No man has made me feel like this before. At least not a man I don't know and have never met. Swallowing to give herself extra time to regain her composure, Dezarae tried to affect an indifferent expression.

"Can you stay awake until I get you some more broth to drink?" she asked, glad he didn't know her well enough to know just how affected her voice sounded.

Still, all he did was stare at her. *Jesus that is one unnerving stare.* "I will take that as a 'Yes.' I'll be right back." Dezarae fled to the solitude of her kitchen and made him another cup of broth. By the time it was ready, her heartbeat had returned to normal.

This time she knocked on the doorframe before she walked in, holding the cup as if it would keep her safe from him and his stare. With determined steps, she moved to the bedside and held it out to him even as his eyes held hers.

"Here, drink this." His gazed flicked from the cup to her face. *My God, he is suspicious.* "What, you think it's poisoned?"

His eyes narrowed as they moved from her face down her chest and back again. They stared into her soul and assessed her. Unnerved her.

"Look." She put the cup up to her lips and took a drink of the warm liquid. "It is fine; now, come on, you need to get some nourishment in you." Dezarae offered him the cup again.

One strong, tanned hand reached up and took the cup from hers. A quivering began in her belly as his fingers grazed against hers. Bringing the cup to his mouth at the very last second, he turned it and drank from the exact spot where she had put her lips. Those gray eyes never left hers as he drained the cup.

What would it be like to have his lips on mine? Guess he doesn't have anything against me yet. Knees trembling from the erotic picture his lips touching the same place as hers had, she took the cup back and swallowed. Now was as good a time as any. "Who are you?"

He blinked and looked almost hesitant. Dark, masculine brows furrowed in thought only to scrunch together tighter before he looked up at her and said in a confused voice, "I don't know."

$\mathcal{T}_{wo}$

Her dark eyes grew big. "What do you mean you don't know?"

A void had settled over him as he saw the information he needed and craved from afar in his mind's eye, but it was just out of reach. "I mean, I don't know who I am. I don't know anything. I don't know who you are or where I am." He gripped the blanket between lean fingers.

"Easy, easy, now. We were never properly introduced so you shouldn't know who I am. Okay. Calm down, my name is Dezarae. Just take it easy." One dark hand reached out to touch him in a comforting gesture, but at the last second she decided not to and withdrew it to rest at her side.

He began to breathe a bit easier. His mind raced as he tried to figure out what was going on. If he could just remember one thing…anything… "So you didn't ask me to test me, did you?" The dark head looked around her definitely feminine room and he asked, "You don't know who I am either, do you?"

"No. I don't." Clearly a bit uncomfortable, she moved back away from the bed, cup in hand. "You should get some rest. It's not like you can go anywhere, anyway." For a brief second, a dangerous glint appeared in his eyes before it was gone, masked under a face of indifference. "Your clothes are still being washed; that's why I said what I said." For the second time in a matter of an hour, she bolted from her own bedroom.

In the kitchen, Dezarae held her hand over her chest and tried to slow the out-of-control beating of her heart. Her gaze took in the rattling of the windows as the storm only increased in intensity. The phones were down; she had already tried to call the sheriff, but she would go in the morning and see if anyone knew her mysterious guest. Assuming the weather would cooperate, that was.

Eyes open or closed, it didn't matter. All she could see was his chiseled body. He wasn't a small man, but he wasn't huge, either. He was full of defined muscles from his head down. Undressing him had been fun; if only he hadn't been near death, she might have enjoyed it even more. Even so, she had appreciated what he offered.

Back in the floral bedroom, the dark-haired, gray-eyed man fought his growing panic. He had no clothes save for the boxers he was wearing, no idea of where he was, how he got there, or what he was doing in this woman's bed. Topping it off, he had no freaking idea who he was.

The more he tried to come up with his God-given name, the worse his head felt. Looking down his near-naked body, he frowned as he located a tattoo over one pectoral. It was of an anchor and a chain and the backdrop was a rebel flag. "Who am I?"

Well, she had been right about one thing. He needed some more sleep and so he snuggled down deeper into the plush mattress on the full-size bed and allowed the gentle smell of some flower he couldn't quite identify to cocoon around him as succumbed to slumber.

He was sound asleep when Dezarae came back into the room.

She smiled as she took in the stranger in her bed. He had curled up against her stuffed tow truck. His face was finally at peace. Moving silently, she left the room and went to make herself some dinner. While it was cooking, she took his clothes from the dryer, folded them, and placed them beside the bed where he still slept. Again, Dezarae reached out her hand like she was going to stroke his face only to again withdraw it. There was something about this man that called to her, but she wasn't sure what. It could have been the real fear she had seen when he couldn't remember his own name, but she didn't know.

After one more glance at his body, she slipped back out of the room with an extra blanket for her own use that night. As she was leaving the room, she didn't notice the slate gaze that settled upon her retreating back, watching the sway of her hips with considerable less mistrust in them.

Glancing at her watch, she knew how long she had before dinner and so, sliding on her coveralls, Dezarae went to the garage and began to work on her vehicle. She was restoring a classic—a 1967 Shelby Mustang GT500, obsidian black.

Her hands were gentle as they moved over the shell of the car. Restoring cars was her passion. She was good at it, as the shop next to her house would suggest, but it was this car that she worked on in her free time, little by little, savoring the experience, for it relaxed her immensely.

So, with a grin, she lifted out the dismantled engine and began to clean parts again, laying them out to dry after she was done. James Blunt played through her garage as she worked. When her watch beeped she stood up, degreased her hands, and unzipped the coveralls, draping them across one worktable, and tuned off the radio before going back into the warm house.

Her home was small with two bedrooms and one bath. It worked for her but with the extra guest she was going to be sleeping on the couch. It was fine, she had done it before.

Pulling the casserole out of the oven, she placed it on the trivet on the countertop. The smell filled her kitchen as she walked to the cupboards and got down some dishes. As she turned around, she froze. Leaning in her doorway stood the man she had picked up alongside the road.

He stood there like he owned the place. He'd dressed only in his jeans that she had left folded beside the bed, the defined abs that disappeared below the waistband of those blue jeans visible to her gaze. Her eyes traveled over the anchor tattoo on his left pec. Suddenly the rebel flag didn't give her shivers; well, it did, but not like it usually would.

He oozed sex as he leaned there watching her with those intense gray eyes that roamed over her body again as if he owned her and the property rights to her. Up and down, slowly, his gaze moved. Burning her, branding her. It was as if he were learning her most private thoughts just from a look.

"I'm sorry I scared you earlier," he said in a deep voice.

"How are you feeling?" Dezarae asked him, ignoring the trembles his voice had created in her body.

"Good." He took a step towards her but stopped as she shrank back. A sad expression filled his handsome face. "I won't hurt you."

It was hard for him to explain how her recoil from him felt. It hurt, but it was more than that. This feeling of wanting to make her feel safe and protected felt familiar to him. But she'd said they didn't know each other.

Still, the fact apprehension had flooded her beautiful sepia face at his forward motion crushed him. He didn't want that expression anywhere near her. So he stayed in the doorway. But his eyes never left her; he willed her to believe him.

How could she when he didn't even know who or what he was? A groan of frustration left him as he realized this situation was bordering on hopeless.

Hearing the groan, Dezarae took a step towards him, immediately concerned for his wellbeing. "Are you okay?" She walked up to him and realized just how much bigger than her he was. He stood about six feet, four inches, and all of it was well muscled.

The man clenched his jaw and nodded abruptly. "Fine. I'm fine."

"Do you feel well enough to eat something?" she asked as she retreated back to the cupboard and took down another set of dishes.

"I think so."

"Well, it isn't fancy but it will stick to your ribs. I hope you don't mind chicken casserole."

"Not at all."

She felt him staring at her, as if hoping she would turn and meet his gaze, but she steadfastly avoided his eyes. After she set the table, she turned and began to prepare a salad as the house shook from the force of the winds.

"Grab a seat," she murmured, opening the fridge to take out the pitcher of cold water she had in there. Turning towards the table, Dezarae sent the man sitting there a nervous smile, wishing he wouldn't gaze at her so.

She dished up the food silently and put the plate in front of him. She then turned her attention to her food, not the bronzed torso muscles he had. Concentrating on keeping her gaze firmly on the plate in front of her, she began to eat. *Stay firm and concentrate on food. Girl, you know he is firm.*

"Where are we?" he asked her as they were finishing up dinner.

"The middle of nowhere. You are about twenty miles from a town called Shadyville. In Montana."

Shadyville. Why did that name seem familiar to him? *Why can't I remember anything?* "Damn it," he swore as his fist pounded on the tabletop.

Unable to help it, Dezarae jumped and squealed, an act that brought him to a halt.

"Jesus, I did it again. I don't mean to scare you. I am just so frustrated that I can't remember anything. I try but it is all just a complete blank."

"I'm sorry. I am just not used to having a…a…a…"

For the first time a half smile cracked that face. Firm lips twitched as he filled it in, "A man in the house." He was glad she wasn't.

"Well…yes, I guess."

"Or a white man?" His eyes grabbed hers and forced a connection.

She nodded. "Especially not a white man."

"Do you have something against white men?" The blunt question was asked as charcoal gray held dark chocolate. *Please say no.*

"Not that I'm aware of. Have something against black women?" she asked in return, her eyes dropping quickly to his left pectoral.

"No, not at all." *If I ever did, I don't remember it and I don't now. I wish she wasn't glancing at my tattoo so often.*

"Well, at least we got that out of the way. I have to tell you," she said as she cleared off the dinner dishes and set down a blueberry cobbler and a pot of coffee. "I don't know if I will be able to take you to town tomorrow if this storm keeps going the way it is."

"And you don't mind me being here?" His head cocked to the side as he accepted the helping of warm cobbler and a hot mug of coffee.

"I'm not going to send you out in the storm, if that is your concern. You didn't even have a coat on. And, while I don't know you from a hole in the ground, I don't want to send you to your death."

"That's good, 'cause it would severely hamper our courting," he said with a bone-melting grin.

A brilliant smile filled her face. "Our courting?"

"Well, I don't always let women undress me down to my boxers, and let me sleep in their bed. So I figure we must be courting."

He saw her begin to tremble. "That is an interesting piece of logic you have there. What makes you think you I am interested in being courted by you?" She arched her brows and stared at him.

He took a bite of the cobbler, washed it down with a swig of the coffee she had placed there, and never once released her gaze. "You just said you didn't have anything against white men."

"I don't, but it doesn't mean you are my kind of man, does it?" she questioned him.

There was a flash of something foreign in his eyes as they moved over her upper torso. Regardless of the circumstances that brought him here, his body obviously wasn't broken as far as sexual reactions. She was making him feel some very intense sensations. And, considering his lack of memory, if there was a woman out there who made him feel something more intense it would kill him. "Oh, I'm your kind of man. I can see how you react to me," he purred as he drew the fork slowly out of his firm mouth.

"So you are handsome, big deal." It was a struggle to keep her true feelings off her face.

He shrugged. "Glad you find me handsome, and I know you think it is a big deal." He winked suddenly. "I think you are enchanting."

"You don't know me."

"True. Tell me about you." His request came out more like an order.

Standing, she removed the dishes and put them in the dishwasher, got it set, and turned it on. "It's late; you should get some sleep." She put her hand out, gesturing for him to leave the kitchen first.

He acquiesced. His body was exhausted still, so he didn't put up much of an argument. As he got to the entrance to the bedroom, he stopped suddenly. Turning to face the beautiful woman trailing him, he reached out one tanned hand and caressed her face. "Thank you for all you are doing for me."

"Anybody would have done it," she said, moving back, as if uncomfortable with the feelings his simple touch evoked in her.

I don't think so. "Tell me something." This time it was a request, not a command.

"If I tell you what you want to know, then will you go to bed?" Dezarae questioned.

"I'll even let you tuck me in," came his saucy reply.

She rolled her eyes, clearly trying not to grin. "Ask your question."

"What is your full name?" One hand started to reach for her before clenching and remaining at his side.

"Dezarae, spelled D-E-Z-A-R-A-E, Phoenix Kerry. Now, get some sleep." It was a gentle push that she gave him to send him in the door. "Goodnight."

Both trembled from the contact but neither responded to it. "'Night." *My little firebird.* He walked into the room, stopping by the bed to turn around and meet her gaze. "Sure you don't want to tuck me in?"

She smirked at him. "I'm sure a strong man like yourself can handle that."

"Glad to you know also think I am strong," he teased back.

Dezarae refused to answer him, just left the room with a shake of her head.

The digital readout on the clock said three in the morning. Body not as sore but feeling just as disoriented, the man who had no name got out of the soft bed and padded silently to the door. His gray eyes easily adjusted to the dark as he stuck his head out into the hallway.

There was another door to his right and he cracked it open, looking for his hostess. Nothing was in there but books and papers scattered all over the room. He walked past the bathroom door and, as he walked into the living room, he found her.

She lay on the couch sound asleep. A blanket covered her from toes to chin. *I can't believe she took the couch and let me have her bed.* A gentle smile crossed his face as he moved silently into the room and knelt down beside her.

"Thank you for saving my life, Dezarae Phoenix Kerry. Thank you," he whispered as his hand trailed down the side of her sleeping face, almost — but not quite — touching the skin that was smoother than silk.

When she moaned softly and tried to burrow deeper into the couch, he reacted. With ease, he slid his arms under her and lifted her off the couch and carried her back down the hall to place her in her own bed. She never awakened.

After tucking her in, he brushed some wayward curls off her face, staring at her like he couldn't get enough. "Sleep well, my little firebird, sleep well." Before he did something he couldn't take back, the man with the gray eyes left the room, carrying the blanket she had used on the couch, and took her place.

$\mathcal{T}hree$

Dezarae woke to the sound of a tree branch snapping. *Well, we either have an ice storm or it is still snowing out.* Sitting up, it took a second to realize she was in her own bed. "What the hell?" Turning on the bedside light, she glanced around.

There was no stranger in her room. She wore the exact clothes she had been wearing when she went to sleep on the couch.

The couch.

So why was she here? *Did I sleepwalk?*

Swinging her feet to the floor she slipped into her slippers and headed for the door. The clock had six-thirty displayed on it. *Where is my mystery man?* A bit hesitant, she moved up the short hallway and stopped.

Sleeping on her couch, which was too small for his big frame, was her gray-eyed Southern stranger. He was crammed onto her furniture in a way that didn't look very comfortable.

Her dark eyes started at his feet, moving up until she halted, for staring back at her were the intense gray ones of his. Blinking rapidly, Dezarae moved into the living room, stopping before him.

"What are you doing out here?"

"Watching you watch me," he replied smoothly.

Dezarae tried to ignore the spread of heat in her cheeks. "I mean, I went to bed here. I left you in my bed."

Those eyes darkened as he muttered, "My little firebird, if we were in bed together you wouldn't be leaving." In a louder tone that she could hear he said, "I moved you back there around three." He sat up, exposing his muscled torso to her, which made her knees weak until her eyes hit that tattoo. "You shouldn't have to give up your bed for me."

She was still having a hard time pretending she hadn't heard his comment. But she had and now that image was burned into her brain, overriding her aversion of the tattoo on his chest. "I took the couch because I can fit comfortably on it," Dezarae stated.

"I've slept in way more uncomfortable places than a couch that I am too long for."

"Really?"

"Yes, really," he assured her.

"Great, that's great!" she said, her dark eyes wide and her hands spread.

Raising a dark brow, he responded sarcastically, "Nice to know my uncomfortable sleeping situations are amusing to you."

Dezarae shook her head as she crouched down in front of him, her darker hand covering his lighter one. "No, that's not it. Not at all. You remembered."

His eyes widened as the truth of her words sank in. "I did. I did!"

"Anything else?"

"No," he said, disappointed even as his body reacted to her touch. "I don't know how or where I know it from, but I know for a fact I have slept in worse conditions. It's just not clear."

"Well," Dezarae spoke as she stood and retrieved her hand. "It's a start. Let's go see if we can find you something to wear." *'Cause I keep looking at your chest and I may find myself looking at that flag in a whole different light. Then again, I already do.*

Dezarae led him down the hall towards her spare room. She had to lead or all she would think about would be how good he looked. Not that walking in front of him changed those images.

It worked out, though, because unbeknownst to Dezarae her visitor was enjoying the view of her in front of him. As he ogled her, she opened the closet to show him a few stacks of folded clothes. "I think you should find something in here that will fit you." Dezarae backed up so he could walk in. "I'm gonna make some breakfast. Feel free to use the shower; there are clean towels in the cabinet."

"Thank you." He turned towards her in time to catch her heated glance as her dark gaze took in his half-naked body.

"You're welcome," she replied, and went to the kitchen to start breakfast.

While the quiche cooked, Dezarae bundled up to go outside. There were still practically whiteout conditions. There hadn't been a snow in the area like this in years.

Standing on her porch, she realized there was no way she was going to town. She could get to her workshop and CB the sheriff at least. That way they would know she had a visitor and would be aware of the accident.

Grabbing the rope, she made her way slowly across her yard. It was a bit of a struggle to force open the side door against the seemingly gale-force winds but soon she was in.

She hit the lights, silently thanking her foresight in having back-up generators installed so the building was always warm, and headed for the CB radio that was at the end opposite to where she was, by the main doors.

Turning it on, she began transmitting. "Sheriff, you out there? This is Phoenix, come back."

A very deep voice reached her waiting ears. "Phoenix, you okay up there, girl?"

"Fine, Dale, fine. Look last night on my way home I passed an accident. There is nothing left of the car except pieces. There was a survivor. He's here w—"

"He? Damn it, Dez, you know better than that. Who is he?"

Dezarae smiled. Sheriff Dale Ship was her surrogate father. He was sixty and didn't look a day over forty. He took her wellbeing very seriously.

"As I was saying," Dezarae began again. "He is here with me. He is about six-four, one hundred–ninety, dark-brown hair cut short, and gray eyes. Oh, and a tat: an anchor, and a chain sitting on a rebel flag."

"Why are you telling me this? Are you sure it was a rebel flag?"

"I know what a rebel flag looks like. Yes, I am sure. I am telling you because he doesn't remember his name. He had a head wound and I didn't find any form of identification on him. See if anyone reports a description like that. I will check in with you later today."

"One more thing," Dale said.

"Go ahead." She waited for him to say what he needed to.

*
**

Ross walked through the house looking for the woman who had taken him in. Showered and dressed in jeans and a sweatshirt he found in the closet, he wandered around Dezarae's home.

"What would a woman like her be living alone out here for? Where is her man to take care of her?" He looked at all these pictures on her wall of cars. Antiques and classics, they were beautiful.

He moved to the front door and looked out into the dark. He could barely make out the glow of a light from across the way. As the smell of cooking food filled the air, he grabbed a thick jacket and stepped out into nature's wrath.

Eyes squinted against the wind, he grabbed the rope that was secured to the porch and began to follow it. His feet were freezing as he finally made it to a large building. Opening the door he slipped inside, grateful to be out of the wind and cold. The place wasn't hot, but it was tolerable.

He brushed the snow from his hair and his ears picked up her voice. It sounded like she was on the other side of the building or in a room, for it was muted. When he heard a man's voice, his gray eyes narrowed.

Stepping out to make his presence known, he took two strides and stopped dead. There were four cars under the lights in various stages of rebuilding. They were also classics, and they were astounding.

In amazement, he walked closer to the first one. It was cobalt blue and gleamed under the bright lights. "Jesus," he muttered.

"It's a 1965 Aston Martin DB6 with a Vantage engine," a feminine voice said.

He looked up to see Dezarae weaving her way across the building to his side. "Whose are they?" One hand gestured to encompass all the vehicles in there.

"Clients. I'm almost done with this one. I'm just making sure the triple twin-choke carburetors and pumps are working properly." She moved down the line. "This is the same thing, only a convertible. Both of them are five-speed manuals. They only made two hundred fifteen of the convertibles. I have a bit more to do on him."

Gray eyes took in the black convertible. The top was removed and he could see the gears and wheel were on the right side of the car. The interior was leather with wall-to-wall carpeting, lots of gauges, and a wood/metal steering wheel.

"You do this?" the incredulous question came.

"Yep. I do." With a smile, Dezarae took him further into the shop to the next car which was a dark green color. "This is a 1964 Ford Fairlane. And down here is my latest addition to the garage."

Wordlessly, he followed her to stop in front of a white car. "What is it?"

"An Oldsmobile Toronado. 1966."

"You repair cars," he stated.

"No, I restore cars. My business is *Phoenix Restorations and Rebuilds.*"

"And you do all this by yourself?"

Chocolate eyes narrowed as she crossed her arms and leaned against the car. "Why are you snooping around out here?"

He seemed taken aback. "What are you talking about? I was looking for you."

"What difference does it make if I do this myself or not?"

"Hey, I was just asking. Why are you being so defensive?" He took a step towards her.

Though he saw a bit of fear creep into her eyes, Dezarae refused to budge. "Because you are asking a lot of personal questions and I don't know you."

"I'm not going to hurt you."

"Look, nothing overly personal, but I have been having some trouble with a few of the locals and I am not inclined to totally trust a man who has a rebel flag tattooed on his chest."

His eyes hardened. "Nothing personal?" He shook his head. "You tell me you are judging me because of a tattoo but I am not supposed to take it personally. How exactly *should* I take it?"

"Like it is. Fact. I am just getting a bit nervous here." Her eyes moved from his tense body back to his eyes.

Taking a deep breath, he held out his hands. "I'll go. I wouldn't want you to feel uncomfortable." He turned around and missed her shocked expression.

"You don't have to go. I just don't want to tell you everything about me," she called as he walked away from her.

"Thanks for everything." Within moments he was gone from the building.

"Shit!" Dezarae ran up to the door and out into the storm after him. "Hey!" she yelled into the wind. "Hey!"

Nothing.

Way to go, Dezarae, send a man to his death just because of a tattoo! She hurried into the house and found him walking out of her room wearing nothing but the clothes he had worn when she found him. Shaking the snow off her head, she held up her hand.

"You don't have to leave."

"I think it would be best." He kept walking towards the door with sure strides.

"Look, you won't survive out there," she insisted. *I don't need his death on my conscience.*

"I'll think of something." He opened the door after barely touching her to get by.

"Fine!" she yelled, as he pulled the door shut after him. "Be an idiot, Johnny Reb, I don't give a damn!" Ripping off her coat, she was totally unprepared for the blast of cold air that hit her when he shoved the door wide open again.

"What did you call me?" he growled, reaching for her and clamping a hand around her.

"An idiot," she muttered.

"No, after that." His eyes were fierce as they bore into hers.

"Um, Johnny Reb," she said quietly, suddenly not as confident as she had been.

He dropped her arm and shut the door with one strong slam. "Johnny Reb, Johnny Reb...Jeb. Jeb, that sounds familiar to me. Jeb, I remember people calling me Jeb." She was the recipient of a winning smile.

"My name is Jeb," he said as he hugged her in gratitude.

As the smell of man surrounded Dezarae, she found her body trembling. How was it that one look, one touch from him could set her to quivering this badly? She moved out of his embrace and smiled back. "Hello, Jeb, I'm Dezarae."

"Hello, Dezarae, I'm, Jeb, an idiot; can I stay?"

"Of course you can." She began to walk away but he latched onto her arm again.

"Hey, I'm sorry my tattoo bothers you."

"I'll be fine, don't worry about it." *Your chest bothers me more. I'd like to lick warm chocolate and caramel off it.* "Let's eat. I have to get to work."

Falling into step beside her, he asked. "Out in the shop?"

"No, I have some paperwork that I have to get done."

"Let me know if there is anything, *anything*, I can do," he fairly purred in her ear.

Swallowing hard, she managed to stutter, "I'll do that."

Four

After breakfast was over and they had both cleaned up, Dezarae sat in her office filling out form after form of tedious paperwork. Her guest, now going by the name of Jeb, was in there with her.

He was silent, though, as he looked through some of her books on classic cars that she had in the room. She worked until her watch read eleven o'clock. With a groan, she stretched and rolled her neck. The desk was clean. Papers had been filed.

"Done?" a deep voice asked from behind her, setting butterflies to fluttering in the pit of her stomach.

"Finally. I hate this part of running a business."

"Anything I can help you with?" he offered as his body materialized beside her.

Don't answer that, Mouth, don't answer that. She shook her head. "I am going to make lunch and then work out in the shop. You are welcome to come along if you want," Dezarae offered.

He arched a brow as one lean finger brought her chin up to meet his gaze. "Why the change of heart?"

She didn't even pretend to misunderstand. "I'm sorry, okay? I took my instinctive reaction to the flag and lumped you into a category. Combined with the stuff I heard from Dale…"She stood and shrugged as her deep, pooling eyes met and held his gaze. "I'm sorry. I was out of line."

Granite eyes bore into hers as another few inches of snow fell outside. "Apology accepted."

Dezarae winked. "Besides, it's hard to court if we aren't together."

He smiled, showing a perfect white smile against tanned skin. "That is very true."

"Well, let's go, then. I told the sheriff I would check back in with him later."

"Why don't you have a CB in the house?"

"I spend more time in the garage than I do here, so it makes more sense." They walked up the hall to the kitchen where Dezarae made some sandwiches and soup that she put in a thermos. "Dale is always after me to get another one for the house."

"Who's Dale?"

"Oh, sorry, he's the sheriff." Finally ready, they bundled up and gathered their food. Talk halted as they walked through the storm to the shop, holding tightly to the connecting rope.

As the door slammed shut and they were shaking the snow from their hair, she spoke again. "I have an extra pair of coveralls you can use."

"What do you want me to do?"

Well, that's a loaded question. "Give me a second. I want to turn up the heat."

"Okay," he said as she walked off to the thermostat.

Jeb watched as the exquisitely lovely black woman sashayed away from him. He knew it was her natural stride because of the fierce way she was fighting her sexual attraction to him. She wanted him and he knew it. But then, he wanted her, a fact she was soon going to learn.

He heard the motor kick in and knew that more heat was soon to follow. She walked towards him and tossed him a pair of green coveralls. Without missing a beat, she slid her body into a second set and he saw she was indeed curvaceous.

Damn, she is stacked!

He pulled on his coveralls and waited for instruction. All the lights were on and she pointed over by a wall. "What?" he asked.

"There is a radio over there, go put on some tunes. I have a whole bunch of CDs, so mix and match."

"What do you want to hear?" Jeb yelled over his shoulder as he walked away.

"I like all the music that's there. Doesn't matter to me," she hollered back.

Dezarae approached the hardtop Aston Martin. Rolling over her tall cart of tools and parts, she lifted the hood and disappeared under it.

Destiny's Child filled the shop as, from under her arm, she noticed Jeb walking back over towards her. "What now?" his seductive voice teased her.

"Eat something. I could use your help in just a moment."

"No rush. I am enjoying the view from here."

Glad her head was under the hood, she blushed. "I know; the cars are nice aren't they?"

"Well, there is a nice back end that I am looking at."

"And you have a nice everything," she muttered as she gave the ratchet a final turn.

"Thank you," he purred in her ear.

Dezarae jumped. "You heard me?" Still, she refused to turn toward him.

"Most definitely." His shoulders settled beside her as he cocked his head and asked. "What are you doing?"

"I, well, *we* are about to make sure this baby runs." Wiping her hands on a rag, she backed out from under the hood and put her tools back.

"What do you need from me?"

"Well, can you cover the seat in that plastic and then get in and start it up?" Her gaze turned mischievous. "That is, if you can drive a stick."

Molten mercury was the only way to describe his eyes. "Oh, I can drive a stick. I promise you that."

She trembled. "Talk is cheap, Jeb. Get in and prove it."

"Let me know when you are ready to let me 'get in and prove it,'" he said as he carefully protected the leather seat and climbed in the right side of the car.

"Ready back there?" Dezarae asked as another blush overtook her body.

"Let me know." His hands lovingly caressed the interior of the car. It was beautiful.

"Hang on." She tinkered more under the hood. "Okay, go now, nice and easy," she hollered to him from where she was.

"Gotcha." Jeb turned the car over and it started but sounded a bit off. "Now what?" he yelled to her.

"Let it run for a bit. I have to do some adjusting. Make sure the brake is on, please," she said as her head peered at him from around the hood briefly before she hid it again.

Jeb sat on the butter-soft leather and just admired the car. His eyes drifted closed as his memories became clearer.

There were eight men together as they walked through the beach town, all of them talking and laughing. "Let me know when you get your hands on an old Jag and then we will talk, Jeb," the large black man in the group said to him.

"I'm just a noncom; you are commissioned. How about you buy me one?" Jeb teased back.

"But you're the newbie. It's customary to buy us a gift."

"Oh, sure, I will get right on that..." The picture faded before a name could be revealed.

Frustrated, Jeb opened his eyes to see a concerned look on Dezarae's face. "You okay there, man?" she asked.

"I had a memory, but I lost it." He didn't want to tell her of what yet, not until he was sure.

"I'm sure you will get it back. Can you rev the engine for me?" She slipped back out of view.

He did and before long the car was purring like a kitten. With a slam, she shut the hood and winked at him. She made a slashing motion with her hand and he cut the engine, climbing out of the car.

"Awesome! I think that is fine. I just have to clean it up and cover it and he will be ready to go. Of course, he will be a she once the client gets him back." She shrugged.

Before he could say anything, a loud squawk came over the CB. "Phoenix, you there, girl? Come back!"

Dezarae smiled as Jeb frowned at the male voice. She eagerly headed over and picked up the handset; Jeb followed. "I'm here, Sheriff."

"Girl, I've been calling for the past thirty minutes. Where have you been?"

"Working on a car. Why, what's up?"

"How you doing?"

"We're fine."

"We? Oh, that man's still there?" Dale snapped even as Jeb's eyes narrowed.

"I'm here," Jeb's masculine voice said as he pressed the talk button, his large hand covering her smaller one.

"Don't you be hurting my Phoenix or you will answer to me."

With a glance to the woman who was beside him, an evil glint took root and grew in his eye. "*Your* Phoenix? I'm the one courting her." Jeb smiled as he heard her gasp seconds before the man on the other end exploded in a string of expletives.

"That's not true," Dezarae interrupted.

"What, didn't I just get finished driving a stick for you?" Gray eyes never left the shocked ones of the woman near him.

"Yes, but that was—"

"I'm coming up there!" Dale thundered.

"No, Dale, it's too dangerous with the snow still falling," Dezarae said.

"What is going on with you two?" the sheriff demanded. "Why does he say you are courting? Why did you say you were courting?"

"Well," Jeb said and smirked, "what would you call it when a woman strips you down to your boxers and insists you sleep in her bed…the same bed she wakes up in later?"

"You aren't telling the whole story!" she screeched as she tried unsuccessfully to reach the handset.

"Oh, I didn't know if you wanted me to tell him how I tucked you in at three in the morning when you were sleeping so soundly." Devilish delight was alive and well in his gaze.

Dezarae was speechless. She stood there and gaped at him. And all he did was wink. "Or how just a bit ago you said it was going to be hard to court if we weren't together."

With a groan, she dropped her head on the table. "He is going to kill me." She gestured to the CB.

"Anyway, Sheriff, she is in very good hands." Jeb turned off the CB and smiled at her.

"What did you do that for?" Her question came as she finally picked her head up to meet his smile.

I felt the need to claim you. "Didn't like how he made you smile. Like you felt safe. That's not his job, its mine."

"Excuse me?" She stood up totally and glanced at him. "What did you say?"

"I said," he replied smoothly, "I am taking care of you now."

"What makes you think I need you to take care of me?"

Shaking his head he said, "Doesn't matter. I'm going to."

*
**

"He never made it. No call. Not anything," the large man said, slamming his fist on the table.

"Any credit card use?" asked the man with an Irish lilt to his voice.

The blond head shook in the negative. "Not a single one, not since he last filled up with gas. And you know Charmane is his whole world, so if he didn't show up..." His voice trailed off, not really wanting to say what he was beginning to fear.

The black man with him nodded and stood, striding towards the door. "I'll page the men."

"Good. Put a 9-1-1 after it, Hondo. We leave as soon as everyone arrives."

"Aye, will do, Harrier, will do." The man immediately left to page the required souls.

Although Ross "Jeb" Connelly was the newest man they had, he was still a member and they were going to find him. Within two hours, a helicopter carried seven men towards Montana to the last known destination of their teammate. They were going to bring him home. One way or another.

*
**

"I don't know why you feel the need to protect me. And, while I find it very chivalrous and cute, I have been fine on my own."

"I can see that." The dark head nodded moments before one tan finger stroked her cheekbone. "Don't bother arguing with me. That is how it's going to be."

The single-minded assuredness and conviction that created his tone made Dezarae fall silent. Not from fear, no, for she felt very comfortable around him. Aside from the intense sexual feeling he stirred up, it was just that it felt nice having someone want to protect her.

So she nodded and walked away, heading over to the sound system, and turned it off, unsure really of how to react to his "almost" claim on her. *For all I know, he could have a wife and kids back home. Better to stay distant and not get attached.*

But she feared it was too late for that. This man was clueless about his past, had almost died, and was heartbreakingly handsome. There was some kind of connection between them that the flirting highlighted.

"What's next?" That deep voice intruded upon her thoughts.

"Going in for the night. It's six," she said, unzipping her coveralls and peeling them off.

Jeb was silent as he watched her disrobe. It was as if she were completely naked, the way his eyes burned her.

"What?" she asked as she tried not to fidget beneath his stare.

He blinked rapidly. "Nothing." His voice was raspy.

"If you're sure." Dezarae folded her coveralls and put them away as he took his off.

"No, I'm not sure," Jeb murmured, standing behind her, reaching his strong arm past her to put away his coveralls as well. He engulfed her in his masculine scent.

Keep your distance, keep your distance. Oh, hell, girl, I bet he can go the distance! Refusing to say anything out loud, Dezarae just turned and found herself flush against his hard body.

Battleship gray clashed with terra firma. Her tongue snuck out to wet her dry lips and another flash of desire sailed through his eyes. "We should be going in," she murmured.

"I suppose," Jeb said softly. His gaze took in her smooth complexion and her wide eyes framed by thick sooty lashes that gave her an innocent yet seductive appearance. Her cute nose endeared him and her full lips made him want to kiss them more than he wanted to take his next breath.

Even though she had been working under a car hood, he could still smell the same floral scent that was on her bedding. And it had the same reaction on him that it had when he was in her bed. He was instantly fully erect, although since he awakened here he seemed to be semi-hard all the time around her.

As they stood there as if they were frozen in time, he noticed her body could fit so perfectly into his. How her curves could press against him so wonderfully. All in all, he wanted her.

Stepping closer until they were really pressed against each other, he leaned his head towards her.

"What are you doing?" she asked in a hoarse voice.

"Kissing you. I may not know anything about myself, but I know this. I am going to kiss you, Dezarae Phoenix Kerry." His mouth was a hair's breadth away from hers.

"So kiss me, then, Johnny Reb," she demanded as she moved her lips closer yet.

"As you wish, my little firebird." His lips covered hers masterfully. Sliding his tongue into her willing mouth, they both trembled as their body temperatures skyrocketed.

Her arms moved up to slide around his neck, drawing him in closer. His arms went around her waist and his large hands settled on her firm derriere, bringing her tighter to his erection.

Tongues dueled. Passions flared. He sucked on her tongue, and her hips bucked against him. He answered with a thrust of his own.

Panting, they drew away from each other, eyes dark and burning with a fire that only was going to be quenched by the other. "Wow," they both breathed at the same time.

Dezarae dropped her arms and slipped under his embrace, then headed across the shop to where their jackets were. *Two more seconds and I would have been begging him to take me on a worktable.* She was ashamed of her actions. She had acted like a floozy.

Jeb was right on her heels. "Dez, wait." He grabbed her and spun her around. "What's wrong?"

She wouldn't meet his gaze. "Nothing." *He called me Dez…*

"Are you sorry it happened?" His question came as he tipped her head to his.

"No." *Now I want more, so much more.*

"Good, 'cause I fully intend on doing that again." His thumb ran over her swollen bottom lip.

$\mathcal{F}ive$

That night Dezarae made dinner. Jeb helped. They worked together as the storm continued to rage on outside, dropping more snow.

Jeb noticed her manner seemed to be a bit reserved. *Maybe I moved too fast for her but I just had to kiss those lips.* "How did you get into this business?" He opened the oven and slid the shepherd's pie inside.

Wiping down the counter, Dezarae spoke. "My father. I grew up in that shop. I think I was 'restoring' cars before I could walk." She tossed the rag into the sink before grabbing two mugs for coffee and pouring some for them both.

After she led the way into the living room, they both sat on the couch, one on each end. Dezarae sat with her legs up in front of her, giving him a wonderful view of her fuzzy red slippers. "It has been in the family for generations. It was passed on from father to son."

He arched a brow and she explained. "I was the only child. Momma died in childbirth with me, so he taught me." A sad smile crossed her face. "Daddy never held it against me. But that is where I got my name from. While he wanted a son, he knew that Momma wanted a little girl. So he named me Dezarae; it means 'to be desired,' or something like that."

He took a sip of coffee. *Well, they were right, I desire you.* "And Phoenix?" he asked.

"You know the legend of the Phoenix right? How it was born, from the ashes?" Jeb nodded. "Well, I arrived after Momma died so he called me Phoenix. He ignored everyone in the family saying he should remarry and have a woman raise me; he wanted to do it. So I went to work with him."

She drank more coffee. "When he passed on, I inherited everything. And I have been here restoring old cars to their former glory ever since."

"And marriage never crossed your mind? A family of your own?" he asked.

"Sure, but if you knew what the pickings were around here you would understand why I am not in any big rush. Besides, I am only twenty-seven. I have time yet. Plus, I don't want a man who thinks he can come in and take over the business. I am fully capable of running it myself."

You sure are. "What about Dale? Isn't he interested in you?" Those gray eyes watched her reaction.

"Sure, but not in that way. He is sixty; and while he looks damn good for his age, that is just a bit extreme for me."

He released a breath he hadn't realized he had been holding. "Oh, so, he is more like your father?"

"Exactly. Of course, he would like me to marry his son." Dezarae smiled at the immediate frown that crossed the handsome man's face.

I don't think so. "And what do you think?"

"I think that Shawn is very nice. One of the more handsome men in the area, and we get along —"

"I thought you weren't in any rush," he interrupted.

The timer went off so, without responding, Dezarae rose gracefully from the couch and went into the kitchen to pull the food out of the oven. "Dinner's ready."

Jeb followed and stood in the kitchen, watching her move. She was poetry in motion. Her hair fell down around her shoulders in gentle waves. She captivated him.

Moving silently, he walked up behind her and placed his arms on either side of her, effectively trapping her between him and the counter. "You didn't answer me," he whispered in her ear.

Shuddering from the breath that skimmed her neck, Dezarae responded. "It's time to eat."

"That wasn't the question, Firebird." His lips moved along her earlobe.

"You never really asked a question. It was more like you made an observation or statement," she corrected, obviously trying not to tremble.

"Allow me to rectify that now. Are you going to marry Shawn?" One hand moved her thick hair out of the way so his lips had access to her neck.

Eyes rolling into the back of her head, Dezarae swallowed. "I don't know," she squeaked.

He nibbled along her smooth skin. "Has he asked you?"

Locking her knees so she wouldn't fall, Dezarae answered the man with the wicked lips. "Yes."

Yes. His whole body stiffened as he pressed against her back. "And you said?"

"I said," she halted. She apparently couldn't concentrate. His lips were distracting enough but suddenly his hands were teasing as well. One ran up and down her arm while the other was tracing the curve of her hip.

"What? What did you say?" he whispered seductively.

"Did you ever want to do something regardless of what the ramifications would be?"

"Are you saying you married him?" The tone grew guarded.

Dezarae continued as if he hadn't spoken at all. "Because the way I feel when you touch me or just look at me makes me want to forget the world outside even exists." Her head fell back to rest against the hard planes of his chest.

"I feel it, too, Firebird. I feel it too." He pulled her so she totally rested against him. "What are we going to do about it?"

Smiling sadly, she looked out the kitchen window and saw the stars in the night sky. "Nothing. We are going to do nothing."

"Why? Why deny what we both want? What we both crave?" Jeb could hear the disappointment in her voice. *Don't give up on us, Firebird.*

"Because you don't know who you are," Dezarae said, pulling away and carrying the dinner to the table.

Gray eyes narrowed to slits. "Jesus! What, you think I'm with the goddamn Klan because of my tattoo?" he thundered, spinning to face her.

"Don't raise your voice to me," she warned. Eyes that normally invited a man in to swim in their chocolaty depths grew unyielding.

"So what if I was with the Klan?! I don't remember who I was!" he kept right on yelling.

"First, you *need* to not yell at me. Second, that wasn't my reason at all." Her movements were jerky as she took a chair and dished herself up some dinner. She totally ignored the man in her dining area.

Jeb groaned in frustration as he rubbed his temples. Silently, he sat across from her and prepared a plate for himself. He wanted her to talk to him, but he knew he owed her an apology.

"I'm sorry I yelled and I'm sorry I jumped to the wrong conclusion. Will you tell me why we are going to do nothing about our feelings?"

"Because you may have a wife, fiancée, or girlfriend," she answered with a wistful smile as she took a bite of food.

"But—"

"I know," she interrupted. "You don't remember. But they would and are probably worried sick about you. I know I would be."

He ate in silence for a while. "And if I wasn't married?"

Brown eyes swirled with heat. "Don't make this any harder."

Oh, it's hard all right. "I don't feel married."

The hand that held the fork trembled as she set it carefully beside her plate. Dezarae met his gaze. "They will have the roads cleared tomorrow and I can get you to Shadyville. We will find out who you are and where you are supposed to be, so don't begin something that has no future and would just wither and die."

He put his fork down as well. Jeb slid his chair back to rise and walk around the table. At her side, he reached for her and drew her out of the chair, leading her to the couch.

Settling his lean body on the furniture, he tugged her down onto his lap. He used one strong arm to anchor her there he cupped her face with his free hand. "Didn't you ever think this was where I was supposed to end up? Here with you?" His hand was gentle as it stroked her cheek. "How do you know this wouldn't have a future, Dez? You are the one who has Phoenix in her name. You must believe that if it was meant to be, dying wouldn't be a concern." His hand drew her face closer to his until their lips almost touched. "For it would be reborn."

Dezarae blinked, her eyes bright. "I can't go through that kind of pain," she whispered.

"I don't understand." His voice, too, was hushed.

"I can't allow myself to feel anything for you. I don't know you and it will be easier when you leave if I don't let myself." Her eyes welled up with tears.

"Don't cry, Firebird. Please don't cry." His fingertips immediately wiped away the first few tears that escaped. "Don't cry. It breaks my heart."

"I'm sorry," she sputtered before the floodgates opened and the tears just poured from her dark eyes.

With a tender smile, Jeb tucked her close to his chest and held her as she cried herself out. One hand pressed her head against his chest as the other one caressed her arm. He remembered comforting someone before; a female with big doe-like eyes. She'd sat in his lap and he'd held her like this. But who? Who was she? Why couldn't he remember her name?

Jeb wanted to know who he was so he could prove to the woman in his arms they were meant to be. Things happened for a reason; he had been told that by someone before. Pushing the fact he couldn't remember aside, he focused on offering silent support to the woman he knew. The one who was real and in his arms right now.

Dezarae cried it all out. The loss of her father, not knowing her mother. Everything. It had been so long since she had accepted comfort from another person. When her father died she had Dale, but he had also been consumed by his grief and it seemed she had done most of the comforting.

Some minutes later, the cotton of Jeb's shirt was soaked with her tears but her sobs had subsided. Every now and then she would sniff but otherwise she just sat there in silence. Her fingers began to pluck the fabric of his top.

"Better now?" he asked gently.

Her head nodded against his chest as Dezarae continued to sniff. "I don't know what came over me. I'm so embarrassed…"

"Everyone needs to cry from time to time," he offered.

"I ruined your shirt," she chuckled, pushing away from his chest.

"Tears never ruined anything." He brushed away the remaining few tears from her face with his thumb.

"Make-up," Dezarae joked.

"You don't need make-up," Jeb said honestly. "It would just hide your beauty from the world."

With a wry smile she shook her head. "My make-up is car grease. I don't dress up much here." She shrugged and started to move off his lap only to be stopped by his steely arms.

"Stay. I like holding you."

Dezarae found herself melting back against him as her brain scolded her. *You shouldn't do this!* "Thank you for letting me cry on your shoulder," she said as one hand began to trail up and down his arm, sending electrical impulses through them both.

"You don't need to thank me, Dez. I'm glad I could help. None of this changes how we feel towards one another, though."

Reality. "We aren't going to do anything," she said as her face snuggled into the curve of his neck. Inhaling, she smelled a purely masculine scent and it made her tremble all over again.

"And we are denying this mutual attraction because of something that may or may not be?" he asked as his hand began to tease the hem of her shirt.

"Yes. That and I am still hungry." Her stomach growled at that moment, agreeing with her statement.

"Well, Firebird. Let's go eat, then." Jeb placed a light kiss on the top of her head before she left his lap and soon they were back in the kitchen finishing up their dinners.

$\mathcal{S}ix$

There was a long debate between them but finally Dezarae won. She would be sleeping on the couch quite comfortably while her handsome guest was in her bed. As they went their separate ways for the night, Jeb hadn't pushed her into surrendering to what they both wanted.

As he stood in the doorway bidding her goodnight, his eyes burned with a passion she knew would affect her like no other ever had. The decision was hers; he wanted her, but it was her call. When she said goodnight and backed away from him, he smiled a smile that should have warned her he wasn't giving up on her, just allowing her this victory tonight. He gave her a small nod and walked into the bedroom without a second look at her.

So now she was lying on her comfy couch, unable to sleep, images of the man who had crashed into her life floating around her mind. His body was full of muscles, all of them hard and honed, with those beautiful gray eyes that saw more than she wanted him to see. He was a beautiful work of art.

"Gorgeous," she muttered to the dark as she pulled her blankets up higher and tried to fall back asleep.

✳✳

"I'm going to miss you too. Always remember that I love you." The *man leaned down and kissed the slim brunette gently.*

Those big brown eyes glistened with tears as her arms slid around his neck and returned the kiss. "Bye," she whispered in his ear.

"I love you, Charmane." One more kiss and he was off running towards the van that had arrived to pick him up.

"Love you too!" The feminine yell reached him as the door slammed shut behind him.

"Charmane," he rasped to the room. Sitting up, covered in sweat, Jeb fumbled for the light. As the glow filled the floral room he realized it had been a dream. A memory, really.

"Who is Charmane?" Dezarae asked from the doorway, her features emblazoned with worry.

"I don't know," Jeb swore, as he couldn't even see her anymore, couldn't recall her.

"Must be someone important to you. You've been calling for her a while now." Dezarae entered the room and walked towards the bed.

"I don't know who she is!" he shouted as his frustration spilled over.

Patiently, Dezarae sat beside him on the bed. "Don't push it; you are getting your memory back."

Dragging a hand through his hair, he flopped back on the bed. "I feel helpless. I feel fucking helpless!"

Unsure of what to say to that, Dezarae grabbed his hand and laced their fingers, giving silent support but not stopping him from ranting. Immediately calmer from her touch, Jeb tugged her back on the bed to lie beside him.

He placed her head on his right shoulder, her thick hair tickling his skin. He placed their joined hands over his heart and the tattoo. He put her hand over it, palm down, and then covered both with his hand.

"I hate feeling like this," he admitted.

"I kinda figured that one out myself there, Johnny Reb," she said, smiling softly.

"What are the chances of pursuing those feelings now?" His right hand rubbed her back.

"About as good as the snow being gone when we wake up."

"That's what I thought." He paused for a moment. "Will you stay with me?"

"Yes, I'll stay," she said immediately.

"Thank you," he whispered, jerking the covers up and turned off the bedside light.

They both slept easier for the remainder of the night. Nightmares were held at bay; memories kept their distance, allowing them both to find the rest they needed. When morning arrived they were still in the same positions as when they fell asleep.

Jeb woke first and lay there content to watch her sleep. Her breathing was deep, even, and soothing. Those thick lashes of hers rested against her dark skin. Moving his head, he looked at the difference in their skin color.

With the hand that was on top of hers, he inserted his fingers between hers. Dark, light, dark, light. They made a stunning combination. It was beautiful. She was beautiful.

Lifting her hand, he stared at her fingers. The nails were short but clean. No polish or shine on them. Natural. Her hands were strong from working on cars her whole life. He ran his thumb over the calluses he'd felt when her hand had rested on his chest.

"You deserve a pampered life, Dezarae. You shouldn't have to work this hard," Jeb spoke softly to the room.

"I like the work; it relaxes me, but thanks for saying that anyway," her voice, husky with sleep, answered him.

"What are you doing awake?" he asked as he moved back a bit so he could look her in the eyes.

"I need to get up, shower, and get ready to go to town." She blushed as she realized they were still in bed together.

"You are very adorable when you blush, Firebird, very adorable." Jeb wanted to kiss her so much but settled to touch the tip of her nose instead.

"I need to get going," she muttered and left the bed without a backwards glance.

Two hours later Dezarae led the way into her garage. It was time to go to town.

A low whistle left Jeb's mouth as he took in the other car in her garage besides her beat-up Land Rover. "Wow. Whose is this one?" His strides took him over to the vehicle that gleamed like a black pearl.

"That? That's my baby. It's a—"

"This is a '67 Shelby Mustang GT500." He stuck his head in the open window. "Four speed manual, V8 engine, I'd bet with two Holley four-barrel carburetors." His gray eyes were wide as he walked around the car in awe.

"Would you like me to leave you alone with him?" Dezarae asked, amazed he had known what kind of car it was.

"Him? Hell, no, a car like this is a woman, needs a soft touch." He was practically drooling.

"Look, buster, this is a he, okay? My car, my sex."

His head shot up to meet her eyes. "Yours? This is yours?"

"Yes. Go ahead and sit in it if you want." She hadn't even finished offering before his large body was slipping behind the wheel. *He must be in love if he didn't respond to my sex comment.*

"This is a work of art," he praised.

"Thanks," Dezarae said as she opened the passenger door and climbed in. "I wish *he* were done but I can't spare the time. Most of my hours are in the shop. So he is kinda neglected."

"This car is not a 'he,'" Jeb insisted.

"Listen here, Johnny Reb," Dezarae teased. "Men get to have their cars be women so why wouldn't I want my car to be a man? If I'm gonna have an orgasm it sure as hell isn't going to be because of a woman."

That got his attention. "Keep up with that kind of talk and you will have an orgasm and I guarantee it will be by a man," he warned.

"We need to get to town," she rasped as she got out of the vehicle.

"Runnin', Firebird?" he challenged, reluctant to leave the car so soon.

"No," she purred in his ear. "I already know this man can make me come, so why would I run from you?" Her dark body moved closer to the car door. "And I am talking about the car." Her lips were right by his ear as she delivered those final words, her warm breath teasing him.

He climbed out of the car and grabbed Dezarae's arm, spinning her back toward him. Not giving her an opportunity to voice her opinion, he lifted her up. Her legs snaked around his waist as his strong hands gripped her ass. His mouth latched onto hers with a ferocity that, instead of scaring her, only inflamed her more.

She wrapped her arms around his neck as she sucked his tongue deeper into her mouth. Pulling back, she held onto his lower lip, dragging her teeth lightly across it.

His hands clenched on her butt cheeks, causing her to let go of his lip with a gasp. "Tell me what male exactly in this garage can give you an orgasm?" Jeb's tone was hoarse as he readjusted his hold so he could move one hand up under her shirt.

"The one with the stick," she panted as his fingers teased her skin.

"Dezarae," he growled low in his throat.

"Yes?" Her question was strained.

The smell of her desire was overwhelming. His free hand slipped from her shirt to the waistband of her pants and over her soaked panties. Her whole body shivered.

"You seem awfully wet. Did your car do this to you?" he asked, deceptively calm.

"No," she admitted. "It was the other male in my garage." Her whimpers grew in volume as his fingers slid under the wet edge of her underwear.

"Tell me," he ordered before his mouth adhered to one of her breasts through her shirt, sucking until the moisture from his mouth was palpable to the tender skin of her full breast.

"You," Dezarae barely managed to whisper. "It was you."

"And don't you forget that, Firebird." He slid one finger inside her welcoming heat.

"Oh, God!" she wailed and her body spasmed with an orgasm.

Slowly removing his finger, he said in a guttural tone, "Let's see your car do *that*." He sucked his finger clean before whispering, "You taste like candy, Firebird."

Eyes closed from the intensity of her orgasm plus a bit of mortification at her response to his touch, Dezarae said, "I...we need to get going."

"Kiss me first. Taste yourself on me. Come, Firebird, kiss me."

Dezarae couldn't ignore him. Hesitantly, she opened her eyes to see nothing but affection in his return gaze. Tenderly, she put her lips on his and began the kiss. Soon it intensified and she closed her eyes in pleasure.

She could taste herself in his heated kiss. Her body pressed harder against his as she felt that need begin to build up inside her again. Dezarae wanted all he could give her.

The kiss ended as he pulled his mouth off hers. Those eyes of his were dark with desire and it was plain to Dezarae as she looked into them. "What?" she asked quietly.

"I don't have that much self-control. We have to stop now, or I won't be able to." With great reluctance, he put her on her feet. "Unlike you, Firebird, I'm only mortal." He brushed his lips against hers one more time. "Let's get going."

$\mathcal{S}_{even}$

Another hour passed before they were ready. Dezarae had gone in the house and got cleaned up while Jeb stayed away from her tempting body.

As he sat beside her in the old vehicle, he watched her out of the corner of his eye. Her face was the picture of total concentration on safely navigating them during the twenty-mile trip to town. She hadn't looked him in the eyes since she'd run from the garage.

She wore a softly colored patchwork sweatshirt and another pair of hip-hugging jeans. Her coat was in the backseat along with the one of her father's that she lent him. Dezarae had her thick black hair pulled back away from her face, allowing him easy access to her side profile.

Please don't let me find out I'm married. His stormy gaze looked out the window at the passing landscape. *Why won't she talk to me?*

"If I apologize for my actions in the garage, will you say something?" Jeb broke the silence that still teemed with sexual tension.

With a brief glance at her passenger, Dezarae sighed. "Have you done something you feel the need to apologize for?" Her dark eyes moved back to the seemingly nonexistent road.

"No, but I will if *you* feel I should apologize." *Hell, no, I don't feel I did anything wrong. Except stop.*

"Then you don't have to." Dezarae fell silent as they approached the spot where he'd busted through the guardrail.

Jeb's gray eyes widened as he saw the mangled debris. It was like he'd tuned to stone. His mouth formed an "o" as the vehicle slowed.

"Did you want to go look?" Dezarae asked in a quiet voice.

"Please." His voice was slightly strained.

Carefully, Dezarae stopped the car, letting it idle. She watched in silence as he pulled on the coat and got out to head down the hill. Allowing him to face this alone, she sat in the car.

Jeb stood at the top of the embankment looking at the burnt remains of the vehicle he'd crashed. "I was lucky to survive," he said to no one in particular.

Making his way cautiously down to the bottom, he walked to stand beside the crushed metal. He looked for anything that might give him a clue to his past. There was nothing he could see.

His mind wasn't jarred by this at all. None of it was familiar to him. Of course there wasn't much left except the car's frame, anyway. Then, coupled with the new snow that had fallen, he knew there wasn't going to be anything for him to find.

Disappointment and frustration welled up inside him. *Will I never know who I am?* Seconds before he yelled in aggravation, a gentle sound reached him.

"You okay?" Dezarae had joined him. Her dark eyes were full of compassion as she looked at him. One gloved hand reached out to rest on his arm.

Jeb couldn't begin to describe the feeling that filled him at hearing her soft voice. "I still can't remember," he answered, pulling her closer to wrap his arms around her.

Dezarae relaxed against his chest. Together they stood there and looked over the remains. After a bit, she patted one of the strong arms around her. "We should get going."

"Thank you," he whispered.

"Let's get going, Johnny Reb," Dezarae said, removing herself from his embrace.

"Right behind you, Firebird. I'm right behind you." Taking the time for one more look over the wreckage, the dark brown–haired man turned to scramble up the hill after his savior.

"How long before we get to town?" he asked once they had begun driving again.

"Once we get to the main road, about ten minutes. If they cleared it." She took a sip of her coffee. "Dale may have some information for you when we get there."

"Okay," he replied in a monotone voice.

Dezarae looked at him in surprise. "Don't you want to know?"

"What if who I am isn't good?"

"Then you change," she said matter-of-factly. Reaching across the car, she patted his hard thigh. "I don't believe you are a bad person."

"But you did," Jeb said placing his callused hand over her softer one to keep it where it was.

"And I was wrong," she insisted.

"How can you be so sure?"

"Because, Johnny Reb, if you were truly a bad person, whether you lost your memory or not, you will still be bad. Evil that is learned can be forgotten, but those who are truly evil always will be." Dezarae pulled her hand free. "I don't think you are evil."

"Why do you still call me Johnny Reb?"

She shrugged. "Don't know. Does it bother you?"

"I guess not." He admitted looking back out the window. *It bothers me you may still think of me as something bad from the South.*

*

"I can't believe this weather," the man swore. "Choppers can't fly and the damn roads are closed."

"Calm down, Cade. We're going anyway. A satellite image shows a break in the system, and we're taking it," another teammate said.

"I just don't like it, Maverick. Not at all."

"None of us do man, none of us do," Maverick responded.

"I know."

"How's the wife?" Maverick asked, trying to lighten the mood.

"Jayde's fine," the man's voice softened. "She wants to know when you're getting hitched."

Maverick just shook his head. It wasn't like he was the only single man in the team, either. For some reason, though, they were all after him to get married.

"It's gonna take one hell of a storm to get me to the altar, Cade. I would marry Jayde or Alexis but—"

"We'd kill you." A deep voice joined the conversation. The leader of Megalodon Team walked in and glared at Maverick.

"See, Harrier," Maverick said, not at all threatened by the intimidating presence of the man there. "You and Cade have the good women."

The two happily married men glanced at each other and grinned. Harrier spoke. "I can't wait to meet the storm that gets you there."

Rolling his eyes in exasperation, Maverick teased, "Hold your breath, man, *please* hold your breath."

**

Dezarae parked in front of the police station. "Come on," she said, climbing out. "Good work, old man," she said to the vehicle as they left it.

Jeb followed. Shadyville wasn't as small as he had believed it was going to be, but it wasn't exactly a huge metropolis. He walked behind her into the building.

"Sheriff," she called out as soon as she opened the door. "Are you here?"

A tall handsome man popped out from around the corner. As his eyes landed on Dezarae, he gave her a huge smile. "Hey, Dez."

She smiled easily at the man. "Hello, Shawn. Where's Dale?"

"He's at the diner getting coffee." He nodded towards the man behind her. "Who's that?"

"This is Jeb. The man from the accident."

Jeb had been watching the man who had asked *his* firebird for her hand in marriage. The second Dezarae had said his name, Jeb disliked him. He had become surprisingly possessive of her in the little time he had known her.

The man was handsome. He was tall, not as tall as Jeb himself, but still tall. He had a thick head of light-brown hair, blue eyes, and a moustache that was neatly trimmed. Within seconds, Jeb knew that he could beat him in a fight; where he knew that from he couldn't say.

The way Shawn kept his blue eyes on Dezarae aroused Ross's protectiveness even more. Still, he stepped forward and offered his hand after Dezarae gave his name. "Hello," he said.

"Hey, man," Shawn said easily, shaking the hand.

The door opened behind Shawn, sending a wave of cold air over them all. It was the sheriff. "Dez," his loud voice boomed. "How you doing, girl?"

"Fine, Dale, fine." She walked over to him and hugged him affectionately.

"Well, come on back." He speared Jeb with a glare. "You, too, boy."

Boy? Boy?! Jeb barely controlled his tongue, but at Dezarae's look he remained silent and followed them. Neither of the other men there missed the exchange.

Shawn stayed up front as the trio went into the sheriff's office.

"Shut the door," Dale ordered as he sat behind his large desk.

Dezarae complied and, when she turned back around, she saw that Jeb still stood. He sat after she had taken her seat.

"So," Dale said, sipping his coffee. "You don't know who you are, then." Eyes the same shade as Shawn's stared at Jeb directly.

"No, sir, I do not. The name Jeb is familiar but nothing more than that."

"Well, I have been checking with missing persons and, as of yet, there is nothing that fits your description." His gaze ran over Jeb. "And I see that Dez gave a very accurate description of you."

Jeb knew she was blushing for she began to fidget in her chair. "I don't mean her any harm," he blurted out.

"If you weren't trustworthy then she wouldn't have let you stay," Dale said dismissively. "She is a good judge of character and I tend to forget that in my overbearing fathering of her." He gestured to a photo on the wall. "That is her father and I. We had been the best of friends forever. Dezarae is my godchild. So I am naturally overprotective."

Jeb looked at Dezarae and was immediately taken in again by her dark beauty. "I can understand that." Since he was looking at Dezarae, Jeb was oblivious to the look Dale sent them. However, when the sheriff cleared his throat, Jeb placed his attention on the older man.

"Got some messages for you, Dez." Dale sat forward and handed her a stack of papers.

"Oh, thanks, Dale." She took them and immediately flipped through them. "Wow, can I use your phone?"

"Of course. You know where it is." He waved toward the direction of the phone.

Without glancing at Jeb, she left the room, shutting the door on the two men.

"Now that she is gone, what in the hell are your intentions towards her?" Dale snapped, leaning forward and pinning Jeb with a glare that should have scared him.

"My intentions? I didn't know I had intentions toward her." *I am such a liar. I just had my hand in her pants this morning and my tongue in her mouth. God willing, I will be doing it again.*

"Are you after her business?"

"No." He shook his head. "Not at all." *Her heart, yes.*

"I won't let you hurt her." The voice grew full of malice.

"I have no intentions of hurting her."

"See that you keep those intentions."

"I will." *You had better believe I will keep them.*

"Good. Now get!" Dale jerked his head to the door.

"Yes, sir." Jeb rose and strode to the door, leaving as silently as he had entered. He walked up the hall and found Shawn and Dezarae talking and laughing amongst themselves. Their heads were bent in close to one another, presenting a total picture of compatibility. Jeb hated it. Hated how intimate they appeared, how that man got her to smile like that. Hated everything it had the potential to mean.

Jeb's anger grew at the thought of her married to that pussyboy. His firebird needed someone strong who could release the passion she tried to hide from the rest of the world. Dezarae Phoenix Kerry needed *him*.

Striding closer, he cleared his throat. If he had been expecting them to spring apart he was mistaken for they barely noticed him, just continued to giggle together over a private joke.

Dezarae turned her head and smiled gently. "Ready?" she asked as she patted Shawn on the arm.

Jeb stopped. "For what?"

"Well, I have to go to the store and pick up some things. I figured you would want to get some different clothes." Her sinful eyes stared straight at him. "Then we need to head back; I have to get to work on some cars. The owner of the Martins is coming for the hardtop so I want to make sure it is spotless."

"I'm staying with you?" he asked her.

A flash of embarrassment crossed her face. "I'm sorry; I just assumed you would be. There is a hotel here in town if you would feel better there—"

"No! No. I would love to stay with you." *In the same bed would be best.* "Let's go, then." His anger had disappeared as fast as it came. She hadn't forgotten about him after all.

"Okay." Putting her attention on the man beside her, she leaned down, kissed his cheek, and whispered something in his ear. He smiled and kissed her back before walking off. "Let's go then, Johnny Reb," she said to the man she was taking home with her. "Bye, Sheriff!" Dezarae yelled as she headed for the door.

*
**

"That was good," Dezarae groaned as she put her fork down. "I ate too much."

Jeb smiled. After shopping she had wanted to grab a bite to eat. "I don't think you eat enough," he told her.

"Oh, trust me, I need to cut back. I'm getting fat," she said.

"If you say so, but I don't see it."

"That's because it's winter and I can get away with wearing big clothes." She drained the rest of her coffee. "It's the coffee. I drink too much. That and I eat too much." Dezarae laughed. "Who cares? Who the hell do I have to impress?"

"I'm very impressed, Firebird. Very." His tone flowed like a double malt liqueur over her skin.

"Well, thank you." She winked at him before leaning back in the booth.

This man had gotten under her skin. While they'd shopped, she had noticed other women from town doing double-takes as they saw him, especially when he was trying on jeans. He had insisted that she come with him. It had never mattered how beautiful the woman was who'd tried to get his attention. He had stayed focused on her, making her feel like the only one for him.

Now, as they sat in the diner, he was once again the object of many stares. Yet still he paid attention only to her. It was an amazing feeling. This man was special and Dezarae knew somewhere someone had to be missing him.

"Ready to go?" she asked, putting money down on the table to cover the bill.

"I hate that you have been paying for everything for me."

"I believe the response is 'yes' or 'no' there," she admonished.

"Yes, ma'am, I'm ready to go." He grabbed her hand and held it until she met his gaze. "And thank you for taking such good care of me."

"Hey, I just stopped and picked you up. You were lucky you weren't seriously injured."

"You are right about that. But I actually was talking about today. For all you got me: the clothes, razors, everything."

"Don't worry about it. I'll work it out of you." Dezarae blurted before she could take into account how her words might sound.

Those gray eyes deepened. "I truly hope you do."

Her body a trembling mass of nerves, she slid out of the booth and was shocked again when he held her coat for her. "Thank you," she muttered.

"Most welcome."

They left with many eyes watching them. It was odd to see Dezarae acting so free with a complete stranger.

$\mathcal{E}ight$

"So when is he arriving here?" Jeb asked the pair of disembodied legs sticking out from underneath the Aston Martin.

Bending her legs at the knees, Dezarae had no idea of the raw lust on his face. "Tomorrow. He is flying a chopper in that is going to carry the car back in a box so it is protected from the elements. He lives in Southern California." She rolled herself out from under the car, grease streaks on her face and looking so adorable.

Standing, she jerked her head towards the car. "Get in and start her up for me, will you? You don't have grease on you."

Not having to be told twice, Jeb slid behind the wheel of the car and turned her over. The car purred to life.

"Hit the lights for me," she ordered. He did and she checked front and back. "Turning signals." Same thing. "Brakes and hazards." He did. "Let it run for a minute, okay? I'll be right back."

Jeb was happy to remain where he was, watching her progress from the rear and side-view mirrors until she came back. "What now?" he asked her.

Still wiping her hands on a rag, she said, "Shut the car off." He did. "We are going down, hang on." She pushed a button and the floor began to drop.

In shock, he sat still in the car as they were lowered to what looked like an indoor racetrack. "What the hell…?"

Dezarae looked in at him. "Look at me. Can you really drive a stick?"

"Yes." His hand gestured around the underground structure. "What is this place?"

"A place for us to make sure the cars run without putting them on the asphalt and getting road grime on them. Or, like this time of the year, when we can't take them out. Daddy had this as long as I could remember but I added some things of my own. Okay, Johnny Reb, this is your chance. Drive it around a few times while I get cleaned up." Her eyes grew serious. "Don't do anything fancy."

"Serious? I can drive it?" His eyes were wide.

"Sure, do a few laps. Go ahead." Dezarae smiled as he turned on the car and carefully drove it off the platform and onto the track.

She cleaned up as he drove around. Finally ready, she waved him in. "What did you think?"

"I think I'm in love," he muttered.

"It is a nice car. Come on, I have to test it out, make sure it runs right," Dezarae said.

Reluctantly, Jeb got out of the car and watched as she slid her body behind the wheel and shut the door. Turning towards him, she said, "Well, come on. Get in."

Eagerly, he climbed back in the car, although this time he was on the passenger side. But still it was good enough for him.

"Hang on, Johnny Reb," she said as she tore off.

Four hours later, they were draping a cover over the spotless, detailed, cobalt-blue vehicle. "Thanks for your help," Dezarae said as she made sure the alarms on the doors were primed before bundling up.

"You have one hell of a setup here. It's amazing," Jeb said in awe. "And you are welcome. Thanks for letting me drive that car."

"No prob. Just, if David asks, you didn't."

"David?" he asked as he slid on his thick coat.

"The man who owns the car."

"I see." *Jesus, don't you deal with any women?*

She opened the door and waited for him to leave before she set the alarm. The night was clear and as they walked towards the house. Jeb walked behind her and stopped as a chill ran over his body. They were being watched.

"What's the matter?" Dezarae asked.

"Go inside," he ordered in a tone that brooked no argument.

Without saying a word, Dezarae headed in, Jeb close on her heels. Inside the door, she found herself alone; he had disappeared.

"What the hell?" she asked the solitude of her home. The deadness in his gaze had frozen her blood.

Hanging up her jacket, she walked to the kitchen and began to prepare dinner. Her movements were restless until she heard her door open again. Moments later, his large body filled the doorway to her kitchen.

"What was that all about?" Dezarae ran her eyes over him as she looked her fill of his muscular body. It seemed that every time she saw him he grew more handsome. He wore some of his new clothes, a black turtleneck and a sinfully tight pair of blue jeans. With the five o'clock shadow that graced his face, he looked good enough to eat. *I bet he would look good enough to eat if he wore a burlap sack.*

"You gonna answer me, Johnny Reb, or just stand there?" Dezarae asked when all he did was stare, the heat in his eyes apparent even to her.

"Thought I'd just stand here and watch you in those tight jeans, what do you think about that?" he teased.

"I think you should get over here and help make dinner. You can make the salad," she tossed back, turning away from his powerful gaze.

"Yes, ma'am." Sure strides took him up to the counter next to her where he ran his hand lovingly over her firm ass. "If you're sure."

Her hands trembled as she chopped up vegetables for the soup. "Get to work."

"You're the boss." He reached around her and grabbed the bowl before settling himself next to her at the counter and beginning to wash the lettuce.

I'd like to be, she thought to herself.

After a hearty dinner, the pair of them returned to the living area to do some reading.

"I'm going to go outside for a bit just to walk around." Jeb announced.

"Okay," Dezarae said, barely looking up from her book.

"Be back soon," he said as his tall body slipped out the back door.

Seconds after she heard the door close, she shut her book. "What the hell is going on with him?" He was acting strange and it scared her. It was as if after coming back from her shop someone had flipped a switch, leaving her with a person who looked like the man she had picked up, but with an edge.

She jumped when her phone rang. Picking it up, she said, "Hello?"

"Hey, girl, how are you?"

"Lateef," she said as she cuddled up on the couch, grabbing her stuffed Corvette and holding it close to her as she smiled. Lateef was a long-time friend and owner of the '66 Toronado she had in her shop. "What's going on, man?"

"I missed you. I miss you," he answered with his deep voice.

"I miss you too, Lateef." She closed her eyes as she pictured him. Tall like her guest and dipped in dark chocolate, he was everything she could ever want in a man, or so she would have thought before she met Jeb. Lateef was a man's man and he knew how to treat a woman. But when her eyes closed at night it was a gray-eyed, tanned, brown-haired man who swam before her. "What are you calling for? What's up?"

"Well, I heard you were having one hell of a storm up there and wanted to make sure you were okay. Couldn't get through the other day; they said the lines were down. How are you doing?" Lateef asked.

"You know me," she said.

"Yes, which is why I am asking. How are you?"

"I'm doing fine, Lateef. I'm fine. We got dumped on but with all those generators I hardly noticed." *I almost slept with a man that came from the storm but, hey.* "How are you?"

"I'm doing well. I have another car for you if you want, and if you have any room."

This perked her up. Another car. "Wow, what is it? Whose is it?"

He chuckled. "We'll get to that. Tell me about you right now. Fill me in."

Covering herself with a blanket, she answered him. "Well, I just got finished with the hardtop Aston. David is coming to get it tomorrow. You should see it; it purrs like a kitten."

"I bet it does. Turn down any more marriage proposals?"

She laughed. "Yes, Shawn asked me again. I don't know why he keeps asking when my answer is never going to change."

"Because he is in love with you. Not that I blame him," Lateef said.

"I don't think I will ever get married, not unless the right man just appears in front of me." A throat cleared, making her look up into the smoky gaze of her guest. Running her eyes up and down his fine body, she continued to talk to the man on the other end of the phone. "What are the chances of that happening to me?"

"Up there? Slim to none. Which is why you need to come visit me here in Cali. Get away from that state, go to some civilization," he said.

"I don't have time for a vacation, you know that. Come on, La-teef, you know me." She closed her eyes on the disapproving stare from Jeb. "Now tell me about this car."

Lateef sighed. "Fine, I know when to stop beating a dead horse. It's a 1966 Lamborghini Miura."

Sitting up, she blinked a few times. "Are you serious?"

"Dead. The man saw some of the pics you sent me of that last show you did and asked me to get in touch for him. I will give you his number and you can contact him. A word of warning, he is a bit...um...rough around the edges."

"Meaning what...he is a rude man? An old curmudgeon?"

"Meaning he is different. Maybe eccentric would be a good word."

"But I can trust him?" Dezarae wondered.

"Yes, I just don't want you put off by his callous attitude. He will not be easy to talk to. You will have to watch your tongue," Lateef warned.

"Me?" she cried. "How come I am the one who is going to have to watch her tongue?" Laughter filled the line. "I know, because I am the temperamental one. Okay, Lateef, I will call him in the morning. Thanks, man."

"You know I love you, darling," he said.

"I love you, too, Lateef. Are you going to be at the show?"

"I haven't missed one yet. And I don't plan on starting."

"Then I will see you there." She paused and added. "I miss you. Take care."

"Always do, darling, always do. Love you." Then he was gone.

"Love you too," she whispered to the dial tone and hung up.

Jeb had done a perimeter check of her house and shop. His motions had been instinctive for him. Whoever had been watching them was no longer there, he'd been sure, but still didn't like the situation, though.

When he'd walked back into her house, he'd heard Dezarae talking to someone on the phone. The thought of her marrying anyone made him sick. He was the one for her just like she was the one for him.

Her affection for the man on the other end had obvious and it had eaten at his gut, even though he knew he had no claim over this woman, for he didn't even know if he were married. None of that mattered; he wanted her, and for longer than one night. Much, much longer than that.

Sitting down in a chair, he'd waited for her to finish her call. His eyes had roamed freely over her body as she'd lain on the couch, snuggled up to a stuffed Corvette and covered by a blanket. He'd watched as her enthusiasm grew at the discussion of a new car for her to work on.

He'd stayed silent until she hung up the phone and put her profound gaze on him. "Friend of yours?" he asked.

Stretching back on the couch, Dezarae smiled. "Yes. Lateef is a very good friend."

"How good?" Jeb's tone was deceptively patient.

Staring at him from under lowered lashes, she answered him. "The best kind of friend a girl can have."

"What exactly does that mean?" His question came as his hands gripped the arms of the chair.

"It means that he is the best thing I have my life," she replied, remaining deliberately obtuse.

"We will see," he promised in a low voice.

"Did you get whatever you needed to out of your system on your walk?" Dezarae changed the subject.

"For now." He stretched his long muscular legs out in front of him. "When's bed?"

She visibly swallowed. "You can go whenever you want. I'm taking the couch."

He shook his head. "I'm not going to let you give up your bed for me." *That and I put some traps around your bedroom window so I know you will be safe there. I will be between you and the door.*

"I fit on the couch. You don't," she insisted.

"Listen to me. You are sleeping in that bed tonight. With or without me but you aren't sleeping on the couch." There was no room for compromise in his tone.

Sitting up, she tossed off the blanket. "What the hell is going on here?" She pointed one finger at him. "You have been acting different since we got back from the shop."

"Nothing," he lied.

Leaving the couch, she walked over to where he sat in her chair and poked him in the chest. "Bullshit! What is going on?" Dezarae had her face right in his.

Inhaling deeply, Jeb found himself surrounded by the subtle smell of Dezarae; it was the smell of sweet peas. He had noticed her soap and shampoo while taking his shower. His gaze raked over her body. The color of his eyes intensified as they filled with desire.

"You smell so good," he groaned before he pulled her onto his lap and kissed her.

Dezarae straddled his lap and began to rock against his hard erection as she kissed him back with all she had. Fingers winding in her hair, Jeb pulled her back from his mouth and said, "You…you could make a monk give up his vow."

"I don't want a monk, I want you," her honest admission fell.

"What about my past?" he asked.

Dropping her head to rest against his, she swore, "You're right. I can't do this. Not without knowing." Dezarae began to leave his lap but he cradled her in it.

"Just let me hold you at least, Firebird. Let me at least hold you," he murmured into her hair.

Nine

A dark van pulled up to the house. The two men getting out were impressive sights. Both were tall, but one was dark-haired, possibly Native American from his coloring, and the other was a tanned Caucasian with brown hair.

Unknown to the curvaceous black woman walking down the steps from the house to meet them, there were five more members of the Megalodon Team surrounding her home and shop. Those men were cold, uncomfortable, and, yet, completely in their element. "Can I help you gentlemen?" she asked as she hit the ground and approached them.

Dezarae looked over the men before her; there was something about their stance and presence that seemed familiar to her. They were both large and imposing. But she hadn't survived and become so successful in this world by being intimidated by men, so she waited for an answer.

The men looked at her. Dezarae's gaze was direct as she met each of theirs. "We are looking for a friend of ours. His name's Ross, Ross Connelly," the lean white man said.

"Sorry," Dezarae said shaking her head. "I don't know anyone by that name. Did you ask around in town?"

Two sets of eyes narrowed as they watched her face. The same man spoke again, "Are you sure?"

Readjusting her leather gloves, Dezarae arched both brows. "Yes, I'm sure. I'm not an idiot. Excuse me. I have some work to do." She got two steps past them when the dark-haired man grabbed her arm. "Hey!" she shouted, trying unsuccessfully to get away. "Let me go!"

"Don't jerk us around, lady." This man's tone was much more menacing than the other one. His fingers dug into the tender flesh of her arm, even through the thick coat she wore.

"Look, I don't know anyone named Ross." She pulled futilely on her arm. "Unless…unless you mean—"

"Let her go, or I kill your friend," Jeb's deep Southern voice rang loud across the yard.

"Him," Dezarae finished quietly.

Jeb was moving towards them, holding another man hostage. "Ross!" Both men by Dezarae exclaimed. "Ghost?" the white man asked the hostage.

"Fine, Cade, he doesn't know who we are," the man said in an emotionless voice.

"Shut up!" Jeb hissed, pressing the knife closer yet to the exposed throat. "I said, let her go!"

When the light from the sun glinted off the knife, Dezarae realized this was no trick on Jeb's part, he really meant what he said. "Let me go," she ordered. "He thinks you want to hurt me." The man dropped her arm and she ran towards Jeb at the same moment four more men with guns materialized out of the snow.

"Let him go," Dezarae commanded as she slid to a stop before her stranger. "Let him go," she reiterated when he ignored her.

Gray eyes were unyielding as the other men moved in closer. "He could have hurt you."

"He didn't. Listen to me," she pled. "Let him go. Hey," Dezarae reached for his face and touched it. "You have to let him go now. Come on, Johnny Reb, let him go. They don't want to hurt me. I think they are here for you."

Jeb shoved the man away from him only to haul Dezarae in close with the same motion. "Are you okay?" he murmured, stroking her face before his gaze hardened as he watched the group of men getting closer.

"I'm fine," she responded, immediately noticing how much safer she felt in his arms.

The seven men exchanged glances. Clearly they had come in expecting to have to save their teammate only to find he didn't know them from Adam.

"What's going on here?" a large blond man asked.

Dezarae stopped Jeb from trying to put himself in front of her. "Do you know him?" she asked the men although focusing on the blond who had spoken.

"Yes, ma'am," that same man answered. "His name is Ross Connelly. He is a Petty Officer in the United States Navy."

Looking to the man beside her, she asked, "Does any of that seem familiar to you? Do any of them?"

"He does." One finger pointed at the lone black man in the group. Jeb frowned and bent his head, wincing and cradling his left temple.

"What is going on here?" the same blond man asked again, he seemed to be the spokesman for the group.

"I think we'd all better go inside." Dezarae said with a frown. Immediately eight men looked suspicious and she held up her hands. "Look, I don't have much time before I have some business to conduct so can we get inside where it is warmer? And I can fill you in on what I know. Please." Latching her hand into Jeb's coat, she dragged him up the steps and inside the small house, leaving the other men to follow.

One by one they entered her house and walked into her living room, which seemed miniscule with all their larger bodies and guns in it. "Please have a seat." She gestured to the open seats as Jeb sat in her overstuffed chair and tugged her down onto his lap, wrapping his arms around her.

"The explanation, please," the blond giant said, leaning forward to rest his large arms on his thighs, his amazing blue eyes reading the situation.

"A few nights ago, I came upon a car that had gone off the road," Dezarae began, ignoring the tightening of Jeb's arms around her. "I found him not too far from the burning car. I brought him here and when he came to, he couldn't remember his name. We got to the point where he said Jeb was familiar, but that is it. Oh, and something about a woman named Charmane is familiar."

"And that's it?" the man asked, frowning as the sound of a chopper closing in became louder.

"That's it. Look, what was left of that car is that mangled mess you had to pass to get up here. He is lucky to be alive. I didn't see any identification and the sheriff has been checking the missing persons for a man matching his description."

Before Dezarae could say anything else, the radio at her side crackled. "Excuse me." She jumped off Jeb's lap and answered the radio. "That you, David?"

"Sure is, darling. You ready?"

"I'm on my way now. You know where to set her down. The area has been plowed. I'll be there to unhook the cable." Glancing at the men in her living room, Dezarae shook her head; this was a strange day. "Make yourselves at home. I have to do some business. Excuse me." Slipping on her coat, she was gone, jogging across the snow toward the large metal building.

Jeb immediately rose to follow and the men let him go. They would get to the bottom of this but that small woman seemed to have a calming presence on him and they wanted and needed that. Eight men walked outside of her house and watched as a helicopter flew into view, carrying a large container beneath it.

"A little more, Charlie. A little more. Great, right there." Dezarae was talking into the headset she wore. As soon as the container hit the ground she scrambled up the ladder on the side and headed for the two latches that attached it to the chopper. On the ground, Jeb swore and headed towards her at a run. "Got it, Charlie, take 'er up," Dezarae yelled.

The chopper lifted higher and the cables were retracted as Jeb reached the container. "What the hell are you doing? Get down from there!" Jeb demanded.

Sliding down quickly, Dezarae brushed past Jeb and headed for the chopper that landed in another plowed area. Two men got out of the bird and waved at Dezarae, who hugged each of them.

"Hey, guys. Charlie, great to see you. David, ready?"

"I have been waiting for this day for a long time now," David replied. He was a stocky man with a dark complexion and beautiful brown eyes.

"Well, she's ready for you." Side by side the two walked over towards the building and entered through a small door while the pilot opened the end of the container. Seconds later, a large metal door rose and everyone there got to see Dezarae pull the cover off that cobalt-blue car.

Ten male mouths fell open. Even Jeb, who had seen it before, was still amazed. David walked all around it in awe. "Dez, she's gorgeous."

Dezarae smiled. "She runs like a dream."

The man seemed almost hesitant to touch his car. But he did and a grin crossed his face as he shook his head and hugged her. "You're amazing. Your daddy would be so proud."

"Thanks." She held out the keys to him. "Here you are. Load her up."

David climbed behind the wheel and turned over the engine, stroking the shifter as she purred to life beneath him. Slowly he drove her on the slats into the container where he, Charlie, and Dezarae secured the car in place after covering her back up.

As they shut and locked the container the two looked at her and smiled. "I can't wait to take her out on those roads. How does she handle?" David asked.

"Like a dream," Dezarae said again.

"What kind of dream?" Dark brows arched.

"A wet dream. You are going to fall in love all over again," Dezarae said with a laugh. "Oh, one thing. Whatever kind of gas you were using...don't. It was leaving deposits in the injectors. It was slowing her down."

"What would I do without you?" He kissed her cheek. "Money's in your account."

"Thanks, David. Hey, Charlie, don't I get another hug before you go flying out of here?" she yelled to the man just about to get back in the chopper. He ran over to her, hugged and kissed her before dashing back and climbing in behind the controls. "Go on, David, I'll secure her. You get in."

"Love ya, babe," he yelled over the noise of the helicopter.

Dezarae waved and climbed back on the container. Talking into her headset she directed Charlie where to go so she could reattach the cables. Climbing down with ease, she waved as the chopper slowly disappeared from sight, carrying with it the precious cargo of one cobalt-blue 1965 Aston Martin. Then she went inside the shop and shut the outer bay door, coming out the small side one.

The men's shocked expressions greeted her when Dezarae returned. With a heavy sigh, she smiled at the men who had come to take Jeb—Ross—away. "Let's go back inside, gentlemen."

This time Dezarae elected to sit in a chair alone, but her stranger stood behind her. Protecting her. "So, what are you all then, some kind of unit?"

"A SEAL Team, ma'am," the huge blond said.

"SEALs, I've heard of them. Some of the best, right?" Dezarae asked. "Look, maybe I should let you all talk alone. I have some paperwork to do." She stood and looked at Jeb. "There's the cobbler if anyone wants to eat. And coffee, you know where everything is." Dezarae slipped away to her office and shut the door.

Jeb took the seat she had left and cast his gray eyes over the group. His head was really beginning to hurt. The amount of images that flashed before him had increased tenfold, as had names. He didn't say a word until he got to the black man sitting on the couch. "Hondo?" The question came as he cocked his head to the side.

"Aye, it's me, Jeb." the man answered with an easy smile. "When I told you to get me a vintage Jaguar, I didn't mean for you to go about it this way."

"How did you find me?" Jeb asked, although he was pretty sure he knew the answer and his headache was getting worse.

"Charmane. She called and said you never made it, never contacted her," Hondo said.

Big brown eyes filled Jeb's mind's eye and the pain in his head exploded in a fiery ball. Grunting in pain, he clamped his hands over his temples and bent forward over his knees. Jeb felt like he was going to be sick.

"Ross, Ross! You okay?" the man closest to him asked.

Wincing from the pain as it receded; he touched the arm of the man next to him. "I'm fine, Ernst, fine. Hey, man, sorry about earlier with the whole knife thing." he answered in a faint slur.

"Meaning?" another member asked.

Gray eyes looked around at the now-familiar faces of his family, his Team. "Meaning, Osten, I can recognize each and every one of your ugly mugs."

"Hoo-yah!" the remaining men exclaimed together.

"I have to get to a phone and call Charmane," Ross said as he smiled at his teammates. Then the smile faltered as he realized he was going to be leaving Dezarae. *At least I'm not married.*

"So, tell us about this woman who saved your keister," Harrier said as he stood up and walked toward the kitchen. "I believe she said something about cobbler and coffee. I don't know about some of you, but my ass is still cold from lying in that snow."

Ross made coffee for them all, totally oblivious to the knowing looks he was receiving. He had just joined the Team when they had gone to Belize to rescue Cade and his wife, Jayde. He remembered looking strangely at the SEAL when he had made her a plate for breakfast and now he was utilizing Dezarae's kitchen as if he had every right to do so.

"Well?" Harrier asked as he ate a bite of the peach cobbler. "What's she like?"

Gray eyes narrowed. "Dezarae is the most amazing woman I have ever met. And if you weren't so in love with Lex, I think I would be offended."

Harrier smiled. "She is very beautiful."

"Harrier..." the warning growl came, to which Harrier just held up his hands. "Dezarae is the owner of *Phoenix Restorations and Rebuilds*. It was her daddy's business and she took it over when he died," Ross explained.

"Jesus, that is this place?" Aidrian asked.

"It sure is, Hondo," Ross said with a smile. He knew how much the ensign wanted an older-model Jaguar. "She is working on three more cars plus her own Shelby Mustang. Maybe she will show them to you."

"Do you think she would mind?" the Irish-sounding black man asked.

"I'll ask her," Ross said.

Ten

"Oh, excuse me," Dezarae's voice fell gently over the eight men in her kitchen. "I just needed to grab something."

All the men looked at her and smiled. "This is wonderful cobbler, ma'am," one of the men said. She smiled in response.

Ross moved to intercept her; his granite eyes searched her face. "Dez?" he questioned as his hand settled on her arm, halting her.

The second his hand touched her, the rest of the room faded into nothingness. He was the only thing she saw. The warmth she got from his gaze, the way it seemed to search into her soul for answers that were only for him, made her flush. With a shuddering breath, she removed his hand and asked him, "What?"

"Are you okay?"

"Why wouldn't I be, Johnny Reb? Of course I am." She made sure there were no tears as she stepped around him and walked to the fridge. "You are welcome to use my phone if you want to call Charmane," Dezarae said as she left the kitchen and walked back to her office.

"We need to get going, Ross. Make your call if you are going to, but there is another system coming and we need to beat it out," Harrier said after a moment of silence.

"She thinks Charmane is my wife," Ross explained as he walked to her phone.

"Why does she call you Johnny Reb?" Hondo asked.

"She saw the rebel flag on my chest under the anchor and chain," he answered as he dialed Charmane's number.

The call hadn't gone the way he had wanted at all. Hanging up the phone, Ross was livid. "Let me just see if Dezarae will show y'all the cars then we can go." His steps were angry as he strode to her office.

A knock on the door surprised her. Dezarae was curled up on her chaise reading about her Mustang. "It's open, come on in," she said quietly.

"Hey, beautiful." Those words reached her before the man saying them had entered fully.

"What do you need?" she asked without looking up, afraid her face might give away her true feelings.

One lean hand plucked the book out of her grasp and laid it to the side, his handsome face filling the spot where her book had been. "I need you to listen to me." He touched her cheek and frowned as she pulled away.

"What about. You're leaving, right?" Dezarae asked.

"Yes, I'm leaving. I have to go." He looked at her full mouth and remembered how it felt against his. "The men would like to know if they could see the cars you are working on."

"Of course. Just let me grab my coat." *What the hell did you expect, Dez? Him to say he didn't love Charmane?* She moved off the chaise and slipped by him before he could say anything else.

Walking up to where the men were by the door, Dezarae said, "My Shelby is in through there. You can go look at him and I will get my coat on and take you to the shop."

"Thanks, Dezarae," that blond man said again. They all filed out into her garage and as the door closed, she could hear the impressed *ooohs* and *ahhhs* from them.

"You're welcome," she whispered as she grabbed her coat, only to have it yanked away from her. Jeb…no, his name was Ross. "What are you doing?" she asked.

"I need to tell you about Charmane," he stated.

"I don't require any explanations from you."

Dropping her coat on the floor, he jerked her smaller body up against his hard one. "I want to tell you about her," he insisted.

Closing her eyes against his masculine scent, she just nodded. "Go ahead then."

"Charmane is—" He was cut off by the door opening and the men filing back in, all of them looked away from the way he was holding her flush to his body.

"I'm ready when you are, gentlemen," Dezarae forced out as she removed herself from Ross's arms.

One hour later she was saying goodbye to the seven members of the SEAL team who had come on a rescue mission for one of their own. They had all climbed in the van and were waiting for her and Ross to say their goodbyes.

Ross took a deep breath and ran his eyes over her body one last time, as if committing every curve to memory. "I don't really know what to say to you at a time like this," he said in a low voice.

"I believe the word you are looking for is 'goodbye,'" she joked.

"I don't want to say goodbye to you." One hand reached out toward her face, only to drop and grab her coat at the last second to pull her in close. With a deep breath he inhaled her subtle scent.

"Come on, Johnny Reb, you have a van full of men waiting on you. Say it and get outta here." Dezarae rested her head against the hard planes of his chest. *I feel so safe in his embrace.*

"Thank you for everything you did for me, Dezarae Phoenix Kerry," he whispered as he hugged her closer. "I'm gonna miss you."

"Get outta here, Johnny Reb." She was fighting back tears.

"Say my name, once," he begged and he didn't care.

Pulling back so she could look up into his eyes she said, "Goodbye. Goodbye, Ross Connelly of the United States Navy. Take care of yourself out there." Dezarae took another step back.

Ross had dropped his arms from around her at the sound of her saying his name. As she stepped further away, however, he seized her again. One callused thumb pad wiped away the first tear that began to fall from her dark eyes. "Please don't cry," he pled. "You know that tears me up." His voice was so soothing.

"Go, you have to go."

"I know." Ross looked over his shoulder at the men waiting in the van before he put his slate eyes back to her. "I will be back."

"Sure you will." Dezarae took his hand off her exposed skin. "Take care." His eyes burned with a fire that made her feel sweat on the back of her neck.

Before she could blink, they were pressed so tightly together there was no light between them. His tongue plundered her mouth, sweeping in and out as he claimed her in front of God and his teammates. They were both breathless when he ripped his mouth away from hers. "I *will* be back. I don't lie, Firebird." He pledged his bond as his lips sealed it with one more fast kiss.

Then he was gone. And when her eyes finally opened, all she got to see was the red taillights from the van as it turned the corner, taking him out of her life.

$\mathcal{E}leven$

The snow was gone. Spring had arrived, bringing with it new life and colors to the world.

I will be back, Firebird. Dezarae heard those words everyday in her head. Each night when she closed her eyes, visions of the gray-eyed man who had come into her life for that brief time filled her dreams. A letter from him remained unopened on the table by her front door.

Dezarae would touch it, hold it, and even smell it as she smiled over his almost illegible scrawl. But she never opened it. She felt almost as if some kind of spell would break if she did.

This afternoon the sun was warm as it beat down. Knowing she had about three hours before it got chilly; her door was open to help circulate some fresh air into the house. Dezarae hung up the phone as she saw the sheriff's SUV pull up her driveway.

Stepping out onto the porch, she waited as he stopped and got out. "Hey, Sheriff. What's up?"

Dale returned the wave but remained uncharacteristically quiet as he walked around to the rear door on the passenger side and opened it. He escorted a person out of his vehicle and walked her up the steps.

Dezarae looked at the girl. She was slender with dark-brown hair and big brown eyes with a panda backpack over one shoulder. The girl had on thin cotton pants, a sleeveless shirt, and a pair of canvas shoes on her feet. Her eyes were very skeptical as she looked at Dezarae.

"Here you go, young lady," the sheriff said.

Glancing between the girl and the sheriff, Dezarae waited for one of them to explain. Neither did. The sheriff grinned at Dezarae and headed back to his Tahoe. "Later, Phoenix," he yelled before he left.

Arching a brow at the female before her, Dezarae waited. Still nothing. Running her hand over her mouth she said, "And you are?"

Tweezed brows rose as the child adopted a very snobbish attitude. "Not staying here," she commented as her narrowed eyes looked over the small home before her.

Ignoring that comment, Dezarae bit back her immediate response and calmly asked, "Who are you?"

"Charmane."

That name was like a punch to Dezarae's gut. Her fantasy man had a child. *Well, at least he wasn't married. Or was he?*

"You know who I am?" the teen asked.

"I've heard the name." Dezarae blinked. "What are you doing here?"

Brown eyes grew defensive. "Daddy said he trusted you, but mama said your kind was inferior to us." She shrugged, unaware of the shards of ice in Dezarae's eyes. "Daddy yelled at her and they fought again, which is why they aren't married. Anyway, Mama's new boyfriend says bad things about my daddy so I came here."

Your kind was inferior. Jesus. "You ran away," Dezarae stated. "Where's your father?"

"On a mission. Not that it matters. Mama doesn't like him associating with me. I may pick up some of his bad habits." The girl was fidgety.

"I see," Dezarae said. "But you won't stay here."

"Oh, no," she rushed to say, appalled. "This is not at all what I am accustomed to."

Hell, no! Adopting a very indifferent attitude, Dezarae shrugged. "Suit yourself." She turned around and walked back in her house. "Just be careful going back to town; it's a long walk." She closed the screen door behind her. "And I hope you walk fast. It will get cold here in about two hours. Not to mention the bears that are waking up from hibernation or the cougars that will think you are food, so be careful out there," Dezarae yelled through the screen as she walked back to her office to get some work done.

Two hours later, a cold wind had kicked up. Dezarae went about her business of making dinner. Another hour passed and as she pulled the macaroni and cheese out of the oven, she said in a loud voice, "You may as well come in and eat something. Unless you aren't hungry."

She smiled as she heard the screen door open. "Go ahead and shut the other door, it's cold enough," Dezarae added. Her guest closed the door carefully.

By the time the teen had entered the kitchen, dinner was on the table. Dezarae glanced at Charmane, inwardly smiling at the almost-defensive look on her face. The girl was trying to be so brave yet she was terrified.

"Grab a seat. You can leave your backpack in the living room," Dezarae said as she grabbed a pitcher of lemonade from the fridge.

The girl did as directed and perched on the edge of her chair like she was ready to bolt. "You were just going to let me leave?" Her eyes grew large as she accepted the loaded plate of food from Dezarae.

"I'm not in charge of you. If you want to leave, go ahead." Dezarae flicked her hand towards the door. "But if on the off chance you want to stay," she continued and shrugged, "that's fine, too."

Charmane didn't know what to make of this woman. Her daddy had spoken so highly of her, everything from her kindness to her cars, it was like he had put her on a pedestal.

She idolized her father and her mother hated that. Her mother took every opportunity to slander him in front of her, even going so far as to wish him dead.

Not Charmane. She wished she could see him more, be there when he came home. But there was no one to watch her, no one who wanted her.

Dezarae wasn't what she'd expected. Even though her daddy had said she was a black woman, Charmane was still a bit shocked.

She dropped her eyes to the plate of food in front of her. It smelled amazing and she was starving. With one quick glance at the woman who was already eating, Charmane picked up her fork and began her meal.

Dezarae held back a grin as Charmane started to eat. Not having much experience with kids, she was a bit out of her league.

It was not the kind of stress she needed added to her life right now. She had enough going on. Two cars were leaving tomorrow and she still had to detail one of them. Parts for the Lamborghini were coming in and she had to get the 'Stang finished for the upcoming show in California.

The sudden appearance of a runaway child didn't help. Rolling her eyes, Dezarae looked up from her supper to see Charmane scraping up every last bit of food on her plate. *I'm surprised she isn't licking the damn dish!* "If you're still hungry, there's plenty more so help yourself," Dezarae offered.

"Really?" the young girl asked.

"Yes, really," Dezarae said.

The child eagerly took more food and was soon stuffing her face quite happily.

"When did you eat last, Charmane?" Dezarae wondered as she refilled the girl's lemonade glass.

"Afternoon, the day before yesterday," she said as she ate more of the macaroni.

Sitting back in her chair, Dezarae just watched the child for a bit. "Why not since then?" she finally asked.

"I ran out of money on the bus," the girl said as she took a long drink of her lemonade.

The bus? "I see," Dezarae said, "and…that would be the bus you took to get here?"

Charmane nodded. "Right, but I didn't get off at the right place and ended up in Idaho so I had to come back and that is why my money ran out." Brown eyes looked across the table at her.

Running a hand over her face, Dezarae couldn't believe what she was hearing. "How did you get on the bus?"

"I bought a ticket at home, printed it out, and went to the station. When I was boarding, I waved at an old woman who waved back and I just told the man there that was my nanny seeing me off." She shrugged. "It was no big deal."

"Wow, well, I must say I'm impressed. That was smart." Dezarae stood up and took her plate to the sink, returning with two pieces of chocolate pie. "You know, though, that you have to call your mother." The child shook her head. "Don't shake your head no at me; you need to call your mother. I'm sure she is worried sick."

Charmane scowled. "My mama isn't at home. She and her boyfriend took another trip." She dug into the pie eagerly.

"So you what…ran away from your nanny?" Dezarae asked as she cut into her pie.

"Yep," Charmane said.

Jesus, this kid has balls. "Well, then, we are calling her," Dezarae instructed.

Those big eyes grew sorrowful. "It doesn't matter, nobody wants me around." She picked at the remaining crumbs of her pie. "Except my daddy."

"Why would you say that?" *Aside from the whole prima donna act I think you are adorable.* "I'm sure many people want you around."

Charmane shook her head. "No, they don't. And you don't want me to stay. I am just good to yell at and hi —" she stopped abruptly and clamped her mouth shut.

Dezarae sat forward in her chair. "Are you saying they hit you?"

Eyes wide with fear, the child shook her head back and forth furiously. "Just that they don't want me around."

Leaning back, Dezarae said, "You need to call your nanny. Go on, make the call." She gestured to the phone. Like a whipped puppy, Charmane walked over and picked up the receiver. "And I will want to talk to the nanny as well, Charmane," Dezarae added.

Thin shoulders slumped even more as she dialed a number. "It's ringing," her dejected tone fell.

Rising, Dezarae took the phone and waited. "What is your nanny's name?"

"Jamie Riley," the reluctant response came.

"Can I speak to Jamie Riley, please?" Dezarae said in her business-like tone when someone finally answered.

"Speaking," a nasally voice said. "Who is this?"

"My name is Dezarae Kerry. I am a…a friend of Ross Connelly and his daughter Charmane is with me."

The gasp was loud. "You have Charmane? Is she okay? Let me talk to her," Jamie ordered.

"I must say I am a bit concerned over the fact that you couldn't keep track of a child, especially Ross's child," Dezarae stated, ignoring the woman.

"That child is a menace, always getting into trouble. No one can keep an eye on her," the voice hissed, full of venom.

Dezarae tsked. "Now, that's not true. She has been here for about five hours now and I have always known where she was. And don't call her a menace."

"Let me talk to her," the woman yelled.

"I think it would be best if you told her mother, if you know where they went, that she will be staying…" Dezarae caught gaze of the young girl and gestured around her home, waiting until she got a smile and nod, "with me until her father comes home."

"You can't do that, that's kidnapping!" Jamie screeched.

"Kidnapping? No, she is free to leave if she wants. I wonder what Ross would think about the treatment his daughter gets," Dezarae threatened the woman. "Would you like to hear it from Charmane?"

"Yes, I would," the response came.

Holding out the phone towards the amazed girl, Dezarae said, "She wants to talk to you."

"Hello?" Charmane said as she took the phone. "I want to stay here with Dezarae. She wants me around; Mama doesn't care and you know it. Besides, now you can do what I know you do in her room when they are gone. I know all about it, Jamie. And you are going to be on our side when Mama comes home or I will make sure you lose your job."

Dezarae shook her head over the girl's attitude. Taking the phone when the child offered it back to her, she said into the receiver, "So it's settled, then. No, don't worry about it. I will send a message letting Ross know where she is. Goodbye." She hung up the phone. *Dear God, what have I done?*

"Why would you do that for me?" Charmane asked hesitantly after a moment.

"I have no idea," Dezarae admitted.

"So, you don't want me, either," the voice grew distant.

"Look, I just assumed responsibility for you, so those damn disappearing games you play, no more as of this second. Now, how do I get a message to your father and tell him where you are?"

Charmane got the information from her bag. "I could just go."

Dark eyes narrowed. "I don't think so. Look, I get that my home isn't what you are used to, but it is all you have unless you want me to call the sheriff and have him put you up until your father comes back. I'm sure a jail cell would be *loads* of fun for you."

The child's eyes grew big. "You wouldn't!"

"Yeah, I would," Dezarae assured her. "I have a lot to do. I have to detail a car tonight, which I can't do until after I get a message to your father, and I have to work on my car so I have it ready to go to the show in California, which I am apparently taking you to now. So I don't need to be worrying about whether or not you will run off. Time to drop your prima donna attitude and grow up. Choice is yours, but make it now." Dezarae crossed her arms over her chest and looked at the skinny child in her kitchen.

It took her less than five seconds to come to a decision. "I'll stay with you."

"Very well," Dezarae said as she looked at the sheet and made the call to leave a message with Ross Connelly.

"I am going to have to put you on the couch until I get a bed up in my office," Dezarae said when she finished leaving the message and walked with Charmane into the living room. "Are you tired now? Do you want to get some sleep?"

Charmane dragged her feet before she asked, "If I don't get in the way, could I maybe just stay with you while you work on the car?"

"Of course, but I think we need to get you warmer clothes. Did you pack anything heavier than that?" Dezarae asked.

"No," Charmane admitted. "I don't do much that requires warm clothes."

"Well, let's see what I have." Dezarae led the way to her room. She noticed the child's eyes roam over her things. Opening the closet, Dezarae grabbed a sweatshirt and tossed it on the bed.

"I like your room," the quiet admission came.

"Thank you, it is the one place I get to be girly." Dezarae looked at her. "I don't have any pants that will fit you. That sweatshirt will at least keep you warmer and we will take you shopping for some clothes tomorrow. Let's go."

Together, the females left the house and walked out into the night, Dezarae wondering what she had done and Charmane wondering if maybe she had found a friend. Entering the shop, Dezarae sent Charmane to turn on some music as she put on a pair of clean coveralls and began to detail the Fairlane. When she was done, Charmane helped her cover it and they went back to the house and into the garage where Dezarae began final touches on her Shelby.

Charmane settled onto the couch that was along the back wall and watched as Dezarae worked meticulously on her car. Exhaustion set in and as she pulled a blanket over her, her eyes began to droop.

It was midnight when Dezarae called it quits. Standing up, her eyes moved to the couch where she saw Charmane sound asleep. "Like that you seem almost sweet, Charmane," Dezarae whispered as she cleaned her hands.

Walking over to the young teen, Dezarae gently shook her. "Wake up, Charmane. It's time to go inside."

Sleepy eyes opened and grew wide as they saw Dezarae until recognition poured in. "I'm tired," she slurred.

"I can see that. Come on, we're going in." Dezarae helped her up.

Within minutes, the child was sleeping soundly on the couch as Dezarae climbed into her own bed and tried to figure out if she should curse or thank the force that had brought Ross Connelly back into her life.

Twelve

Strong hands held his head as Ross sat in the back of the dark bar alone at his booth. His beer before him sat untouched, as were the burger and fries on the plate. He was miserable.

"Mind if I join you?" a voice asked as a man slid into the other side of the booth without waiting for a response.

The hands dropped to the table and a sharp retort was bitten back as he saw who it was. Gray eyes took in the only black man on their Team, Ensign Aidrian O'Shea, better known as Hondo. "Do I have a choice?" the man asked, wanting to be left alone in his misery.

"Nae, not really." The man shook his bald head as he reached for the beer and took a swig. "What's up with you, man?"

"What do you mean?" Ross asked, being obtuse for a reason; he didn't want to talk about the root of his problem.

Hondo slid the plate of food over to himself and began to eat. "I mean, e'er since your accident, you've been different."

The faint Irish lilt never ceased to bring a smile to Ross's face. It didn't fit the first impression one got looking at the man. Hondo stood six foot, three inches and was an ex-football player from his days at Annapolis. He had dark skin and black eyes.

"How have I been different, Hondo?" Ross asked his friend.

"Take tonight, for example." He shoved more fries in his mouth and ate them. "You used to be out with the men carousing for women, not sitting here in the corner booth of a bar alone."

"I don't want just any woman, Hondo. Not anymore." Ross reached for his plate and yanked it back to him, eating some fries himself. *I want my firebird.* "Don't you ever want something like Harrier and Cade have?"

Hondo scoffed, "I'm a warrior, man. I do war and blood. Not mushy love stuff."

"Mushy love stuff, huh?" another voice said as two more men slid into the booth.

Ross looked at the two married men of the group, Lieutenant Commander Scott "Harrier" Leighton and Lieutenant Tyson "Cade" Kincade. "Do all y'all think I have changed so much?" he asked the three men.

"Yes," they answered as one.

"So it's a unanimous decision that I should go get laid?" he asked as his gray eyes moved to each of them.

"I think you should follow your heart," Harrier said.

"Me too," Cade added.

"Grab a hooker and get your damn jollies off, man; it's been three months," Hondo said bluntly.

"It hasn't been three months, Hondo. But the last woman I was with, I called her Dezarae," Ross admitted. "Not exactly flattering."

All three men just stared at him until the waitress came around and they all ordered beers, burgers, and fries. She was an attractive woman who flirted with them all, but no one bit.

"I dinna know you had it this bad, man," Hondo apologized after the woman left.

Harrier and Cade just nodded in understanding. Ross looked between them, "Was it this bad for the two of you?"

"Yes, but I think it was easier for me, since I was in the jungle with Jayde," Cade said. "And Lex is Navy so that was another obstacle for Harrier."

"But neither of you gave up," Ross pointed out.

"True, we got the women we loved. And from the way you were defending her when we got there, and then touching her, looking at her, it's a safe bet your feelings are pretty strong for her," Harrier added.

"Nothing ever felt so right as it did being with her," Ross said. "But I'm not exactly a catch of the day." At the men's confused looks he continued, "I have a child and an ex-wife who makes every day of my life a living hell. I'm the lowest-ranking guy on the Team, and I don't make or have much money. Add onto that, we can leave at anytime; it's not precisely a winning combination. Oh, yeah, and I'm white with a rebel flag tatted on my chest!"

The three men nodded their heads. "All that is true, Ross, but how do you know she cares about that?" Harrier asked.

He shoved his hands through his shorn hair. "I don't, but I have a hard enough time seeing Charmane now. If I were to add Dezarae into the mix, there would be no way. My ex, Joy, wouldn't allow it." Ross fell silent as their food and drinks were delivered. "I have to think of Charmane first, not my wants."

His teammates stayed quiet. It would be hard for Ross to get custody of his daughter. Judges rarely ruled in favor of the father and even less so if he was a military man.

Hondo looked at his young friend. "It will work itself out, man, and you have to believe that."

"I wish I could. She's all I see; she's everything I ever wanted in a woman," Ross admitted.

"We kind of figured that out ourselves. You talk in your sleep, man," Cade teased him.

Ross blushed. "Sorry."

Taking pity on him, Harrier jumped in. "Hey, don't worry about it, Cade can't say a word. Remember Belize, Cade? Loud squeaking bed frame?"

Cade burst out laughing. "How true. Okay, I will let it go." The others joined in for they all remembered hearing Cade make love to his wife in the lone bedroom of the safe house.

Moods lightened, the men enjoyed a fun evening. They stayed late at the bar, eating and drinking. By the end of the night the whole team had arrived and just had "guy time."

Somewhere in the Indian Ocean

The men jumped from the helicopter onto the flight deck of the aircraft carrier. They all headed into the situation room, faces grim with their upcoming mission, where the captain met them and waved them inside.

"Gentlemen, sorry your trip home has been delayed. But as you know there has been a situation brewing over the border of Rwanda and Burundi. There is a peacekeeping mission down there and they need extraction immediately," the commanding officer of the carrier said. He brought up a picture on the overhead. "These are your objectives. All of them need to be brought back safely."

The members of the Megalodon Team looked at the fifteen people in that photo, committing each person to memory. "What are the rules of engagement, Captain?" Scott asked.

"Expect trouble. Both sides want this group. You can fire if fired upon." The CO fell silent for a moment. "I have to tell you, the odds don't look good here."

The eight men looked at each other and grinned. "That's why we are the ones called in, sir," Scott said. "When do we leave?"

"One hour; you will have to hump it in to where they are being hidden. Go check your gear, grab some chow, or whatever." The captain dismissed them with a salute.

Ross decided to grab a bite to eat when he saw an ensign talking to another sailor and pointing at him. Eventually the officer walked over to him. "Petty Officer Connelly," the somber voice came.

Standing at attention, Ross responded, "Yes, sir."

"At ease, sailor. You have a message," the ensign said, handing him the paper with the message.

Taking the folded paper, Ross said, "Thank you, sir."

"Carry on," the ensign said before walking away.

Sitting back down, he opened the note and read the words over and over not believing them.

```
Charmane has run away. Have notified authorities.
                ~Jamie Riley
```

He felt sick. Standing up, he made his way to his gear, not seeing anything but the eyes of his daughter.

Two of his teammates were there when he arrived at his locker. "What's wrong, Jeb?" The question came from Chief Petty Officer Ernst "Ghost" Zimmermann.

Wordlessly, he handed him the note and began to repack his gear. "Oh, hell. Man, I don't know what to say about this," Ghost said as he passed the note to the other man there.

"There isn't anything to say, but thanks, Ghost. Thanks anyway," Ross spoke in a monotone voice.

"What are you going to do?" Dimitri "Merlin" Melonakos asked.

"The only thing I can do, pack for the mission and pray my little girl is okay," Ross answered. *I can't believe that stupid woman let my daughter run away!*

The whole team knew about the note by the time they were boarding the helicopter. Ross was subdued but ready for the mission. Scott wasn't sure if he should go, but Ross had said, "I will go home after the mission."

So as they took their seats and the door was closing Ross prayed he would see his daughter one more time. Suddenly the door stopped closing, slid back open, and that same ensign was running up to the chopper.

"Commander," he yelled to Scott. "I have another message for Petty Officer Connelly, sir. It just came over the wire."

"Jeb!" Scott shouted into the interior of the chopper, not sure he wanted him to read it, but he knew if the situation were reversed he would want to know. "Message is for you."

Ross moved up to take it from the ensign and saluted him before the man stepped back and shut the door. Maneuvering back to his seat, Ross hesitated a moment before opening the note.

```
Please let Petty Officer Ross Connelly know that
       his daughter has been found safe.
She is staying with one Dezarae Kerry and will wait
            there until his return.
```

Gray eyes closed with relief and then flew open to read it again. *Dezarae? His Dezarae? Charmane was with Dezarae?* A smile crossed his face as he realized that soon he would be with his daughter and his firebird. Another teammate yanked the note out of his hand and read it to everyone else. All the men congratulated him and then began to tease him about seeing Dezarae again.

As the helicopter flew deeper into Africa, the teasing ceased and the men got ready to night jump. Even as the cold air rushed past them as they fell through the dark sky, Ross had a smile on his face, for his heart was once again beating contentedly. And he knew that soon, soon he would be able to hold Dezarae Kerry in his arms again.

Three weeks later they were finally on their way home. Eight men had dozed as the transport plane carried each of them to whatever awaited them upon their return. Upon landing, Ross waved goodbye to his friends and hopped on another flight that was taking him to Montana.

Taking him to his daughter and the woman he loved. A silly grin was plastered on his face the whole flight.

Thirteen

Dezarae grinned at the child who, yelling, ran past her as she chased the dog that had her shoe in his mouth. Turning her dark eyes to the handsome man next to her, Dezarae laughed. "Your dog is a menace, Tank."

"He is, but what are you gonna do?" Tank commented easily as he helped put the ramp up on the truck.

"Beats me," Dezarae said and climbed into her Shelby Mustang. Carefully, she drove it up into the back of the semi that was in her driveway. Tank had climbed up in the back and helped her secure the vehicle in place.

Looking across the gleaming hood of her car, Dezarae smiled. Tank Williams was a bear of a man. He was solid muscle and was as dark as the car they were securing. Standing well over six feet, he didn't look up to many others.

Tank was the owner of a construction business and worked alongside his crew instead of merely delivering orders. He was the big brother Dezarae had never had and she loved him to death.

"Thanks for staying out here for me, Tank," she said as she tightened her last tie down.

"It's my pleasure, hon. Just make sure you do well at that show." He grinned at her. "Oh, by the way, I am adding on to your house while you are gone."

Her head snapped up. "What?"

"You heard me; your house is getting an addition. It's too small," Tank insisted.

"My house is fine," Dezarae protested.

"You need at least two more bedrooms. Don't bother arguing; it's going to start as soon as I get your ass out of here," Tank said as he jumped down with ease from the back before turning and lifting Dezarae down.

As her feet hit the ground, she shook her head. "Why do you insist on spoiling me like this?"

He kissed her briefly before stepping away. "Because I love you."

"I love you, too, Tank," Dezarae said as together they walked towards the garage that had packed bags waiting by the open door. "Charmane! Let's get going."

"Coming!" the girl yelled, sprinting towards them.

Dezarae looked at the girl running towards her. The past week had brought about amazing changes. The haunted look that had been in Charmane's gaze was no longer there, she was smiling more and had put on some weight. Charmane was a very easy child to deal with.

"Ready to go?" Dezarae asked as the young teen skidded to a halt in front of her.

"Yes, ma'am. I'm ready!" Charmane was clearly thrilled about going to California.

Nodding, Dezarae said, "Well, go get in the truck. We have two more cars to pick up along the way and don't want to be late to meet Sam." Sam was the owner of the other two cars and was driving down to California with them.

"Okay, Dez," she said, grabbing two bags and taking them with her.

Tank picked up the other two bags and carried them as he walked with Dezarae to the tractor. "You two be careful, now," he ordered as he tossed the bags up with ease to Charmane, who put them in the back of the sleeper cab.

"We'll be fine, Tank," Dezarae assured him. "I've been doing this a long time."

His hands settled at her hips. "I know, but allow me my worrying."

Scrunching up her nose, she nodded. "Okay, see you in a week."

"You driving just the car back?" he asked, not releasing his hold on her.

Dezarae winked at the girl watching them from the cab. "Yes, Sam is staying for the whole show and he wants to keep the trailer with him. I have to return here so I said I would be fine driving back. Besides, it will be a great time to road test the car." She patted Tank on the cheek. "I gotta jet, thanks again, Tank."

"Kiss," he said.

Dutifully, Dezarae stood on her toes and kissed his lips. "Love ya," she commented before she stepped out of his arms and climbed easily into the truck and started it. Both females in the cab waved out the windows as the eighteen-wheeler pulled out of the driveway and headed for California.

*
**

"Great job, Phoenix!" the cry came from another guy at the show.

"Hey, thanks, Jack. I loved your car. Nicely done!" Dezarae said as he shook her hand and hugged her.

"Well, she was nice but your Shelby kicked her ass," he said with a smile. "Who's this pretty woman with you?" Jack nodded at Charmane.

Dezarae made introductions, "This is my friend, Charmane Connelly. Charmane, this is Jack MacKenzie. He owns that dark purple Benz that we saw."

"Nice to meet you, Mr. MacKenzie," Charmane said politely as she stared at the man in front of her. He was a little shorter than Ross but he had jet black hair, green eyes. His body was fit and he wore clothes like they were tailored for him only.

Jack reached for her hand and bowed over it, kissing the back. "You are charming, please call me Jack." He winked at Dezarae as the girl blushed. "I insist that we have dinner together tonight."

"Charmane? What do you think?" Dezarae asked the girl.

"Could we eat along the water?" she questioned softly, her love for the ocean evident.

"I think that could be arranged," Jack responded. With a smile at Dezarae, he said, "Seven at my slip?"

"We'll be there. See you tonight, Jack," Dezarae agreed.

"Later Phoenix and Ms. Charmane," Jack said with a wave and walking off.

"Why do people call you Phoenix?" Charmane asked as she watched the handsome Jack MacKenzie saunter off into the crowd.

Following the young girl's line of vision, Dezarae smiled, "It's my middle name and part of the business name. He is very handsome, isn't he?" she whispered into Charmane's ear.

"I...I...I was just wondering about him," Charmane stuttered.

"A lot of women do, he is good looking." Dezarae put her arm around Charmane. "Let's go get the car; we can do some sightseeing before dinner."

Charmane leaned on the edge of the yacht as it sailed slowly across the bay. She smiled as she took in the view of the sun was setting across the water. Life was never like this when she was with her mother.

Dezarae was an amazing person; she let her be a child but didn't let her get away with foolishness. The older woman never talked down to her or assumed she was too stupid to understand what she was saying. Charmane liked her a lot and would willingly stay with her while her daddy was gone.

"Do you want any more dinner?" Dezarae yelled across the deck to her.

"I'm coming, Dez," the answering voice said.

"No rush, we just weren't sure if you were done or not. Take your time," Dezarae sent back. She and Jack had moved to sit on some lounges. "I love it out here, Jack, and from the looks of the smile on her face, so does Charmane."

"It is my pleasure, Phoenix, totally my pleasure," Jack responded as they accepted two cups of coffee from one of his crew. Another man stood watching over Charmane, just in case. "Why don't you stay out here?" He took her hand in his. "With me."

Squeezing his hand, Dezarae smiled at him. "That is one of the sweetest things I have ever had said to me, Jack, but you know we aren't cut out to be a couple. We are way better as friends. We tried the couple thing before, remember?"

He chuckled sadly. "I remember a fool of a man who was dumb enough to let his arrogance and pride get in the way and let you go." With one last caress, he released her hand as Charmane walked up and sat down at the end of Dezarae's lounge.

Her brown eyes darted between the two adults she sat with and she asked, "You two used to date?"

This was not exactly a conversation Dezarae wanted to have with the daughter of the man whom she dreamt about nightly. "Yes, Charmane, we did," Dezarae said bluntly.

Charmane heeded the warning in Dezarae's gaze and stayed silent about it. "Thanks for bringing me out here tonight," the young girl said.

"Anytime you wish to stop by and visit, my dear, you are most welcome," Jack replied as he bowed his head to her. "I believe they are ready to serve dessert if you want to go with Daniel there and pick out what you want."

"Dez?" Charmane asked her.

"Go ahead; it's your last night in California. Enjoy yourself," Dezarae said with a wave of her hand. She shook her head as the child bounded up off the seat and eagerly went with the man who waited for her.

As Charmane disappeared around the corner, Dezarae left the lounge and walked over to the edge of the yacht, leaning against it with hands around the warm mug. Her dark eyes moved over the water as the night crept upon them.

Jack stood too and walked over to her. "I was such an ass to let you go, Phoenix." He turned her toward him.

"Jack," she protested. "Don't."

He trailed on hand through her loose hair and down the side of her face as he watched her expression. "You don't love me anymore, do you," he said as an observation instead of a question.

Dezarae removed a hand on the cup and placed it over the masculine one that was on her face. "Not in the way you may wish, but I do love you. I will always love you." Her voice dropped to a whisper. "But not like that."

With a wry smile, he nodded. "Of course not." His thumb moved over her lip as he stared into her eyes. "You know I will always be there for you right, Dezarae? Always. If you ever need any-thing...you call me. *Anything.*"

Tightening her grip on his hand, she smiled through the tears that had formed in her eyes. "I love you, Jack," she said as the first tear began to fall.

He began to chuckle and brought up his other hand to wipe away the tears from her face. "Don't cry, Phoenix, I love you too." Jack took her coffee cup and set it on the deck of the yacht before facing her again. "Ahh hell, come here." He pulled her into his embrace and held her, his hands moving comfortingly up and down her back.

"I'm sorry," she whispered.

"For what?" Jack asked as he moved back from her to look into her eyes.

"Crying, being a baby." Dezarae wiped away some more tears until his hand brushed hers away and took over the task.

"Don't apologize. I love holding you." His lips moved over her forehead.

Dezarae allowed his strength to surround her. Her eyes closed as they stood like that for a while. Her arms had moved around his waist.

"Hey, Dez, I brought you some..." the voice trailed off.

Dezarae opened her eyes and saw Charmane standing there staring at them. "What did you bring me, Charmane?" she asked.

"A p...p...piece of cake," the child stuttered.

"Great," Dezarae pulled back from Jack, kissing him on the cheek. "Thanks for the hug."

Jack smiled a smile that men get when they knew they had lost their love. "Anytime. Just so you let me know when you want to sell your Shelby."

"Don't hold your breath, Jack MacKenzie. I love that car," Dezarae said as she sat next to Charmane at the table.

Jack took a seat across from Charmane. "So do I and I want to buy her."

"My car is a he. I don't drive women," Dezarae quipped as she put her fork into the marbled cake that was in front of her.

The next morning, Jack hugged Charmane as she climbed in the front seat of the Mustang. "Great to meet you, Charmane. I hope to see you again," he said, shutting the door for her.

Dezarae shut the trunk on their luggage and walked up to the driver's door of her car. Jack was waiting for her. With a big sigh, she smiled at him and went unhesitatingly into his arms as he opened them.

"Bye, Jack," Dezarae said as she hugged him tight.

"Bye, Phoenix. Her daddy must be something special. I hope he is smarter than I was." He stepped back and captured her chin in his hand before he kissed her. It was gentle and when he stepped back he said, "Love you, Phoenix. Call me about the car."

Dezarae kissed him on the cheek and jumped in the car. "Love you, too, Jack. And I don't think so on the car."

"Bye, Jack," Charmane yelled out the window as Dezarae turned the key and the powerful V8 engine roared to life.

"Bye, squirt, drive safely," he responded with a wave.

Dezarae waved out the window as she put them on the road headed for Montana.

"He still loves you, doesn't he, Dez?" Charmane asked as they drove.

With a shrug, she answered. "I think he believes he loves me. Why?"

"No reason," the teen responded quickly.

"Right. Did you have fun?" Dezarae questioned.

"It was a blast. I wish that daddy could have been there. That would have made it perfect," Charmane stated.

Yes, it would have. "I sure he wishes he could be with you as well," Dezarae said, truly believing it.

The city gave way to empty interstate, so Dezarae opened up her car and let it go. She had music playing softly and after two hours she looked over and saw Charmane peaceful in her world of sleep.

"You are one lucky girl, Charmane, to have a daddy like Ross Connelly," Dezarae admitted.

Dezarae drove straight through; she was anxious to get home and begin work on the Lamborghini. They stopped for meals, gas, and bathroom breaks but otherwise pressed on, the women growing closer as the stunning 1967 Shelby Mustang left the miles in the dust.

Fourteen

A green Ford Explorer pulled into the driveway and parked. All four bay doors were open on the shop that was under a new sign that read Phoenix Restorations And Rebuilds. On the backdrop of it was the legendary bird itself, wings outspread as it rose from the flames. There were two vehicles in the shop.

Eyes took in the house that seemed to have a new addition to it. Suddenly Ross was nervous. His hand ran through his short hair before he put his hand on the Explorer's door handle to get out and froze.

Out from the shop ran a young teenager. She wore blue jeans and a white tee shirt. Following at her heels was one huge, ugly-looking mutt. It was the face of the child that made him stop dead in his tracks. On it was one of the biggest smiles he had ever seen.

Following behind her was Ross's dream woman. Dezarae Kerry. Inside the leather interior of his vehicle he allowed his eyes to ogle her uninterrupted. She wore a pair of skintight jeans that made his body twitch in response. Her shirt was a cutoff sweatshirt, gray in color. Her hair was free around her face and her dark skin was flawless.

She was on the phone but as her dark-chocolate eyes fell on the vehicle, she hung up the phone, clipped it back to her pants, and crossed her arms, staring in his direction. Eyes narrowed as she waited for him to get out of the vehicle until a yell got her attention.

"Dezarae," a masculine voice yelled to her from the house.

Her head jerked away from the vehicle in her driveway as she shouted back, "What is it, Tank?"

"Come here, will you?" the voice asked.

"Sure." She looked back to the unmoving car in her drive. "Be right there." Cocking her head, she turned and walked to her house where a large man stepped out to greet her.

That was when the driver of the Explorer got out. The second that man touched Dezarae Kerry.

Dezarae didn't know what to make of the vehicle in her driveway. No one was getting out, but she felt like she was being watched. Intensely. She had been on her way to see who it was when Tank had yelled for her.

Deciding that person would get out if he or she wanted to, she walked to her house, which had grown considerably since she had gone to California. Tank and his men had added fifteen hundred square feet onto it. They had given her three more bedrooms and another bathroom along with a master bath for her. All they were doing now was cleanup.

Charmane had been moved into her old bedroom, which was fine until they figured out which one Dezarae wanted for her office. So as she walked up the steps and Tank put his hand on her arm, she heard the slamming of the car door. Charmane went running by with Haley, Tank's mutt.

"Daddy! Daddy, you're back!" the screech came.

Dezarae swallowed. Ross. Her knees were trembling and she felt faint.

"You okay, Phoenix?" Tank asked.

"Fine, Tank, I'm fine." She took a deep breath. *Liar.* "I guess I should go explain why his daughter is here instead of with her mother."

Tank laughed, "I think I will go inside. Good luck." He slipped away.

Dezarae cursed him under her breath as she turned and met a sight that brought tears to her eyes.

Ross was holding his little girl in his arms, crying.

Ross couldn't believe it when Charmane ran up to him. She was not the same girl he had last seen with her mother. That girl had been skinny and reluctant to let him go. Her eyes had been dull with sadness. This girl was healthy, full of life, and smiling as she jumped into his arms.

"I missed you so much, Charmane," he said as he held his daughter close.

"I missed you, too, Daddy, I missed you too," she cried as they hugged.

Pulling back, he looked down at his pride and joy, "Do you have any idea how scared I was when I got the message you had run away? You can't do that, Charmane," he began to scold.

"I know, Daddy, Dez already told me that I could have put you in more danger because of it. I'm sorry, please don't be mad at me," Charmane begged.

"Baby, I was so relieved when I got the message that you were okay. I will have your word that there will be no more running away," Ross said.

"Promise, Daddy." Her arms tightened around him. "I can't wait to tell you what I have been doing!" she said, once again excited.

"Let me go talk to Dezarae first, okay?" he said.

"Okay, Daddy, don't be long." She backed away from him and yelled, "Dez, Daddy wants to talk to you! I'm going to be with Tank inside; I want to show Daddy my room when you are done, okay?" Charmane ran off into the house after taking one more hug from her father.

Ross turned those gray eyes onto the woman who had ruined him for all other women. She was the only one for him now. Her movements were slow but sure as she went across the yard to where he stood by his vehicle.

"Hello, Johnny Reb," her quiet voice reached out and touched his soul.

"Hello, Firebird," he drawled.

For a minute, they could only stand there. Their eyes moved up and down each other, each absorbing what they could see of one another.

"Glad to see you're okay," Dezarae said. Ross wore a pair of tight blue jeans and a black button-down shirt, of which the top three buttons were undone. On his feet were cowboy boots,

"Are you?" he asked.

Her eyes narrowed. "Of course I'm glad you're okay."

"I meant are you really glad to see me?" Ross clarified.

"I guess so," she said, shrugging and not meeting his eyes. "I hadn't really given it much thought."

"Liar." He stepped closer to her and reached out to touch her cheek, smiling as her lids fluttered shut at first contact. "You thought about me all the time."

"How do you figure that?" Dezarae asked, opening her eyes.

"Because, Firebird, I thought about you all the time too," he admitted.

"Shut up and kiss me," she murmured.

"Call me by my name," he ordered as his body stepped in closer to hers.

"Kiss me, Ross," she said.

He did. His other hand moved up to capture her face and he held her immobile as he lowered his mouth to hers. He nibbled around her lips before sliding his tongue inside her mouth to dance with hers.

Dezarae purred as she moved her hands up around his neck and pulled him in closer to deepen the kiss. Her strokes matched his and soon there nothing in the world existed except the two of them.

Passions rose as flames exploded with new life. Drawing back, Ross looked into her fathomless eyes and saw what he had prayed for so badly—her love for him. His gunmetal eyes moved down to her swollen lips and he kissed them once more before pulling her into his strong embrace and holding her.

"Thank you for taking care of my daughter," Ross whispered into her hair.

"You're welcome." Dezarae moved her hands from around his neck to settle around his waist. This was heaven, her being in his arms again. Inhaling deeply, Ross felt as if suddenly his world was right as the scent of this woman filled his soul.

"I have to go see my daughter," he said as his hands rubbed her back.

Dezarae suddenly jerked away from him and pulled on her clothes, trying to cover up her nervousness. "Of course," she rushed to say. "Charmane is in my old room. Go on in."

He reached for her, frowning over her reaction. "What about you?"

"I...I...I have some things to do in the shop," she stuttered before she bolted.

Ross watched her hurry to her shop, look at him once more, and disappear into the building. His eyes narrowed; it was as if she were embarrassed for kissing him...and enjoying it.

Ross shook his head and went inside, determined to deal with that later. Knocking on the doorframe of the room he had stayed in, Ross saw his daughter sitting at a desk and writing. "Whatcha doing, baby?" he asked, stepping into the room.

It definitely belonged to a teen now. There were teen idol pictures on the walls, but what surprised him were the classic car posters.

"Homework," Charmane said with a smile for her favorite man in the world.

Homework? "You're in school out here?" Ross asked, amazed.

His daughter laughed, a sound that almost brought tears to his eyes. "Of course, Daddy. I have straight As. Dez called my teacher and had him send my stuff so I didn't fall behind. I'm caught up, but since you're here now, I thought if I got some extra done we could do something fun together.

Dezarae did all of this? Ross sat on the bed and patted the space next to him, "Come sit with me, Charmane."

Immediately she scampered over to him and cuddled up next to his body. "Did you come to take me with you, Daddy? Are you staying here with us?" Charmane asked. "Tank built all this extra room when we were in California so it won't be crowded."

Stay here with us? It sounds like Charmane likes it here. "Why did you come here, Charmane?"

"I wanted to be around someone who didn't say bad things about you," his daughter said.

"Dezarae let you stay, just like that?" he asked.

"Sorta," she hedged until he cleared his throat. "I was really rude to her and said I couldn't stay here so she left me on the porch and told me to have a nice walk back to town," Charmane said as she picked up a stuffed panda. "Then she told me about bears and cougars and left me alone out there for about three hours."

She saw her father frown. "Dez made dinner and told me to come in and eat something. She said I could go any time since she wasn't in charge of me but that I could stay if I wanted." Charmane laid her head on her daddy's lap.

"She made me call Jamie and tell her I was okay. Then she said I was staying with her until you came home." Her voice got more excited as she relayed the details to her father. "I can eat more than half a plate of food and Dez always treats me with respect…well, after threatening me with jail."

Ross's eyes narrowed. *Jail?* "Why would she do that?"

"Because after she said I could stay, I said I might just leave. She said, no, not since she'd assumed responsibility for me. So I made my choice." Charmane's voice softened. "I really like her, Daddy. A lot."

Me, too, baby. Me too. "What's this about California?" Ross asked his daughter as he twirled some of her brown hair in his fingers. His eyes, however, had focused on something outside the window — Dezarae, who stood close to a very large man.

"We went to a car show, she drove an eighteen-wheeler there." The awe was evident in her voice. "We took three cars, went sightseeing; her car won some award, and we drove back here in her Mustang. Oh, yeah, and we had dinner on a yacht in the bay that belonged to an ex-boyfriend who is still in love with her."

Yacht? Boyfriend? Ross wanted to get something straight with Ms. Kerry: she belonged to *him*. Nobody else. "Sounds like you had fun. Tell me more about this yacht," he said deceptively.

Unbeknownst to Ross, however, his daughter had plans of her own. "Well, the guy who owns it is named Jack MacKenzie. He is not as tall as you, but still tall. Handsome, black hair, green eyes, nice smile."

"What do you know about his smile?" Ross demanded.

"I know he smiled a lot when he held Dezarae in his arms and kissed her on the yacht in the sunset."

Ross tensed, becoming even more upset when his daughter grinned. "So you stayed how long on this yacht?" Ross prompted, not really sure he wanted to hear more.

"Only for dinner and dessert." She paused as she looked up at her father's clenched jaw line. "When I came up from the galley with dessert they were standing together and he was kissing her. He seemed to do that a lot," Charmane said.

"I get it, Charmane," he growled. "I think I need to talk to Dezarae again. You finish your homework and we will go to dinner tonight. Just the two of us."

"Okay, but what about Dezarae?" Charmane asked.

"Well, I guess we could ask her along," Ross said. "Where is her room?"

Charmane walked him to the door and pointed. "At the end of the hall."

Ross went through the new addition, not really seeing it at first. Then he spotted Dezarae's bedroom at the end and he walked in and stopped. Her room was done in royal purple and silver. Large windows offered a magnificent view; however, he walked over to the dresser and began looking at the numerous photos she had there. Most of them were of her in various stages of childhood. Ross figured the man in them was her father. Many of the photos had classic cars in them as well.

He picked up a silver tri-fold frame. All the pictures in there were of Dezarae and she was stunningly beautiful, elegantly dressed up in each one. Ross realized his hand was shaking as he looked upon her photo.

"You are so beautiful, Dezarae," he spoke softly to the pictures he held.

Hearing footsteps coming his way, he set the frame back and stood nonchalantly with thumbs shoved through the belt loops on his jeans. He tried to keep his expression bland but couldn't stop the flare of heat searing his eyes as she came into view.

Dezarae walked to her sanctuary, needing to find a moment to herself that didn't involve Tank, Charmane, or Ross. Especially Ross. Seeing him had brought back such deep emotions, and she was mortified she had kissed him like she had where his daughter could have seen them.

Entering her bedroom, she had her eyes closed and used her foot to shut the door behind her. Dezarae sagged and rested her head on the smooth wood.

"Something on your mind, Firebird?"

The slow Southern drawl jerked her upright. "What the hell are you doing in here?" Dezarae demanded as she prayed her heart would slow before it jumped out of her chest.

"I needed to talk to you," Ross answered pushing away from the wall he had been leaning on to prowl closer to her.

"Now?" she asked as she moved cautiously away from the door.

Steel eyes narrowed. "Something more important to do this second?"

"I just don't think you should be in my room, especially with your daughter here. It's not proper."

Ross arched his brows in disbelief. "As opposed to necking with some guy on a yacht in front of her?"

Dark chocolate eyes grew large. Her mouth moved but nothing came out.

Strong arms crossed over a hard chest as he stared at her. "The only man you will be kissing is me," he vowed.

Her knees trembled at his forceful words. "Look," Dezarae began, "why don't you go to the living room and I'll meet you there and we can talk." *Because in here all I think about is you putting me on that bed.*

His gray eyes moved up and down her body, becoming smoldering coals as he looked at her. "I think we will talk here." Ross sat in a chair, sending her a look that dared her to defy him.

With a groan, she ran her hand over her face and slid down the wall to sit on the floor. "All right, you win," she conceded. "What did you want to talk about?"

Fifteen

Ross wanted nothing more than to pick her up, toss her on the bed, and show her exactly what he wanted to do to her. Show her what kind of a man she had turned him into. But for some reason, she was still trying to fight her attraction for him.

"Us," he said, watching her, waiting for her to look at him instead of the floor. "Charmane, and then, us again."

Dezarae picked her eyes up from the floor and put them on the man who lounged in her chair. "Us?" she questioned. "There is no us."

Not yet. "Why are you so determined to keep me at a distance, Dez?" he honestly wondered.

"It's better that way. If there are no feelings involved, then no one will get hurt."

Ross grumbled something unpleasant under his breath and then said to her, "Feelings *are* involved. Charmane loves you, and I..." He fell silent; something in her posture told him now wasn't the time.

"You are grateful for what I did for you months ago. There are no real feelings between us. We don't know each other," Dezarae insisted.

Swinging his legs to the floor, Ross put his elbows on his knees and laced his fingers. "So would you object to us getting to know one another better?" he asked.

"No, I wouldn't." Dezarae said with a shrug.

"So you aren't hesitating because of my skin color or my tattoo?" Ross got off the chair and crouched down in front of her, demanding she meet his gaze.

"I...I...I don't know, Ross. I honestly don't know," she admitted.

"This Jack guy you were kissing, is he white?" Ross had reached for her chin, holding her head up. *I will not be mad she was kissing another man. I will not be mad.*

"Yes," she said.

"So it can't be that." *I lied — I'm pissed.*

"What difference does it make? Now that you are here, you are going to take your daughter and go...hell, I don't even know where you are from!" Dezarae cried in frustration.

"I am from Virginia. My full name is Ross Murdock Connelly, I have a twelve-year-old daughter, I'm a divorcee, and I am a thirty-year-old Navy SEAL." He pulled her to her feet and walked them both over to the large chair. He sat first and then settled her on his lap. "I'm on leave for the next ten days and I want nothing more than to spend it with you and my daughter." His hands teased her skin. "Can I stay?" Ross cleared his throat and amended, "Can *we* stay?"

"Of course you can stay," she said on a sigh.

I'm one step closer, Firebird. "Wonderful," he murmured into her ear.

When she moved to get off his lap, Ross's his arms locked around her, holding her immobile. "I have to go," she protested.

Ross didn't want to let her go. "We're not done talking."

Dezarae turned in his arms to look at him. "What else is there to talk about?"

"This." Fast as a striking rattler, his mouth was on hers. His large hands held fistfuls of her hair, keeping her in place.

As his tongue slid between her full lips, she moaned deep in her throat. Dezarae fidgeted on his lap. Ripping his mouth off hers, Ross pulled back just enough so he could look into her molten eyes. "There is something between us, Firebird. You know it and I know it. I am not going to let you ignore it."

Heart pounding, Dezarae just stared into his gray orbs, and he could imagine them saying, *I could love you, Ross Connelly.*

"Good," he murmured, seconds before his lips dominated hers again.

"Daddy!" Charmane's yell came from down the hall. "Where are you, Daddy?"

Dezarae jumped off his lap as if the hounds of hell were after her. "Jesus, you shouldn't be in here!" she said, panicked.

Ross stayed right where he had been sitting, eyes narrowing as he watched her movements. "Why not?"

"She is your daughter...we are in here...you shouldn't be..." Dezarae was totally flustered.

Ross smiled as his eyes followed her. "My daughter loves you and would be thrilled to find us together."

"We aren't together!" Dezarae hollered. Stomping over to the door, she flung it open, shoved past Charmane who was about to knock, and stormed down the hall.

His daughter stuck her head in the open door and saw him sitting in a chair, looking as if he belonged in the room. "What's the matter with Dez, Daddy? Why is she so upset?" A frown crossed her face. "Does this mean she isn't going to dinner with us tonight?"

Dinner? I was thinking about putting my tongue down her throat, not asking her to dinner! "I haven't asked her yet." *And I have a hunch what her answer is going to be.*

"Well, I'll go ask her," Charmane said, seconds before she furrowed her brow and harrumphed. "Later, I guess; she is with Tank."

That got Ross's attention. His head whipped around and he scowled as Dezarae laughed easily with the giant of a man she stood beside. Forcing a smile, he stood and looked at his child. "Let's go get my bags; I have some down time and Dezarae said we could stay here. So I guess I will take whichever room Tank isn't using."

With a smile that could rival the cosmos for brightness, Charmane squealed and hugged her father. "She has a guest room but Tank isn't staying here. He comes in the morning and leaves at night. Well, he stayed when we were in California but he was watching the shop."

Walking up the hall beside his child, Ross listened to her talk as if she really lived and belonged here with Dezarae. Nothing was Dezarae's; it was all "we" and "our."

Side by side they walked outside into the afternoon sun and over to his vehicle. Opening the back, Ross pulled out his sea bag and another bag. Charmane took the small one and he swung the large green bag over his shoulder with ease.

"The guestroom she has right now used to be her old office since they are just finishing up cleanup right now," Charmane explained as they walked back in the house.

"I'm sure it will be fine," he assured his daughter. As she opened the door to his temporary room, his mind settled on her mother and he frowned. He had to deal with Joy sooner or later.

"What's wrong, Daddy?" Charmane asked, fixing her big doe eyes on him.

"Just thinking I need to talk to your mother. Don't worry about it." He tried to play it off but couldn't miss the look of dejection that crossed her face.

"Oh, I guess I have to go back there now that you are home," she said quietly.

"I don't have anyone to watch you while I am gone, baby; you know I want you there when I come home. But—"

"But Mama won't let me stay with you. She never says anything good about you. I hate it. I hate her!" Charmane yelled as she ran from the room.

"Way to go, Ross," he muttered to himself as he tossed his bags in a corner of the small, yet comfortable, dark-blue room. "Way to go."

*
**

"I don't know how to thank you, Tank," Dezarae said as she walked with him and the few remaining men from his crew who still remained.

"It was our pleasure, Phoenix, truly it was," Tank responded as he pounded on the door of one of the trucks in farewell as the man left.

"All of you are so wonderful to me." She smiled at the men as they got in their vehicles.

"We all love you." Tank picked her up and spun her around in a circle, causing her to squeal.

She laughed. "Put me down, Tank!"

"Someday I'm just gonna toss you over my shoulder and carry you off somewhere," Tank warned as he set her back on her feet.

"Why would you want to do that? You know I'm ornery." She winked.

"That's true." He opened the door of his 3500 Dodge Heavy Duty truck and climbed into the cab after getting his dog inside. "Okay, babe, I will be over tomorrow to check on you." His eyes narrowed briefly. "And your guest."

"I know you will." Dezarae wrinkled up her nose and stood on the running board of his truck to stick her head through the window and kiss him. "See you then. Love you, Tank."

"Love you, too, Phoenix," he said, returning her kiss and driving away once she jumped down. She waved to him until he was gone from sight.

"Dezarae!"

Turning around, she saw Charmane running towards her, tears streaming down her face. Automatically, Dezarae opened her arms and let the child run into them. "What's going on, Charmane?" she asked as her arms closed around the trembling girl.

"Daddy doesn't want me, either!" she bawled.

Rolling her eyes, Dezarae reassured her that her father wanted her, "He came all this way to find you and spend time with you. Why would you think he didn't want you?"

"He said he had to call Mama." Her tiny body shook with the force of her sobs.

"Of course he has to call your mother. She needs to know he is with you and you are fine." Looking at her porch, Dezarae saw Ross step out from her house, stop, and watch them. She waved him closer.

"Mama doesn't care," the child protested.

Dark chocolate met gunmetal as Ross moved closer. "I don't know your mother, sweetie, but I know your father loves you very much. You were the one name that he could remember when he had his accident. You, he remembered you." Dezarae set Charmane back from her a bit and looked into the young teen's face. "You need to work this out with your father, not me."

"He is inside; he doesn't care," Charmane sobbed.

"That's not true, baby," Ross interjected. "I'm right here." Dezarae turned the child toward her father and gave her a little push. As Ross's arms took the place her arms had been moments before, Dezarae smiled sadly at the memory of her own father and she walked to the shop.

Two hours later, Dezarae stretched and rolled the stiff muscles in her neck. She had been cleaning up two of the bays where the cars had been. When it came to her shop, Dezarae was fanatical about keeping it clean.

"I'll give you a massage if you think it will help." Ross's deep voice flowed over her like cognac.

Without turning to face him, Dezarae just gathered her hair in one hand, moved it off her neck, and said, "Come on, then."

His hands were gentle yet firm as they settled on her shoulders and began to massage her tension away. "How does that feel?" he asked.

"Wonderful," she moaned. "Where's Charmane?"

"Showering and getting ready to go to dinner." His hands stilled on her body as he leaned over one shoulder and whispered in her ear, "Want to come with us?"

And feel like part of the family? "No, this is a good time for you and your daughter to spend together. Besides, I have a ton of work that I have to catch up on."

"She would like you to come," he murmured into her ear.

What about you? "No, I have to get ready for my next few cars. And I have a lot of data that I have to put into the computer." She shrugged her shoulders. "Why did you stop?"

He chuckled as he began to move his magic hands. "You know, this would be so much better if we were naked and on a bed."

"Life would always be better with 'if' in it, Johnny Reb." Dezarae closed her eyes and allowed herself to relax.

"So, are you saying you don't want a repeat of what happened in your garage?" His challenge rang firmly in her ear.

Twisting out from under his touch, Dezarae looked at him, amazement on her features. "I can't believe you said that to me." Her dark eyes picked up on Charmane coming across the yard.

"I want more than that, Dez. I want to make you scream my name out loud. I want to make love to you. With you. All night and then some." His eyes burned with a feral heat as he spoke. "You are mine, Firebird, you are mine."

Charmane walked into the shop before Dezarae could formulate an answer. "Ready, Daddy? Are you coming Dezarae?"

Her expressive eyes moved to the child among them. "I'm not coming, Charmane." She looked back to Ross, "Not yet, anyway. I have to stay here and get some work done. I'll see you both later on."

"Bye, Dez," Charmane said as she pulled her father out of the shop with her.

"Bye, Charmane. Have fun with your daddy." Dezarae waved as they moved towards the vehicle. Once they were in the confines of his green Explorer, then and only then did she allow her tears to fall.

Sixteen

Where is she? Ross frowned as he left the room. "It's eleven at night, where the hell would she be?"

Low voices coming from the open door grabbed his attention. Silently, he padded to the partial opening and peered in.

Sitting together on the bed in the large purple and silver bedroom were Dezarae and the one Ross had been searching for, Charmane. His daughter wore a nightgown while Dezarae wore an old tee-shirt and a pair of pajama bottoms.

Charmane sat perfectly still in front of Dezarae as she got her hair braided. They were talking softly as hushed music played in the background. Charmane was telling her about their dinner.

On one hand, Ross wanted to listen and observe their interaction with one another, but on the other... he wanted to be a part of the closeness he was witnessing. Even when Charmane had been a baby, he had never sat with her and Joy. She hadn't wanted him near her or the baby.

So now, he opened the door further and slipped inside, unable to stay away from his daughter and the woman who had brought life back to him. "Ladies," he said in a quiet voice, "mind if I join you?"

Head immobile, Charmane answered him, "Hey, Daddy! Dezarae is braiding my hair. Come in and sit down."

"Evening, Ross," Dezarae said in her naturally low voice. "Grab a seat."

"I was on my way to check on you Charmane and I couldn't find you," Ross said. He sat in the chair where he had so thoroughly kissed Dezarae earlier, his body lounging in it so he could easily watch the women on the bed.

"Sorry, Daddy, I asked Dez earlier to braid my hair before bed. I didn't mean to worry you," she said softly.

"Don't worry. I found you." He winked at his daughter. *I have to find a way to get you away from your mother.*

"So you did," she said moving her head to look at him, only to have a silent Dezarae gently but firmly put it where she wanted it to stay. "Sorry, Dez," Charmane apologized.

"So, then, what happened?" Dezarae prompted the girl to go back to her story.

For the next thirty minutes, Ross sat in silence and watched his daughter bond with a woman more tightly than he had ever seen. He knew Dezarae didn't want him to talk and he was willing to watch and listen. His gray eyes never left the women on the bed.

He stared at the way Dezarae was so patient with Charmane. How she smiled and nodded to things that were said to her. How her soulful eyes moved to him from time to time and ran over his body as if testing the water.

Ross sat up in the chair when Dezarae whispered something to his daughter, causing her to look at him and laugh. "What is so funny?" he asked as his tall body unfolded gracefully from the chair and approached the bed.

"Nothing," they both said at the same time.

"Humph," he grumbled and narrowed his eyes at them. "Why is it that I don't believe you?"

"Overly suspicious?" Dezarae teased.

"Of two women who look at me and laugh? Now why would that make me suspicious?" Ross wondered sarcastically.

"Beats me," Dezarae said. As he took another menacing step towards her bed, she added, "Charmane is ready for bed now." She smiled at the child and said goodnight to her.

As the twelve-year-old led her father out of the room, Dezarae waggled her fingers at Ross as he left with a promise in his gaze. Shutting the door behind them, Dezarae quickly brushed her teeth and headed for bed herself. She had a busy day ahead of her.

Two hours later, she was lying awake and looking up through the skylight over her bed. "Damn him," she swore. "Why the hell would I think he would actually come in here tonight?" Dezarae flailed her arms and legs like she was having a tantrum, moaning in frustration as she rolled over, punched her pillow, and tried to fall back asleep. "Why the hell do I care?"

"Because you want me. No matter how hard you try to deny it, you want me, Firebird."

"Ross," she breathed, unwilling to look in his direction. "What are you doing here?"

He chuckled. "After that fit you threw, you are going to pretend you are shocked I came?" Out of the shadows, he materialized beside her bed.

Of course he would be around to see that. "Why are you here?" Dezarae tried to keep her heartbeat slow and sound unaffected by his scent. Nevertheless, she rolled towards him.

"Because you called for me," he said as he sat down beside her on the mattress.

"I did no such thing," she protested even though her body shuddered with anticipation.

"You have been calling for me since the day we met. The same as my soul has been calling out for you." He leaned over her, halting millimeters away from her mouth.

Dezarae parted her lips to dispute and found his on hers. Ross slid his tongue into her mouth as he simultaneously rolled her onto her back. Never breaking the kiss, he jerked the blankets off her and took their place, covering her with his own body.

Strong hands settled on either side of her head as the kiss intensified. Tongues stroked one another as the age-old ritual began.

Dezarae moved her hands up his back, urging him closer. The feel of his hard erection against her was mind-blowing. Her body dripped; she was so wet for him. His chest was bare, for she could feel the warmth of his skin through her shirt.

She whimpered into his mouth and her hips bucked against him. *Now!* She wanted to scream that word at him, but Dezarae also didn't want the toe-curling, spine-tingling kiss to end.

Reluctantly, he pulled his mouth off her full one. "Tell me now, Dez," he said in a raspy, desire-filled voice.

Dezarae didn't hesitate. "Stay with me tonight."

Ross sighed as he lay on his side and rolled her to face him. Their lips met again, gentle this time. Despite the urgency present, something deeper had blossomed between the night lovers.

Dezarae held his head between her hands as they explored each other's mouths. He tasted so good. It was like having a fine cigar, only to be handed a snifter of top-of-the-line brandy to go with it. She teased his tongue, drawing it back into her mouth to suck on it.

Ross's whole body was alive for her. Every inch of his skin tingled, burned, felt more alive than he had ever known possible. His body was painfully hard and with each upward thrust from Dezarae his control slipped another notch. He had never dreamed passion could be this intense.

His large hand leading the way, Ross felt her outline in the dark. Her body was perfect, each generous curve she had would fit him like none before. Toned muscles didn't remove from her sexuality — they added to it.

Ross knew she was strong and he loved that about her. His gray eyes opened and he found himself staring at the woman he knew he had fallen in love with. Her dark beauty was barely visible under the full moon that shone upon them.

"Look at me, Dez." His command was silky but concrete.

Thick lashes rose, exposing the melted-cocoa eyes. They were so dark it was like looking at black pearls. Slowly, she released his mouth and just gazed at him. The only noise in the room was their heavy breathing.

"I want to make love to you, Firebird." Ross began as his hand moved up to touch her face.

"Yes," Dezarae said and she put her lips back on his, only to release a frustrated groan as he pulled away.

"I want the lights on," he mumbled against her mouth. "I want to be able to see all of you naked. Beneath, beside, and above me."

"All of them?" she questioned.

"All of them," he confirmed, nibbling around the edges of her mouth. His fingers began to slide under the bottom of her shirt to tease her skin.

Ross could feel her indecision. "Firebird, I already think you are perfect. I just want to be able to look at you when we make love for the first time."

"Why would you say something like that?" Her voice was truly amazed.

"Like what?"

"What you said. I already said yes. There is no reason for you to lie to me." Skepticism filled her tone.

Dezarae suddenly had doubts. She knew she wasn't the slim girl she had been. While not fat, she definitely wasn't what one would describe as being attractive by society's standards. Her belly wasn't flat; her arms were strong, as were her legs from doing what she did for a living.

Looking away from Ross, she felt him leave the bed. Seconds passed before the room was filled with a blinding light as he had turned on the large ceiling light. His body, clad in only pajama bottoms, stood beside her at the bed and pulled her up to a sitting position.

His eyes were like flint. "What the hell would make you think that I was doing such a thing?" Blinking furiously against his anger and the light, Dezarae didn't answer him right away. His hand latched around her arm and he repeated his question.

"Oh, let's not kid ourselves here, Ross," she said, regaining control of her senses. "We both know I am not your type of girl. I want to have sex with you; I said so. Don't pretend this is anything more than what it is. I don't need the sweet, flowery words; I know you don't mean them." *I would love for you to, but I am not disillusioning myself.*

With a smooth movement, Ross pulled her up from the bed and took her over to stand in front of the large mirror she had on her wall. He went behind her and stared at her in the reflection.

His eyes still shot sparks, but his voice was controlled when he spoke. "You don't know a damn thing about me, Dezarae Kerry. You don't know what my type of woman is or what turns me on. But I am going to enlighten you."

Ross settled his hands on her hips. "Look at the mirror," he ordered. "Don't take your eyes off us." When she nodded her understanding, he continued. "You *are* my kind of woman, Dezarae. Everything about you is intoxicating to me. Your passion for life, your work, everything you do turns me on. I can't wait to get beneath that surface and really see what kind of passion you have locked up inside of you."

His hands began to move up under her shirt, exposing the dark skin as the thin material was bunched up along the way. "The sparkle you get in your eye as you drive around your racetrack or work on a car…" With one swift movement, he pulled her shirt off, throwing it to the side before holding her arms, not allowing her to hide her body. "How fearless you are climbing on top of containers to unhook them from the helicopter—no matter how foolish—all of that tells me you love life."

He placed light kisses along her shoulders, enjoying the smooth skin as his hands made like they were going to touch her full breasts, only to land on her ribs at the last second. "How can you not think you are beautiful? Look at what I see. I see the smoothest skin God ever created. Breasts that were made for a man to hold, cup, kiss, and suckle upon until you carried his child. Made for *me*."

Ross slid his hands up under her breasts, allowing his thumbs to graze the already hardened tips. His eyes became molten mercury as he ran his tongue along her neck. "Imagine how it will feel to have my mouth on you instead of my fingers, to have my tongue swirling about the hard tips of your luscious breasts." His forefingers joined his thumbs to roll her nipples between them and he seemed to revel in her tremble.

"Do you know what turns me on?" he purred into her ear as his hands moved down to slide beneath the waist of her pajamas. "Knowing that you are wet with desire for me — not the guy with the yacht, not Tank — but *me*. That turns me on." One finger slipped across the apex of her thighs and felt the wetness.

"I need you to believe that I am not lying to you. I am telling you the truth. I want to make love to you — not have sex, make love to you — because I — " Ross broke off, spinning her in his arms and kissing her like she was his everything.

Bare chest met bare breasts and as he dominated the kiss. Dezarae slipped her hand down the front of his pants, closing around his throbbing erection. She smiled as she felt it jump at her touch. "Make love to me, Ross Murdock Connelly of Virginia," Dezarae moaned into his mouth.

"Your wish is my command, Firebird," he responded and he swept her up into his arms. He carried her back to the bed. Setting her down on the comforter, he undressed her, not allowing her to hide any part of her body from his gaze before he removed his last article of clothing.

Lights on, illuminating the lovers, he once again covered her body with his own.

Seventeen

"You are a work of art," Dezarae murmured as her hands eager-ly moved over the naked body on top of her, then sliding through his dark-brown hair that was cut close to his scalp.

Ross kissed her silent and allowed one hand to slip over the neatly trimmed thatch of black hair nestled between her legs. Two fingers ventured forth and easily slid inside her wet body.

Dezarae shivered as her first orgasm took her. The same as it happened in her garage, all it took was one touch and she was seeing stars. Whimpering, she arched against his hand, taking his fingers in deeper yet.

Ross obliged her, moving his wrist, sending his fingers in and out of her aching body. His mouth pressed harder onto hers before he nipped her tongue and moved down to suck on her bare breast.

"Ahhh!" Dezarae released to the room. Her hands held him to her chest as he worked her nipple into an even tighter point. Flames licked her body as the hold she tried to have on her emotions broke. "Please," she begged.

"What do you want?" Ross asked, his words vibrating her al-ready extremely sensitive nipple.

"More."

"More what?" His two fingers fluttered inside her.

"More…more…more of you," she babbled as her thighs tigh-tened around his wrist.

"Okay." He slid in a third, her body stretching at its intrusion.

A sound between pleasure and frustration left her mouth. It felt so good having him in her, but she wanted more. "Please," Dezarae went back to begging.

"Tell me what you want." He licked a path from her breasts up to her mouth. "Tell me," he coaxed.

"I want you," she managed to say as her body began pushing against his hand.

"What do you want from me?" Ross rasped.

"I want you inside of me," she panted.

He flexed his fingers as his lips moved to her ear. "I am."

"Ross," she whined.

"Dezarae…"

"Love me," she pleaded.

She saw his eyes soften and her heartbeat accelerated in response. He quickly removed his hand and she opened her legs wider to accommodate him. "All night, Firebird, all night." Ross slid his erection into her warm wetness. He groaned as her internal muscles gripped him. "Ah, Jesus, you feel so good."

Dezarae felt another orgasm take over her body as he filled her to completion. Her eyes shut and she released a hiss of pleasure. She opened them again as he didn't move, just sat there buried deep within her. "What?"

"Just give me a second, Firebird. If I move now, it will be all over before it begins." He had begun to sweat with the intensity of the sensations and attempted to control the urge to take her and find his own release.

Looking up at the man above her, Dezarae swallowed. He was so handsome to her it hurt. His gray eyes were shut as he tried to regain his control. Strong jaw clenched with determination, he flexed his muscles as he held himself over her. Moving her hands from the bedspread to his face, she kissed him.

Ross opened his stormy eyes the moment he felt her lips on him. Her tongue began to stroke along his and he moved his hips in time with her motion. Her body quivered around him as his penis moved in and out of her.

Dezarae began to suck on his tongue as her pelvis bucked up to increase the speed of his thrusts.

Drawing away from her tempting mouth, Ross murmured into her ear, "Not yet."

A heat had begun to blossom inside her. Dezarae started to squirm beneath his hard body. Her hands rested on his back as her legs wrapped themselves around his lean waist.

Ross ignored her prompting. Making each stroke excruciatingly slow, he sank into her completely before withdrawing all except the head of his rigid manhood. And then back again. "Do you burn for me, Firebird?"

While she wanted him to suffer like she was, her craving to find release was too intense. "Yes! Yes! Yes!" she yelled with frustration.

Sitting up, Ross watched her flushed body wriggle beneath him. Her mouth was open slightly, lips shiny with remnants of their kisses. Her breasts moved with every stroke of his and each response of her own. "Good," he said arrogantly as his hands grabbed her full hips.

Dezarae locked her hands around his forearms when he increased his speed. Her teeth clamped on her bottom lip as she tried to keep quiet. Harder and faster came his pleasuring thrusts. Mews formed at the back of her throat only to escape as his fingers dug into the flesh of her hips.

"Ross," she cried as her breathing changed again.

"What, Firebird?" he grunted as he increased his speed more.

"I'm gonna come."

"Then come for me."

Back arching, her fingers dug deep into his arms. If she had nails, she would have drawn blood. Dezarae screamed her release to the bright room.

Ross drove deep and hard into her for three strokes before pulling out his unprotected length and coming all over her dark belly. His body was shaking and he had no energy left except to collapse beside her.

For a moment, the room was filled with the sound of breathing as it slowly returned to normal. They lay like that for about ten minutes.

Dezarae turned her head to look at the man beside her. No one she had ever been with before had made her feel this way. The fact he had not come inside her gave her conflicting emotions. The part of her that always looked for the bad in situations figured it was because of her skin color. Her rational side was grateful, especially since she wasn't on the Pill.

Still, part of her wondered what it would be like to have a child with Ross. Shaking her head to get rid of that image, she sighed as his eyes landed on hers.

"You just about killed me, Firebird," Ross said happily as he traced her cheekbone with one finger.

Blinking at him, she smiled. "Thank you."

"Why are you thanking me for doing something I have wanted to do since I woke up in your bedroom?"

"I was talking about protecting me. I'm not on any form of birth control." Her eyes held his steady.

He sent her a gentle smile. "I wasn't sure." His eyes narrowed as his voice dropped, "And get that damn reason out of your head."

Dezarae's eyes widened. "What thought?"

"The one that you gave yourself about me pulling out of you. I, for one, happen to love the color of your skin." He kissed her hard before rolling off the bed and walking naked to her bathroom to get a cloth to clean her up.

Unsure how he had known what she was thinking, Dezarae remained where he had left her. Watching him approach, she eagerly took in his naked body. *I could look at him all day and them some.* "What makes you think you knew what I was thinking?" she asked as he began to clean off her belly.

Ross didn't answer her; he was too absorbed by the smoothness of her skin. The hand that didn't have the washcloth in it began to make abstract designs on her belly. Soon the washcloth had dropped to the floor as his lips began to kiss along her stomach.

Dezarae felt that familiar fire erupt again as his body settled between her legs and she felt his breath at the juncture of her thighs. With a squeal, she tried to move away from him but one strong arm held her in place as his tongue slipped between the lips to taste her.

"Ross," she cried, her earlier question forgotten as he began to make love to her with his mouth. Dezarae shuddered as he worked her into a panting mess.

His fingers and tongue teased her, pleasured her, and allowed her not a moment's rest. Her hands dug into the bedspread as wave after wave of release engulfed her body.

Ross slid his hands under her ass as her hips lifted with her orgasm. He held her to his mouth until she stopped coming, his tongue sweeping inside her, encouraging more tremors. When she stopped he pulled away and lay on his back, rolling her on top of him.

As if bench-pressing, he lifted her up and set her back down on his fully enlarged penis, both of them moaning in pleasure as her body welcomed him back into her. Gray eyes settled on her face as she began to ride him at her own pace.

Dezarae watched the man below her through slitted eyes as he stared at her. The intensity in his eyes was a bit unnerving; his emotions were there if she wanted to accept what she saw. Not ready for that yet, she chose to remain oblivious.

She moved up and down his long shaft while his hands clenched and unclenched as he tried to allow her to maintain their speed. Dezarae loved feeling his penis stretch her body and he moved easily in her slick heat. Finding a pace she enjoyed, Dezarae closed her eyes and gave herself over to the sensations that flowed through her body.

Ross pressed his lips to the space below her ear. "I love you, Dezarae." He mouthed the words as his hands left the bed and grabbed onto her hips.

Her eyes flew open and she looked at him. *Did I hear him say he loved me?* Dezarae met his gaze and he smiled at her, thrusting faster. *It must have been my imagination.* She closed her eyes and allowed him to escalate the rate at which she moved above him. Her body ground down on him as she lost herself to the passion that flowed between them.

Gray eyes darkened. "I'm about to come, Firebird."

Dezarae stopped moving and sat on him, making sure he was as deep as he could be. "Then pound the hell out of me and come." Her eyes blazed with the need to find her fulfillment.

With a growl, Ross rolled them over so she was once again on the bottom and proceeded to do just what she had said. He slammed into her, shaking the whole bed with each powerful thrust. Harder. Faster. Deeper. Again and again.

"Oh, God, *yesssss!*" Dezarae wailed as her body shuddered and exploded into a million little pieces.

Ross almost came inside her when her body convulsed around him, trying to milk his essence from him. Barely pulling out in time, he came all over the ebony goddess beneath him as he shouted to the room.

Like before, he collapsed beside her, their hearts pounding at the same hurried rate. Dezarae still trembled as her body came down from the high it had experienced.

Ross buried his face into her neck and breathed in her scent. The feeling this woman gave him was surreal. He knew Dezarae was his soul mate. There had never been anything remotely close to this with any other woman he had been with. Their connection went way beyond just the physical.

After a while, Ross rose up to look at the woman who could make him hard as steel with a whiff of her soap, a look from her inviting eyes, or even the sight of her smile. Her eyes were closed and her breathing even, telling him she was asleep.

Getting out of bed, he gently cleaned his seed off her belly before covering up her enticing body with her bedding. He looked at the clock and realized he had fallen asleep with her. It was almost five-thirty in the morning.

Sliding his clothes back on his fit body, he moved silently back over to her bedside. Brushing a thick lock of hair back from her face, Ross smiled as she tried to nestle into his hand. "I wish I could stay the entire night with you, Firebird, but I don't think you're ready for that yet. God knows I am," he whispered as he brushed a kiss along her lips.

Ross grudgingly left her sleeping there alone and snuck down the hall back to his room and climbed into his bed, immediately missing the warmth of the woman who had shared her passion with him earlier. Heaving a sigh, he closed his eyes and tried to get some sleep before his daughter got up.

The beeping of her alarm clock intruded into the nicest dream she had ever had. Ross Connelly had made sweet love to her. *Damn, six o'clock hour ruining my dream.* Shutting off her alarm, Dezarae winced at her sore muscles. "Why the hell am I sore?" she asked as she walked to the bathroom.

Dezarae found the hickey on her breast. "Sweet Jesus, what have I done?" *It hadn't been a dream after all.* A smile crossed her face as she shrugged her shoulders. "Had one hell of a night making love." Shaking her head, she corrected her statement. "Having sex."

Climbing into the shower, she grinned as her mind ran through all they had done last night. Dezarae felt relaxed and ready to face her day. Ross had only been in her room for a few hours, but her body trembled at the thought of what all night would be like.

Twenty minutes later, she was clipping her phone to her belt and walking out the front door to meet the truck that had pulled up in her driveway. She ruffled the head of the monster dog that jumped out the second the door opened and said, "Morning, Haley." Then she grinned up at the behemoth that got out of the truck next. "Morning, Tank."

The man plucked her up off the ground and kissed her. "Morning, Phoenix, ready for the day?"

Kissing him back as he put her down, she answered, "Sure am, Tank. Are your men coming up also?"

"They will be here by seven; they want breakfast," he said with a wink.

"It will be ready by then. Come on inside." Together they walked into her house unknowingly observed by a Navy SEAL who shook with fury at their easy camaraderie and the familiar and accepted way Tank touched Dezarae.

$\mathcal{E}$ighteen

Ross was the last one into the living room. It took him a while to calm down after seeing Dezarae and Tank together. But as he heard the laughter and his child's delighted voice intermixed with the deep barks of the dog, he gathered his emotions and walked into the room.

There was a large table covered with food and around it sat ten men, Dezarae, and Charmane. One empty spot was left between Charmane and Dezarae. All the men looked at him when he entered and each offered up a "good morning."

"Morning, Daddy," Charmane said as she accepted a plate of biscuits from the man beside her.

"Morning, baby," he said, walking around the table to kiss her on the cheek before sliding into his chair. "Morning, y'all." Ross looked at each man present and nodded. Gray eyes slanted to the woman beside him,. "Morning, Dez."

"Morning, Ross," she responded in kind, barely sending him a glance.

Introductions were made and breakfast resumed. The atmosphere was lighthearted and cheery. The men were polite and included his daughter in the conversation. It was no wonder Ross noticed a change in her demeanor; here his daughter was treated like family.

After breakfast, Ross stood with two of the men as he watched over his women. Charmane, without being asked or told, helped Dezarae clear the table and put things away. "Y'all seem to be really fond of Dezarae," he observed. Dezarae wore another pair of her tight jeans and a loose blue shirt.

The men, Mike and Joe, smiled at each other before answering him. "Yes, we all love her. I hear you met her a few months ago?" Mike asked.

"Yes, she saved my life." Ross admitted as he saw two more men help Dezarae clean up.

"What are your intentions with Phoenix?" Joe asked.

None of your damn business. "I am just here to get my daughter and spend some time with her," Ross evaded.

The honking of a semi truck interrupted whatever the men were going to say. Dropping the rag she held, Dezarae said something to the man next to her and shouted to the rest of them, "Thanks so much, guys. You're the best! I'll chat with you before you go. You know where coffee and stuff is so help yourself." Then she bolted out of the kitchen, her hands brushing over Ross as she moved past him to go outside.

Jogging across the yard, Dezarae opened up the doors to her shop while the truck turned around. She couldn't wait to see the cars that were inside the semi. Lateef's friend had sent the Lamborghini as well as a Porsche and a Citroën. Then there was the newest car for her own personal collection—a Lotus Elan.

"Hey, man," she yelled as the driver jumped down from the cab. "How are you doing, Ben?"

"Good, Phoenix, I'm doing good. How about yourself?" he asked as he gave her a hug.

"Not too bad. Let's see what you brought me." She walked with him to the back of the truck.

"I brought you a bunch of junk. I love seeing the cars when you finish with them, 'cause, Lord knows, when I bring them, they need help." He swung open the back doors and lowered the ramp.

Dezarae walked up the ramp and swore under her breath. It broke her heart to see beautiful cars in less than stellar condition. "Well, let's get them down."

As they were working, Ross and Charmane left the house to investigate what Dezarae was doing. They walked up to the truck and Ross stopped Charmane from getting closer. A plume of black smoke exploded out of the trailer.

Before he could run up and see what happened, a car rattled down the ramp, the engine coughing and burping every inch. He made out Dezarae sitting behind the wheel and maneuvering the car carefully to sit outside of her shop.

The engine died with a wheeze and blew another huge collection of smoke; and as Dezarae walked out of the cloud fanning her face, Ross noticed she was laughing. "Well," she yelled as her body trotted back up the ramp, "now I know why I got it so cheap!"

The man walked back to meet her at the top of the ramp and Ross got a good look at him. *Jesus, didn't she hang out with any ugly men?* This man was stocky with lots of muscles underneath his olive skin. His hair was inky black and when he smiled, he showed a set of perfect teeth. Ross hated him in a second.

"Hey, Dez!" Charmane shouted.

Dezarae turned and looked down at the person who called her: Charmane and, next to her...Ross. "Hey, Charmane." Looking at the man beside her, she made introductions. "Ben, this is Ross Connelly and his daughter, Charmane; they are staying with me for a few days. Guys, this is Ben Embree."

"Nice to meet you both," Ben said with an easy smile.

"Nice to meet you, Mr. Embree," Ross said, the naked possessiveness in his gaze making Dezarae squirm with delicious heat.

"Please call me Ben." He winked at Dezarae and disappeared back into the truck.

"Anything I can do to help, Dez?" Ross offered.

"Sure, come on up. Charmane, you need to stay out of the way for us," Dezarae said to the girl.

"Can I watch?" the child asked.

"Sure, just keep back," Dezarae answered as Ross loped up to meet her.

"Are you sore?" Ross whispered to her as the next car was started from the inside of the truck.

"Shut up," she hissed and moved to the side as Ben backed the car up past them. Then she disappeared into the truck, Ross right on her heels.

"I just wanted to make sure you were okay this morning," Ross said as he helped her free the next car.

Dropping the strap that anchored the car she looked across the dented and peeling hood of the Porsche. "I'm fine. Thanks for your concern."

"Thank you for last night," he murmured as he walked around the car to her side.

"What are you doing? I thought you were here to help."

"I want a good morning kiss first," Ross said, gathering her in his arms.

"Let me go," she demanded. "Charmane is right outside."

"She's outside. Kiss me, Firebird."

His command wound around her soul. Unable to resist, she stretched to fuse their lips together. Her tongue slipped into his mouth and touched his, igniting more flames between them. Dezarae wrapped her arms around his neck and he lifted her straight off the ground, his hands under her ass as he backed her against the side of the truck.

"Well, that explains the glare I got when you introduced me," Ben's voice broke into their little world.

Tearing her mouth off his, Dezarae tried to get out of Ross's arms to no avail. "Put me down," she insisted.

His hands flexed on her ass and he said, "One more kiss."

Quickly she put her lips to his and gave him what he wanted. Ross immediately took control and the fast kiss dragged on until Ben cleared his throat. This time Ross did let her stand on her own.

"Not one word, Ben," Dezarae warned as she opened the door to the Porsche only to hesitate. "Ross, you take this one; put it in the next stall for me."

"Sure." He slid behind the wheel and started the car. It sounded better than the first one she had driven off, but looked worse. Carefully, he backed the car down the ramp and into her shop.

"Well, now," Ben said as he watched the car go down the ramp. "Tell me what this is all about."

"It's about you minding your own business," Dezarae snapped, still embarrassed he had seen them kissing.

A strong arm settled around her shoulders as they walked up to the Lamborghini. "Just looking out for you."

Her anger was gone in a second. "I know. I am just mad at myself. I don't seem to have any control when it comes to him."

"Doesn't seem like he has any, either," Ben joked and released her, walking to one side of the car to loosen the ties.

"Yeah, but I am just a passing fancy for him, Ben. But my heart is already involved and it scares me."

"Are you sure about that? Him only viewing you like that?" He looked at his friend, doubt filling his brown eyes.

"Of course," Dezarae responded immediately.

"I wouldn't be to sure if I were you." He dropped the last tie. "Okay, done on this side."

Climbing into the car, she started it without answering her friend and backed slowly out of the truck and into her shop. Ben was putting the ramp back and Ross was helping him when she reemerged from her building.

"Want something to eat, Ben?" Dezarae offered.

"I would love something," he answered as he shut the doors and secured them. "Thanks for the help," Ben said to Ross.

"No prob," Ross said. Charmane came back over, followed closely by Haley.

"Well, go on inside. I will be right there I just have to put this in my garage," Dezarae said as she frowned.

"Why don't we just push the damn thing? That way, you don't die from the stuff it's coughing up," Ben suggested.

"Sounds like a plan." Reaching into her pocket, Dezarae pulled her keys out and tossed the keys to the teenager. "Charmane, move my truck will you?"

"Okay," she yelled happily and ran to the garage.

"Are you insane?!" Ross demanded.

Dezarae spoke before he could shout to his child. "She has driven my vehicle before. She learned how one day; and while she is a bit jerky, she can do it." She touched his arm, bringing his attention to her. "My Shelby is in there. Do you really think I would let her drive if I thought she was a danger to herself or my own baby? Have some faith in your child."

Ross nodded as he watched the garage door open and her vehicle move out slowly. Dezarae was right; his daughter could drive. They watched her parked it to the side of the garage before shutting it off and jumping out. "Here good, Dez?"

"Perfect," Dezarae answered and got in her car, putting it in neutral. Holding the wheel, she braced herself to push as Ben took the back and Ross took the passenger side. "Ready?" she asked the men.

"Ready," Ross answered.

"Let's do it," Ben said.

They pushed the car into the garage and Ben spent some time looking at her finished Mustang. Charmane was telling him all about the trip back from California in the car.

"What kind of car is this?" Ross asked softly beside her, looking at the vehicle he'd helped push.

"This is a 1962 Lotus Elan, my new project. What do you think?" Her hands gestured to the car.

"I think you will return it to all its former glory," he offered. *It looks like something the cat dragged in.*

"I know it's not much to look at now, and, Lord knows, it doesn't seem to run very well, but imagine it finished. I was thinking a ruby or blood red. A few coats of wax and an engine that purrs like – "

"Like you last night as I slid in and out of your body?"

"Just like that," Dezarae said in a breathy voice. "You know how I like things with sticks."

Ross was rock hard in a second. "I want you," he murmured as he pointed to something else on the car as his daughter continued to chat with Ben, wanting to give off the impression they were talking about the car.

"I want you too, Johnny Reb. I am so wet for you right now." Dezarae leaned close to him. "I would love for you to take me up against the table, just rip down my pants and take me from behind."

"Dez," he growled, his erection throbbing painfully in his jeans.

"What a shame I have to go make something to eat for Ben," she said as she walked off and spoke louder to the other man. "Food will be ready in a few, Ben."

Ross watched her leave, mesmerized by the sway of her full hips. Ben and Charmane followed immediately after, leaving a hard, horny Ross alone in the garage with her car. Adjusting himself to try and relieve some pressure, he was about to go inside when his phone rang.

*
**

Dezarae waved goodbye as Ben drove away in the semi. She hadn't seen Ross since the garage. Tank and the men had left not long before Ben, her house done and cleaned up. So now Charmane was the only buffer between her and Ross.

The phone at her side rang as she was walking to the shop. "Kerry," she answered and picked up the packet in the Lamborghini that contained the owner's color choice and personal preferences.

"Girl, what do you think?" Lateef's deep voice asked.

"I think this man is shameful for letting them get to this point. I just got the packet and am trying to figure out what order to do them in," Dezarae said, looking over the three new cars in her shop.

"Well, he is looking forward to seeing how they turn out. What did you think of him when you talked?"

"I think eccentric was being polite," Dezarae responded as she recalled talking to the man who owned the cars she had gotten today.

Lateef laughed. "Well, call if you need me. I gotta run; hot date, you know."

"You? With whom?" she asked, skeptical.

"Oh, you don't know her. I work with her," he hedged.

"Uh-huh, what did I tell you about trying to pass those blowup dolls off as real women? Come on, now, Lateef, you are attractive; you could get a real woman."

"I would whup your ass if you were closer," he snarled.

Dezarae laughed. "Me and my ass are trembling. Have fun, babe, talk to you soon and hey…Lateef. Thanks."

"You are welcome, my dear." He was gone in the next second.

Nineteen

Closing the screen behind her after finishing up in her shop for the day, Dezarae saw the preteen watching a movie. "Hey, Charmane."

"Hey, Dez." Her brown eyes smiled as she looked at her friend. "I finished my homework; is it okay if I watch this?"

With a slight lift of her shoulders, Dezarae answered, "That is between you and your daddy. I'm not in charge of you anymore." She moved down to the hall. "I will be in my room if you need me. I have to change clothes."

Entering her room, Dezarae peeled off her dirty shirt and tossed it into the hamper as the door shut behind her. Walking to her closet, she took out a clean pair of pants and a sweatshirt. It was going to be cool tonight and she didn't want to be shivering the whole time on the wagon ride she and Charmane had planned to take.

In her bra and panties, she headed to her bathroom and turned on the shower as her remaining clothes hit the floor. The shower she took was quick but when she opened the door to step out, she froze.

There, leaning on the marbled bathroom countertop, was Ross Connelly. He had on an indecently tight black shirt that only enhanced his defined chest and a pair of jeans that looked painted on him. No shoes were on his feet, only a pair of socks.

"What do you think you are doing here?" Dezarae asked as she reached for the robe that was by the door.

The eyes that met hers were haunted, not at all the ones she would have expected to see. She did get to see the heat flare up in them before it was gone, though, but something was seriously wrong for him to be this deadpan.

"What's going on, Ross?" Nothing but concern filled her voice as she walked to stand in front of him. Still silent, all he did was look at her with a need in his eyes and she opened her arms. Ross sagged against her, his face in her neck. Unsure of what to say to him, Dezarae allowed him to lean on her for a while.

So in the bathroom, full of steam from her shower, Dezarae comforted the man who had taken over her heart.

Ten minutes passed before he pulled away and looked into her sympathetic gaze. "I'm sorry," he mumbled, brushing a wet strand of her hair away from her face.

"What's wrong?" Dezarae wanted to know.

Closing his eyes briefly, Ross opened them to see she was still watching him. "Nothing is wrong; I'm okay, now."

Not wanting to hear that answer from him, she nodded; but she was less willing to pry into something he didn't wish to share. "Okay, then, do you think you could leave so I can get ready for tonight?"

His eyes got a wicked glint in them as he said in a husky timbre, "I think you are dressed too much for what I have in mind."

Holding him off with one hand, she smiled. "Sorry, I was talking about the wagon ride after the festival today in town."

"Wagon ride? As in sitting with a date kind of wagon ride?"

"I guess you could go with a date. I am."

"Who the fuck is your date?" he growled.

Dezarae didn't blink. "Your daughter."

Shocked, he frowned. "Charmane is going?"

"Why not? We had planned on it since we didn't know when you were coming back."

"Will you be my date and sit beside me, keeping me warm?" His breath teased her neck as he prowled around her.

"No," she managed to get out.

"Why not?" He trailed one hand over her hip, grabbing her ass as he moved on.

"Because Charmane should be your date."

"Can't I have two?"

"Sure, but not if one of them is I." Dezarae's senses were swimming. He had stopped behind her.

"Well, that settles it, then. I will just have to take you now," he whispered in her ear. One leg nudged hers apart as he jerked up her robe.

"What are you doing?" Dezarae asked even as her body flooded with anticipation of upcoming events.

"Giving you what we both wanted in the garage," he said, putting her hands on the smooth countertop and opening the tie of her robe at the same time. "Look at you," he said.

Dezarae did as she was told. Her body was leaning over the counter, her breasts hanging down, almost touching the smooth cool surface, and the bottom of the robe was bunched up around her waist. She jumped as she felt his fingers slip inside her wet channel.

"You *are* wet for me, Firebird," he said as he withdrew his two fingers and sucked them clean. "And you still taste like candy." His hand gathered her hair and set it over one shoulder.

She could feel his erection poking her. Dezarae almost groaned in relief when she felt him prod the entrance of her vagina. Her body pressed back against him, encouraging him to proceed.

"It was wrong of you to tease me in the garage," he reprimanded.

"Wrong," she agreed.

"Oh, Dez," he murmured in his sexy voice, "I want to make slow love to you."

"Yes," she said as her body pushed back on him more.

"No, I can't do that." Ross moved his penis away from her.

"Ross," she pled.

"What?" his raspy voice asked.

"Please." Dezarae searched for his gaze in the mirror.

"Oh, don't worry. I just said I couldn't make *slow* love to you." With that, he drove home in one swift stroke, sending Dezarae forward. The tips of her breasts dragged across the cold marble, which created another type of tremble through her.

"Ah, hell," she drew out. "More, Ross, more."

"Watch me as I move in and out of you," he commanded, increasing the intensity of his pounding.

Her eyes were on him as he had sex with her in the bathroom. His lighter hands grasped her shoulders, holding her so her breasts skidded across the counter with each thrust. She was biting on her lower lip as her orgasm grew closer. "Harder, Ross, harder."

He obliged her.

She was just about there when from the other side of the door came, "Dez? Are you in there?"

It was Charmane.

"Answer her," Ross mouthed. He slowed his strokes but didn't stop. The second she tried to get him to stop, he drilled into her once, hard. When her eyes opened after closing from that delicious stroke, he shook his head no.

"Dez?"

"I…I'm in here Charmane. Just finishing up from my shower," Dezarae lied as Ross rewarded her with two more hard thrusts.

"Well, then, I guess you haven't seen my daddy. I wanted to tell him about tonight," the child said.

"I'm sure he will be fine with you going tonight. In fact, he may even want to come…come with us," Dezarae offered as he brought her closer to her release.

"I'm gonna go look for him," Charmane said.

Dezarae bit her lip to contain a moan of pleasure. "Okay."

Ross leaned in and whispered, "I want to come with you. Want me to stop?"

"Not now, she's gone. Damn you, Johnny Reb, let me come," she muttered.

"Don't call me that," he growled as he stopped moving altogether.

"Ross," she wailed, totally unconcerned about whether she could be heard or not.

Dropping his hands from her shoulders, he gripped her hips and held her up more as he pounded into her. "What, Firebird?"

"Let me come," she begged again.

"Will you be my date tonight?"

"Yes, anything. Just let me come!" Dezarae ground out as she pressed back against him.

"Anything?"

"Anything," she promised.

"And I can claim it whenever I want?"

"Yes, yes!" Her voice was hoarse.

"Very well, Firebird," Ross said before he began to piston his hips, driving deep into her craving body.

The only sounds were their grunts as they both reached the pinnacle at the same time. Ross barely managed to pull out in time, but he did and his ejaculation covered her ass as they both quivered from the intensity of their climaxes.

Dezarae collapsed on the countertop, the marble cool against her heated skin.

Breathing heavily, Ross stripped off his clothes and walked to the shower, turning it on. Then he walked back to Dezarae, removed the robe completely, and put her in the shower with him.

He quickly washed off the traces of their lovemaking and got them out of there before Charmane got suspicious. With Dezarae wrapped in her robe again and he with a towel around his waist, Ross kissed her.

"You go first and make sure she isn't around, and then I will sneak to my room," he said.

Eyes still heavy from her explosive orgasms, she nodded and walked out, leaving the bathroom door slightly ajar. "Charmane," Dezarae called. "Did you find your father? What did he say?"

"I didn't find him, Dez," the girl yelled back.

"Well, maybe he went outside to take a walk around. I know he did that when he was here before," Dezarae suggested as Ross left the bathroom and leaned against the wall by her bedroom door.

"I will check by the shop, thanks, Dez." They heard the screen door slam and Dezarae inhaled sharply while watching, through her window, Charmane run towards the shop.

When Dezarae looked at Ross to tell him to hide, he was no longer there.

"See you in a few, Firebird." Then she was left holding the towel he had used and watching as his firm yet naked ass moved up the hall.

***

Ross laid Charmane in the backseat of Dezarae's Land Rover. She was exhausted. The wagon ride took a lot out of her since she wasn't used to being so active. Carefully closing the door, he looked up to see Dezarae talking animatedly with Shawn. Frowning, he walked over to them and slid his arm around her waist. "Ready to go home?" he asked, intruding on their conversation.

Shawn merely glanced at him. "I will see you tomorrow, then, Phoenix, okay?"

"Sure thing, Shawn, around noon good?" Dezarae asked, not even acknowledging Ross.

"See you then, Phoenix. Goodnight, Mr. Connelly," Shawn said with a smile and walked off.

"Think you could be any more possessive?" Dezarae asked the man who held her close.

"I could be much more possessive; now, let's go home." He kissed her cheek, oblivious to the stares of the townspeople.

Rolling her eyes, Dezarae walked to her vehicle and smiled as she saw Charmane sleeping soundly in the backseat. "Why *are* you being possessive?" she asked as he slid in on the passenger side.

"I want that wannabe deputy to know that he needs to stop asking you to marry him."

"My relationship with Shawn is really none of your business, thank you very much." Dezarae started her old Rover and began the drive home.

Ross glanced back to make sure Charmane was still asleep. "Everything about you is my business. He isn't the man for you and you know it. You need someone who is going to bring out your passionate side even when you aren't working on one of your cars. He can't do that for you."

"And I suppose you are that man, Johnny Reb?" Dezarae asked as she looked across the dark interior of her vehicle at him.

"Firebird, I am the only man for you." His answer was firm with his conviction. "And don't call me Johnny Reb."

"I'm not the one going around with a rebel flag tattooed on my chest."

"Keep sassing me, woman, and I will put one there as my body covers yours," he threatened playfully.

"You need to hush with that kind of talk. Now, will you tell me what had you so upset earlier?" Dezarae asked.

"I got a call from my ex-wife," he muttered, distaste fully evident, so into his memory he neglected to make sure he child was still sleeping.

"What did she want?"

"Well after cussing at me for a while she threatened to take Charmane away from me forever if I was going to insist on having her around…" he trailed off, not sure he really wanted to repeat what his ex had said.

"My kind?" Dezarae supplied. "Charmane told me what she had said before."

Ross clenched his fists to keep from hitting the dash of her vehicle. "I'm so sorry about that."

"Hey, from what Charmane said you disagreed with her," she said, though she did shiver slightly.

"I don't know why I ever married her," he swore as he reached for her hand.

"Because you had to be a father to Charmane." Squeezing his hand, she let go and held the wheel again. "She loves you so much you know."

What about you, Firebird? Do you love me? "I am so lucky to have her. But that doesn't help me out of my situation. My ex wants to get my parental rights revoked. I don't know what I would do without Charmane in my life."

Dezarae pulled the vehicle into the driveway and stopped outside of her garage. "Then don't let her win. Keep your daughter."

"I'm a Navy SEAL, Dezarae; courts don't exactly find that good for a single father," he snapped.

Opening the door, she looked at him as he was illuminated by the dome light. "I know you are a SEAL. But you are also a father; that has to count for something. Go put your daughter to bed and meet me in the kitchen. We can talk about this some more." Dezarae shut her door and opened the front door to the house, letting Ross pass her while carrying his daughter in his arms.

Twenty

Ross walked into the kitchen and stopped. His gray eyes moved leisurely over the woman who was cutting slices of lemon meringue pie and placing them on the table. The coffee was already poured and he knew his would be the way he preferred it—no cream and three sugars.

Looking up, Dezarae licked a bit of pie off her finger and smiled. "Grab a seat."

"Sorry I snapped at you in the car," he said as he sat across from her.

"Look, I don't know your ex-wife, but surely there has to be something you can do." Her eyes grew serious as she leaned towards him. "I don't know whether I should tell you this because I don't know if it is true or not."

Ross had swiped his finger through the pie and was sucking it clean but stopped and gave her his undivided attention. "Tell me what?"

"When Charmane first came here, she was talking about how nobody loved her or cared about her. I figured for a teen who ran away, that must be pretty normal venting." She fiddled with her fork. "While we were eating, she was practically licking the plate and seemed extremely surprised I said she could have more. She was skin and bones when she arrived here."

Dezarae took a sip of her coffee. "But when she told me she hadn't eaten in about a day and a half because her money ran out, I figured that was it." Hesitating, she set her cup down and played with her plate. "Then, when I said she had to call her mother, she didn't want to. Again, I assumed it was because she had run away, entirely logical. But when I asked her why she thought no one wanted her around, she said all she was good for was to yell at and," Dezarae paused, "to me, it sounded like she was going to say hit, but when I asked her, she almost flipped out."

Ross was so angry his eyes were almost black. The feel of hot liquid on his hand made him realize he had just broken one of her mugs.

"Oh, my God, are you okay?" Dezarae jumped up and got a rag to get the coffee and see if he were bleeding.

"Why didn't you tell me this before?" he asked in a voice that was deadly calm. His hand lay limp in hers as she wiped it clean.

"Because I was hoping she would tell you if something was wrong. I don't know for a fact she was going to say that, but she seemed very skittish after she began speak." She held up one piece of the broken ceramic mug. "This was another reason."

"I have to get her out of that house or I am going to kill her mother," Ross said.

"Killing the mother of your child isn't going to help either one of you." Dezarae moved on to his leg and began to blot away the coffee.

"Stop," he ordered, grabbing onto her hand. "I don't care about the damn coffee."

"Look," she retorted. "I am just trying to keep busy because I don't know what else to say." Dezarae jerked away from his hold and stood over by her sink, rinsing out the cloth.

Ross ran his hand over his face. Pushing away from the table, he moved to stand behind Dezarae. "I'm sorry, Firebird. It's just that, even if I do manage to get custody, then I have to find someone in Virginia who I can trust her with...to take care of her. I'm just frustrated."

"I don't know what to tell you; I'm not a mother or a father, obviously, but it is painfully clear you love her. Why don't you have more say in the matter of her well being?"

Taking her hand, Ross led her into the living room and settled them on the couch together. "Joy is all about appearances and she is fucking the judge who presides over our case. All she wants is money and I don't make that much being a SEAL. She gets part of my salary, anyway, and child support, which I have no problem paying; but the judge has always seemed to have his mind made up before I get there."

"What about your teammates? Do they have suggestions for you? Are any of them married?"

"Two are married and the rest are off limits for you, Firebird. I don't need you flirting with them." His lips grazed her cheek. "They have given me advice but I am the lowest-ranking person on the team and the only one with a child. Well, the only one with a child who isn't married. Scott and Tyson have children."

"I don't see what your position on the team has to do with anything except that you are still doing your damnedest to provide for your child," Dezarae defended him vehemently.

"It means I get paid the least. I am the newest member as well."

"And you can't just quit because you signed a contract."

"Right, besides, Charmane has full health and dental benefits this way." His head dropped to the back of the sofa. "I don't know what to do. I just don't know what to do."

"Have faith."

Have faith. "I'm trying, Firebird. I'm trying." Closing his eyes, Ross sat in the dim light while holding the woman of his dreams.

"What are you two doing, sleeping together?"

Charmane's voice brought them both wide awake with a start.

Dezarae's eyes flew open to meet the disgustingly amused gaze of the man she lay upon. Blushing, she rolled right off him and onto the floor. "Ouch!"

"Are you okay, Dezarae?" Ross asked, helping her to stand.

"Why were you two sleeping on the couch together?" Charmane demanded, not willing to be ignored.

Turning his gray eyes to his daughter, Ross would have sworn he saw a smile lurking on her face before she narrowed her eyes and glared, waiting for a response. "We must have dozed off last night. We were up talking." His gaze followed Dezarae as she slipped silently from the room as he answered his child.

"*Ummm-hmmmm…*and what happened in the kitchen? There is a broken mug on the floor."

I forgot about that. "I broke a mug last night." Ross stood up and looked down at his daughter. "We need to talk, Charmane."

The seriousness in his voice made her blanch. "I was only kidding with you two. I don't care if you sleep with her," Charmane babbled.

Cocking his head to the side, Ross watched as fear totally overtook her. "I am not *sleeping* with Dezarae," he insisted. *Way to go Ross, lie to your daughter!* "I don't want to talk about that. I want to talk about you and life at your mother's."

His observant eyes didn't miss any of the myriad of feelings that flew across her face. When they stopped moving, it was like looking at a marionette. No emotion showed on her face; she was just blank.

"Okay. Everything there is fine." Her voice was monotone, as if she were reading from a teleprompter or some script that only she could see.

"Charmane," he said, his voice extremely gentle as he took his daughter's hand and had her sit beside him on the couch. "I am trying my best to get you out of that house, but you need to tell me everything that is going on. I will never hurt you. You have to believe that, baby."

Her eyes filled with hope before it was washed away in a blink. "Everything is fine, Daddy. I am fine." She looked away from him and out the window.

"Look, Dezarae told me what you almost said." His strong hand turned her face toward him. "Do they hit you?"

A cold, clammy sweat covered her body and she began to shiver. Her mouth moved, but no sound came out. It took her three tries to get out the word, "No."

She was lying. *I am going to kill them for laying a hand on my child.* Ross gathered her close to his chest and held her. "Baby, I am so sorry. I will find a way to get you from her. I swear it," he vowed as tears began to fall down his lean cheeks.

"Can I stay here with Dezarae?" the small voice asked.

Wiping away his tears, he answered her honestly. "I don't know, baby. Dezarae is a very busy woman."

"But she likes me, Daddy, I know she does. And I don't cause her any trouble. I am getting good at helping her out in the shop!"

"That is a lot to ask of her. I don't know, Charmane, I just don't know," Ross said, even though he had been thinking about that himself for a while now, ever since he'd received Dezarae's note from when Charmane had run away.

She pulled back from his embrace and looked him straight in the eyes. Her voice was solemn when she said, "I feel safe with her, Daddy."

That seals it, then. I have to ask Dezarae if she would be willing to watch over Charmane when I am gone. Ross smiled down at his daughter. "Even if she said yes, baby, and that is a slim chance, it still would take some time to get your mother to agree to it."

"Can't you just kill her or make her disappear?" Charmane asked, glowering and sucking her teeth.

"I don't ever want to hear you talk like that again. Are we clear?" he said fiercely.

She averted her gaze from him. "Sorry, Daddy, I won't say it again."

"Good. Now, I have to get up and shower. I'm sure Dezarae has something to do today, so what do you want to do?" he questioned as they both stood.

"I like hanging out with Dezarae. But maybe we could run some errands for her in town, you know, to help her out." Charmane suggested as they walked down the hall.

"Sounds like a plan to me, baby." Ross stopped at the door to his room. Grabbing Charmane, he hugged her tightly. "I love you, honey."

"Love you, too, Daddy." She returned his hug and scampered off back towards the living room.

*
**

The green Explorer pulled into the driveway and parked by the house. Ross and his daughter got out and began to unload the bags of groceries they had bought. As Charmane took in the last two bags, Ross saw that one bay door was still open at her shop.

Sticking his head in the house he shouted to Charmane, "I'm gonna go let Dezarae know we are back. You going to be okay putting things away?"

"Fine, Daddy," Charmane answered.

With an easy gait, Ross made his way over to the shop. He looked in the door and stopped. Dezarae and Shawn were in there together working on a large Bronco. Shawn was polishing a new brush guard while Dezarae was wearing goggles and sawing through the metal on top of the vehicle with a huge, sexy smile on her face. The back part of the roof had already been removed, allowing her to stand inside the vehicle as she worked.

Ross could only stand there and watch. The pure passion that filled her face amazed him. Her hair was shoved up under a cap and the muscles in her arms effortlessly held the heavy piece of machinery. Legs were braced as she cut a precise line through the roof.

"You want to keep the windshield, Shawn?" Her question rang through the shop as she turned off her saw.

"What do you think?" Shawn asked, looking up at her.

Hoisting the saw over her shoulder, she thought for a moment. "I think you will want one. Taking this off road, you are gonna want a bit of protection from the branches."

"Sounds good to me," he said, smiling as she nodded and pull-started the saw, once again intent on her task.

Ross walked in and moved to where Shawn was back to work. Gray eyes took in how the man wore jeans, hiking boots, and a shirt that showed off his muscles. Ross didn't like that at all. "What's going on?" he asked as he stopped by the shining brush guard.

Blue eyes looked up from where they had been focused. "Hey, Ross," Shawn said easily. "Phoenix is helping me with my Bronco."

A loud crash grabbed both men's attention. The top was off; Dezarae killed the saw and smiled at Shawn first and then turned her attention to Ross. "Hey, Ross. Thanks for getting food." Her dark eyes moved back to the blue ones of her friend. "All we have to do is smooth these out and attach your winch and guard and you are ready. Oh, and I have better tires for you. Twenty-inchers."

"You, Phoenix…you rock!" Shawn said as he walked over to her and took the saw, allowing her to jump out effortlessly.

She nudged him. "My pleasure, sorry that it took so long to get in the winch you wanted."

"You will receive no complaints from me." He set the saw back in its appropriate place.

Ross interrupted, not liking how they were ignoring him. "How long has this been going on?"

"We have been doing this for a month now," Dezarae said. "Our schedules don't always work well together and with the show happening, I wasn't around to do it."

"Can I help with anything?" Ross offered, not wanting to leave them alone together any longer.

"Sure, you can help us put on the guard and winch," Dezarae said.

"Works for me," Ross responded as he moved next to his woman.

Twenty-One

Three hours later, the Bronco hit the floor. "There you go, Shawn. Looks great." Dezarae smiled.

"Sure looks different, don't it, Phoenix?" Shawn asked.

"Good thing you wanted it to!"

"Thanks so much, girl. It is more than I could have dreamed." Shawn kissed her on the cheek and jumped into the driver's seat, his hands moving lovingly over the interior.

"You are most welcome, my friend. Most welcome." Dezarae stepped back next to Ross and waved as Shawn started out of the shop.

"I put the money in your account, Phoenix. Thanks again!" Shawn yelled over the roar of the engine. Then he was gone.

"Bye, Shawn," she whispered as her eyes took in the man beside her. "How did it go in town?"

"I missed you," Ross said, pulling her into his arms.

Leaning easily against his hard chest, Dezarae smiled. "You weren't gone that long. And I saw you this morning."

"Yes, what a lovely way to wake up, you sprawled all over me." He inhaled the smell of cut metal and Dezarae, and she felt him harden against her hip. Who knew a car shop could turn a man on like this? There weren't even pictures of women in bikinis on the walls. "Are you saying you didn't miss me?"

"I'm saying I was working. Which I have to get back to, so if you will excuse me." She moved out of his embrace and began to sweep up the metal particles.

Ross let her go and watched her, not making a move to her at all. She looked up at him, seeing the crease furrowing his brows and the slight clench of his jaw.

"What's the matter with you, Johnny Reb? You look really confused."

His frown deepening, he glared at her. "Why are you still calling me that?"

"I don't know. Does it really bother you?" she asked as she used the broom to prop up her arms.

"Yes, I don't want you to think of me in a bad way."

Dezarae arched an eyebrow. "What way am I supposed to think about you?"

"As your lover, boyfriend…"

Chocolate eyes went wide. "Lover? Boyfriend?"

"What?" Ross narrowed his eyes at her. "That doesn't sound like a plan to you?"

"I think that we're getting ahead of ourselves a bit, don't you?" Dezarae said. "I mean, we aren't even dating. So I am not going to think of you as a lover."

His eyes flashed gray diamonds. "I wanted to go on a date with you. I *want* to date you. And I am *damn* sure we are lovers. I don't know what else you would call what we have been doing with one another during hidden moments." He stalked up to her, anger radiating from every pore of his body. "I am your lover, Firebird. I am your lover and your boyfriend. Just as you are my lover and my girlfriend."

A small grin flitted across her face. *God, I could fall in love with this man so easily. Who am I kidding? I am in love with him.* "You are very sure of yourself there, Mr. Ross Murdock Connelly."

"I have every reason to be, Ms. Dezarae Phoenix Kerry. We both know it is true." He crossed strong arms over his torso and dared her to refute him.

"Don't you think you should ask a girl first? I mean isn't that how it used to work, a man would *ask* a woman if she wanted to be his girlfriend. He didn't dictate it to her," Dezarae said as she crossed her arms as well, bringing his attention to her full chest.

One half of his mouth turned up in a sexy smile. "Is that what you need, a man to *ask* you to be his girlfriend?"

Her eyes glinted with mischief. "Well, a man would be a great start. And then yes, I would like him to ask, not assume."

The forge was lit beneath the steel of his eyes, making them heat up. "Oh, your man is here, no doubt about that. And we are about to take care of the asking." Dropping his arms from his chest, he reached for one of her hands and pulled her closer to him. In his slow, Southern drawl Ross asked, "I don't have a piece of paper to write it on and put the boxes for the checkmarks, but would you be my girl, Dezarae? Will you be my steady?"

Biting the inside of her lip to keep the tears at bay, Dezarae graced him with a full-blown smile. "If I had the paper, I would check yes." She blinked her fathomless eyes and leaned in to kiss him.

Ross met her halfway, easily drawing her in closer to his body. He caught her sigh in his mouth as his hands slid down to cup her denim-clad ass.

Dezarae wrapped her hands around his waist, allowing his solid wall of strength to support her. She whimpered as her body pressed closer and closer to his. A flood of wetness coursed through her as her body responded to his touch.

"So this is why I couldn't find anyone in the house." Charmane's voice filled the garage.

Dezarae tried to bolt out of Ross's arms but he held her immobile. Shaking his head at her slightly, he turned them both to face his daughter. "Dezarae agreed to be my girlfriend."

Mortified beyond belief that Charmane had caught them kissing, Dezarae put her face into his chest, only to pull away as she heard, "Wonderful! I think you two make a great couple."

"See, Firebird, she loves you," Ross whispered as he smiled at his daughter.

"I have to get to work," Dezarae said, using her only means available to escape.

"Well, we will let you do that, then. Call if you need help," he said as he tipped her face up for a quick kiss. "Let's go, Charmane, she has work to do. You and I will begin dinner."

"Okay, Daddy." The young teen smiled widely at Dezarae's flushed face before she turned and ran after her father.

Finally alone in her shop, Dezarae sat down at her desk. Her body was a conflicting mess of emotions. "Oh, Papa, I wish you were here. I need some advice," she said to the framed picture of her father that sat on the desk.

With a sigh, she stood and looked at the cars in her shop. A grin crossed her dark beauty. Although in rough shape, they were wonderful vehicles.

Her eyes fell first upon the 1955 Citroën DS. A French car, she imagined a pale jade-green color for it. It wasn't a project she'd normally choose for herself because Citroëns were pains to work on; the fenders had to be removed just to change a tire, not that it was a problem to remove that one bolt, just annoying. But the money she would get was well worth it.

Then they moved on to the 1965 Porsche 911, German engineering at some of its finest. Top speed was one hundred thirty-two miles per hour and went from zero to sixty in nine seconds. This car she imagined a pearly-gray color.

The 1971 Lamborghini Miura SV drew her eyes next. The top speed was over one hundred seventy-four miles per hour and it could go from zero to sixty in six-point-eight seconds. With five-speed manual transmission, this car begged to be driven fast. A shiny metallic-blue and silver was preordained for this car.

"God, I love my job," she said as she spun around in the shop. "I love my job!" She then walked over to the '55 Citroën. "Well, Frenchie, I guess I'm gonna start with you." Slipping on her coveralls Dezarae got to work, dismantling the beat-up vehicle.

She needed to fix the swiveling headlights, and the rear panels had some dents in them that needed to be taken out. The hydropneumatic suspension was shot and needed a new pressurized hydraulic system, for it ran the power-assisted steering, brakes, and semi-automatic gearshift. The fiberglass roof also needed work.

It was with a smile that she opened the hood and looked at the engine.

She didn't know how long she worked until Ross's voice took the place of the music that played throughout the shop. "Come inside and eat, Firebird. It's late."

Looking over her shoulder at the man who seemed to suck all the air from her body, she smiled. "Hey, Ross."

He smiled at her grease-streaked face and the sparkle in her eyes. "Dinner's ready. Charmane cooked and she says it's time to eat." Ross moved towards her and looked under the hood at the mess that was there. "You know you look adorable covered in grease."

"Wow Jo...Ross, you really know how to sweet talk a gal," Dezarae teased.

Ross's smile softened. "If my daughter wasn't waiting for us with dinner, I would sweet talk you right out of your coveralls."

"Oh, I don't think you need to sweet talk me out of them. I will take them off for you right now." Dezarae unzipped her jumpsuit and shoved it to the floor. "You will have to do some fancy chittin' and chattin' to get me out of these clothes, though."

Kissing her hard and quick, Ross picked up her discarded coveralls and draped them over a stool. "Don't tease me, Firebird," he warned.

"Isn't dinner waiting?"

"You know you are going to be my dessert." He kissed her again, smacked her on the ass, and led her out of the shop into the cool evening.

"I can hardly wait," she drawled, looking at him from under lowered lashes.

His hand gravitated back to her ass as while walked in the house. "That makes two of us," he said in a low voice as Charmane looked at them.

"What took you so long to get here?" Charmane asked as they took their seats.

"I had to drag her out from under the hood of her car," Ross answered.

"Sorry," Dezarae said. Having someone cook for her was new. "Looks great."

Charmane smiled. "Thanks." The dinner consisted of a large salad, spaghetti, garlic bread and a wonderful-smelling sauce.

The food was wonderful and Ross helped Dezarae clean up; Charmane sat in the living room and watched television.

"Do you usually lose track of time like you did today out in the shop?" Ross asked as he began to wash the dishes.

Holding a drying towel, Dezarae nodded. "Quite often. I get so into my work; that is why I have a bed out there... and a small fridge with water and some snack food in it."

Shaking his head, he continued to wash. "You are going to kill yourself working this hard."

"I am not working that hard. No harder than anyone else." She put away the dried plates.

"Do you ever wish you could give it all up and start over doing something else?" Ross asked, putting his eyes on her.

"Nope," Dezarae said immediately. "There is something magical about taking a car that is dented, rusty, and not running properly and making it like new. I get such pride from watching people look at the car they left with me in a new light. I don't know anything else, and I feel close to my papa when I am out in the garage or shop. We had great talks out there." She smiled as she dried more dishes and put them away.

"What about a family?" he questioned as he drained the sink and began to wipe off the counters and table.

"I have one. Dale and Shawn. Tank. Shadyville is my family." Dezarae reached for dessert plates and set them down on the clean table.

Ross laid out the silverware and took out the lemon meringue pie from the fridge. "What about a family of your own?" He then switched gears. "Charmane, dessert is ready," he called to his child. "Turn off the television and come eat."

"What, like a husband and kids?" Dezarae asked as she held the plates for him to put the pie on.

"That is the usual definition of a family. Yeah, like that." Ross waited while she gave a plate to Charmane.

"I don't know. I suppose, eventually, somewhere down the road. But I am happy with my life the way it is." She shrugged and took a piece for herself, sitting down at the table.

"Don't you want kids, Dez?" Charmane asked as she ate a bite of pie.

"Someday. I don't think I am ready now," she answered the child.

"Oh," Charmane said.

Dessert ate as Charmane talked about things she wanted to do with her father tomorrow. As they finished, Dezarae took the plates and placed them in the sink, saying, "I will wash them later. I have to go close up the shop and look over my Elan." With a smile for Charmane, she added, "You cook a mean meal, Charmane. Thanks." With a wave, she headed out of the kitchen and into the rapidly darkening night.

It was eleven-thirty at night. Charmane was in bed and Ross walked through the dimly lit living room to the door that took him to the garage. Standing in the doorway, he leaned on the frame and observed Dezarae as she worked on her car. Oldies music played throughout the space.

She wore another pair of nondescript coveralls, but Ross seemed to think of sex regardless. Then again, anything she wore took his mind down that road. At the present moment, she was at a workbench, working on the engine she had hoisted out of the car.

Dezarae labored over each piece carefully, cleaning it and making it shine. The actions must be automatic for her, he mused, since she was singing along with the music as she toiled. "Are you just going to stand there and stare or come closer and hold a conversation?" Her question surprised him.

"Didn't want to disturb you. Charmane's asleep. Do you know what time it is?" he asked as he moved to grab a stool and sit on the other side of the bench so he could watch.

"I reckon it's late," she said, never taking her eyes off her meticulous cleaning. "And you disturb me less sitting here instead of lurking over me like a damn vulture."

"This is a mess. Tell me about the car." He reached across the table and touched her cheek so she would look at him.

Her eyes briefly moved to his face and she smiled before ducking her head to watch her hands. "Well, what do you want to know?"

"More than the year," Ross answered.

"Do you remember what year it is?" she quipped, setting down the piece she had been cleaning.

"Yes, ma'am. It is a 1962 Lotus Elan," he said snappily.

Rolling her eyes, she got off the stool. "It is the Elan 1500, actually." She moved over to the car. "Its engine is a 1558-cc engine. Four-speed manual transmission, goes over one hundred miles per hour." Dezarae grinned, "Or it will. Considering the crap it was coughing out today, I would be happy with twenty miles per hour."

Walking to the front of the car, she pointed at the headlights. "These are pop-up headlights, a rarity in the 1960s. The body is fiberglass for the lighter weight. The car will have a beautiful wooden dash when it's done."

"It's only a two-seater?" Ross asked, standing beside her to look at the hunk of junk in front of them, trying to envision it as she did.

"They did introduce a +2 model in 1967 but I haven't gotten my hands on one of them yet. Maybe someday." She smiled at the man beside her. "They also have a convertible version. In 1971, they introduced the Elan Sprint, which is normally found with a five-speed manual transmission. That one can shoot from zero to sixty in seven seconds."

Dezarae blushed and shook her head. "I'm sorry. I get carried away sometimes. I forget that not everyone loves the history of these cars like I do."

"Don't apologize. It is very obvious you love what you do. But do you think we can go to bed now?" Ross asked, stepping closer to her. "I want my dessert."

Body trembling, she nodded and moved away from him to turn off the stereo. "I'm kinda wanting mine as well," she said as he stopped her by the door and kissed her.

"I don't have any condoms," he muttered against her lips. "I didn't want to buy them with Charmane right there."

Pulling away, she met his gaze and wondered, "Why are you telling me this?"

"Because, as much as I want to make love to you, it is harder and harder for me to pull out of you and not come inside your warm body." His eyes held hers. "So if you don't have any, all I can do is hold you."

"What kind of an idiot was Joy to let a man like you go?" Dezarae reached up and touched his face gently. "You are such a kind man."

Grabbing her hand, he held it against his cheek. "I am kind to you because I care about you." *Because I love you. But I can also be a very violent man.*

"Let's go to bed. We'll think of something." Hand in hand they walked inside and straight to her bedroom, closing the door behind them.

Neither of them saw the brown eyes that watched the affectionate couple head off to the same room before the door closed completely and the child went to sleep with a smile on her face.

Twenty-Two

"I love you, Dezarae," Ross said as they lay in her bed. She was sleeping on his chest, her breaths coming nice and even.

Ross stroked her hair. He had been awake for over an hour. His mind was running too fast for him to sleep anymore. How to solve Charmane's situation and what to do about Dezarae plagued him to no end.

What did he have to offer a woman like her? He knew she wouldn't want to move; her business setup was damn near perfect. But, he knew without a doubt he would get married again—to Dezarae Phoenix Kerry.

He felt such completion in her presence. Such focus. Such love. "I love you so much, Firebird," Ross whispered to the room.

His face grew grave as he wondered how to approach Dezarae about watching his daughter. Would she think that was his motivation for sleeping with her? She wasn't very trusting. *Should I tell her I love her before I ask?* Ross shook his head. "She wouldn't believe me."

Dezarae stirred against him and covered his rebel flag tat with her hand before she sighed and was still once again. "I can't ever let you go, Dez," Ross said, kissing the top of her head.

With a glance at her clock, he carefully untangled their bodies and got out of bed. Pulling on his pants, he picked up the rest of his clothes and walked to her sleeping body. Ross leaned down and brushed his lips over hers. "Sleep well, Firebird. Sleep well." Silent like the warrior he was, Ross slipped away.

Beep. Beep. Beep. Beep.

That damn alarm! Fumbling around, Dezarae finally hit the button that shut off the annoying noise. Flopping over on her back, she sighed as she looked out her skylight. "There are some days that six just comes too damn early." With a small frustrated sound, she climbed out of bed and headed for the shower.

"Jesus," she complained as the shower's spray pounded down around her. "I am so sore." Regardless of the stiffness in her body, she smiled as she recalled the passionate night she had shared with Ross.

That man released each and every one of her inhibitions. "I think I need to start doing yoga," she said with a smile as she washed her hair. Dezarae didn't even remember him leaving last night.

Done in the shower, she got dressed for the day, opting today to wear sweats and a baggy tee shirt. Pulling her thick hair back into a ponytail, she walked up the hallway to her kitchen. Both rooms her guests occupied had their doors closed and so she grabbed a quick glass of juice and headed out in the early morning to her shop.

Disengaging the alarm, she entered the shop and opened up the bay door in front of the Citroën. "Morning, Frenchie," she greeted the car. Slipping on her coveralls, Dezarae turned on the music and lights and got to work.

"Damn it!" she swore as the blood poured from her finger. Dezarae got out from under the hood and walked to the sink to clean the wound. The gash was long but not that deep, so she bandaged it up and went back to work, ignoring the blood-soaked rag she left lying there.

The final adjustments to the pushrods on the engine done, she stood up and stretched. Rubbing her finger, Dezarae grabbed the keys and sat in the vehicle. "Here we go. Come on, Frenchie, don't let me down." With a flick of her wrist, the engine turned over.

Her ears picked up the slight hesitation it still had. Leaving it running, she got out and went back under the hood to make the final adjustments. Within fifteen minutes, she had the engine purring like it was just off the assembly line.

Shutting it off, Dezarae picked up the replacement hose for the hydraulics. She had found a substantial hole in the current one. This car was not as hard as she had assumed it was going to be.

Lying on her back under the car, she labored away until a loud roar scared the beejeezus out of her.

"DEZARAE!!!" a masculine voice yelled.

Rolling out from under the car, she searched frantically for the person who made such a racket. "What?" she said urgently as her body jerked upright. "What's going on?"

Ross was standing by the sink, holding something in his hand. "Are you okay?" he demanded as he practically ran over to her.

Standing, Dezarae gave him a quizzical look. "Why wouldn't I be okay? What the hell is the matter with you yelling like that?"

"I found this." He waved the bloody rag in front of her. "What happened?"

"Look, this is a shop. I work on cars, and there are times when I get cut and bleed. I sliced my finger." She held up her left hand and showed him the neatly bandaged pointer finger. "I washed it and I bandaged it." Snatching the rag from him, she tossed it into a trash barrel.

"I'm sorry," his reply came as he pulled her in close. "I came in looking for you and you didn't answer me and then I saw the blood. I panicked."

With a sigh, she shook her head. "I am not going to break. I am actually pretty strong for a woman. You can't come into the shop yelling like that."

"I've been properly chastised. I'm sorry. Forgive me?"

With that drawl, I will forgive you anything. "Of course. What did you need me for?" Dezarae asked, stepping away from him and moving back to the car.

"I came to see if you were going to get some lunch or not?"

She slipped back under the car. "Well, I'm not really that hungry so I will pass. Besides, I am almost done with the hydraulics and I want to get that done before I stop. Feel free to help yourself to anything in the house."

"You need to eat something," he insisted, taking a deep breath before he lay down beside her and wriggled under the car.

Dezarae laughed. "What are you doing under here?" She turned her head to look at his gray eyes.

"I want to spend some time with you. And since this seems to be what holds your attention, I figured this is where I have to be." Wrinkling up his nose at her, he added, "Not very romantic, if you ask me."

Rolling her eyes, Dezarae put her attention back on the job before her. "Why are you trying to score points with me? I would think you would want to be with your daughter."

"She is finishing up the last of the work her tutor sent her and I was in her way," Ross said.

"So you came out here. Should I be upset that I was your second choice?" she teased.

"Never second, Firebird. Never second," he vowed.

"Don't worry. I am not upset." Her hands moved consistently for a while and she grunted before saying, "There. That should do it." Dezarae wheeled herself out from under the car and stood up to wipe her hands on a rag.

Ross lay on his back looking up at the hand reaching down to assist him. "You know, I think we could use you on the Megalodon Team," he said as she helped him get to his feet.

"The what?" Dezarae asked as she released his hand and grabbed her water that was on the workbench.

"The Megalodon Team. It's the nickname of our SEAL Team," Ross explained, taking the water bottle from her and enjoying some of the cool liquid.

Grabbing a low-wheeled stool, Dezarae settled in front of the left headlight and began to reconnect the wiring. "What does it mean? Megalodon?" she asked as she worked. "Here, come over here and hold this in place for me. You can sit on this stool," Dezarae said.

Ross sat as she vacated her seat. Then she climbed into the open hood area and sat straddling the car over the left wheel. Her head bent, she continued to adjust the lights. "Well, what does it mean?" Dezarae asked again.

"The Megalodon, *Carchardon megalodon,* is the ancestor of the Great White Shark. It was the deadliest predator in the water. It attacked swiftly, precisely, and always…deadly," Ross answered as his hands moved the light to where she pointed.

"So you're a fish?"

He chuckled. "Do I look like a fish?"

"Well…" she drawled.

"Dez," he warned.

"Okay, fine. But why call your team that?" Dezarae paused and tsked herself. "Duh, because the SEALs are fierce, dangerous, and deadly." She nodded. "I get it. Cool." Moving his hand away, she looked at the headlight and said, "This one is good. Help me with the other one."

Ross rolled over while Dezarae got off the car, walked around, and climbed back up. He held the light like he did the first one.

"So is being a SEAL like they show in the movies? You know, where the man gets the woman of his dreams and carries her off into the sunset." Dezarae looked at him.

"Not exactly like they show in the movies. As far as the SEAL getting the woman of his dreams, I'll let you know." He winked at her.

Dezarae trembled. "You do that." Her hands stopped moving and she put her dark eyes on him. "Don't take this the wrong way, Ross, but don't you think you should be focusing on your daughter's situation with your ex-wife instead of me?"

"I did call her before I came out here. I am meeting her in two days. Can I leave Charmane with you that day?"

"Of course, if you think that best." Her touch on his hand was light as she positioned it where she wanted.

"I don't want her anywhere near my baby," he growled.

"Hey, temper, man, temper. I am not the enemy here," Dezarae said, only half-joking. She finished putting the light in and got off the car. "Thanks for the help."

"I just get so pissed at the thought of her raising her hand to our daughter. You know, she may hate me and that is fine. But to do that to your child...unforgivable." His voice was full of disgust.

"I don't think there is anything that I can say to make it better for you. I'm sorry." She touched his arm affectionately.

Ross smiled and touched the end of her nose gently. "It's not your fault."

Some of it is if she is being worse because you and I are friends. "I can still feel bad for the situation, can't I?"

"Only if I get a kiss for it," he responded, trying to tease that sad look off her face.

"One kiss." Dezarae leaned in and kissed his cheek before stepping back and turning her attention back to the car.

Ross mumbled as he walked out the bay door, "I should be jealous, but at least it is a car and not another man that keeps her attention so intently."

"Dez," the feminine voice broke into the concentration of the woman who was dutifully working on the car in her shop a few hours later.

Looking up, Dezarae saw Charmane leaning across the workbench, staring at her. "Hey, Charmane. What can I do for you?"

The girl smiled as if sharing her own private joke. "Daddy sent me to get you. He said that I'm not to take no for an answer. You have to come eat. Even though you missed breakfast and lunch, he isn't about to let you miss dinner. He cooked."

"He cooked? Your father cooked. Tell me, Charmane, is he a good cook?"

The child shrugged. "I don't know, when I would visit him he would order out."

Oh, boy. "Well, I guess we should go then. Just let me lock up. Will you close the big door for me, please?"

"Sure!" Charmane ran off to do that while Dezarae stripped off her greasy coveralls.

Turning off the stereo, she kissed the portrait of her father goodnight and waited by the side door when Charmane came running back up to her. "Ready?" she asked the child.

Charmane nodded. "Ready."

Setting the alarm, Dezarae and Charmane walked out into the evening. The day had flown by for Dezarae as she had worked on the car. There were a few things she had to order for the interior, but it was moving along much better than she had anticipated.

A little unsure of what awaited her, Dezarae was almost hesitant to walk into her own house. The smells that greeted her, however, made her mouth water. A surprised look on her face, Dezarae opened the door and went inside.

The sight that met her stopped her in her tracks.

A table had been set for two in her living room. A pair of silver tapers sat in crystal holders, the flames bouncing off the intricate cuts. The lights were down low and she heard soft romantic piano music in the background.

"The wine's been poured. The food is ready. All that is missing is the woman I want to take on this date," Ross's seductive Southern voice poured over her. "Will you be that woman, Dezarae?"

She looked to her left and smiled as her gaze fell upon Ross who stood dressed in a white turtleneck and black slacks. "Like this?" Dezarae gestured to her clothes.

"You look beautiful to me but go ahead and change. I'll wait."

Dezarae slipped down the hall and into her room. It didn't take her long before she wore something else and headed back up to the living room.

Ross stood as she walked into the room and his breath audibly caught in his throat. Dezarae had let her hair down around her face, her curls softening her appearance. She wore a cream-colored dress that was simple in design with a deep v-neck and wide shoulder straps. It fell to just above her knees, showing off her silken legs.

Her feet were in a pair of open-toed heels the same color as her dress. There was no makeup on her face but the grease was gone. The smell of sweat peas reached him before she did.

With a shy smile, she shrugged her shoulders. "I hope this is okay."

"It is better than okay." Ross moved to her side and escorted her to the table. "You look beautiful, Dez."

"Thank you," she whispered as sat and he slid her chair in closer to the table.

With a quick kiss along her exposed neckline, he murmured, "No, thank *you.*"

Twenty-Three

Ross noticed the change in Dezarae as he took his seat. Her demeanor was shy, a trait he found totally endearing in the normally self-confident Dezarae Kerry.

Charmane walked in silently and set plates of food down, continuing until there were no more to bring to the table. Then, with a smile she walked away, leaving them alone with one another.

Dezarae took in the food before her. Crab-stuffed mushrooms, mandarin hazelnut salad, halibut with mushroom and shrimp sauce, bow-knot dinner rolls and garlicky greens and beans. "This looks amazing," she said as her chocolate eyes met the handsome Navy SEAL across the table from her. "What's the reason for it?"

With a smile, Ross took a sip of wine and answered, "I thought you deserved it."

"Thank you. If it is as good as it looks and smells...I've died and gone to heaven!"

Ross toasted her with his glass. "We also have ginger pudding for dessert."

Her eyes closed as the first bite of crab-stuffed mushroom entered her mouth. "Are you sure you cooked this?" Dezarae questioned.

"What, don't you think I can cook?"

"I must say I am surprised." She raised her glass to him and said, "Pleasantly so, yet still surprised."

"Oh, I'm a man of many talents, Firebird. Many, *many* talents," Ross said smoothly.

With a roll of her eyes and a shake of her head, Dezarae returned to eating.

The question was on the tip of his tongue, but just wouldn't come. He couldn't ask her, not tonight. Ross ate quietly while he watched the ebony beauty across the table from him.

"What are you so focused on over there, Ross? You seem serious." Dezarae asked and then she sipped her wine, leaning back in the chair.

"Just thinking about how beautiful you are," he said as his eyes roved freely over her face.

"And that brought a scowl to your face?" Her eyebrows rose. "You seem like whatever it is, you aren't happy with the thought."

Damn, she is quick. "I am very happy with my thoughts. I didn't mean to scowl."

"Right." She nodded. "I won't pry don't worry. I can respect your privacy."

"I didn't mean to imply—"

"Hey," she interrupted him and raised her hand. "Let's not do this. I don't want to ruin a perfect evening."

A flash of white crossed his face as he smiled at her. "Right you are. Let's not ruin tonight. Are you ready for dessert?"

Her eyes burned hotly as she remembered being his dessert last night. "I'm ready. Can I get it?"

"No." He waved her back and stood instead. "This is your night to be pampered."

"Be careful. I could get used to this," Dezarae said with a grin.

"I surely hope so," he muttered as he walked to the kitchen and got their dessert.

Elbows on the table, Dezarae watched the man who had supplied this wonderful dinner for her. Every second she spent in his company, her feelings grew deeper and truer.

It scared her.

What did she really know about him? It didn't matter, she realized. He made her feel safe and special like no other man before.

After dessert, the pair merely sat quietly and listened to the romantic piano music. Their gazes locked. A soft smile crossed Dezarae's face as she spoke. "Thank you for the best meal I have had in a long time."

"It was entirely my pleasure."

"What about Charmane? Did she get to eat?" Dezarae asked as she stood and began to gather the dishes.

Standing as well, Ross responded, "She ate before she came to get you." He picked up his dishes and leaned in to blow out the candles.

Walking into the kitchen, Dezarae set down the dishes and began running dishwater. "And dessert?"

"I'll go get her," Ross said.

"You do that," she muttered as her hands plunged into soapy water.

After Charmane had her dessert and Dezarae finished washing the dishes, they sat around the kitchen table playing cards.

"Gin!" Charmane announced with a grin as she laid her cards on the table.

"Humph." Dezarae shook her head. "Tell me again why I agreed to play this?"

Dezarae still wore her dress, although her shoes had long since been discarded. Ross had his sleeves pushed up over muscled forearms and his shoes off as well. He was playing footsie with Dezarae as his daughter soundly whipped them at the game.

"Come now, Dez," Ross chided playfully as he winked at his daughter conspiratorially. "You don't expect to win at everything do you?"

Pressing on his foot, she retorted, "Everything? No, but a game here and there would be nice."

Charmane began shuffling the cards. "Can we play again, Daddy?"

Looking at his flesh and blood, Ross said, "It's getting late, baby. You need to go to bed." He glanced at Dezarae. "What do you think?"

Dezarae was speechless. *Why does he want my opinion on her bedtime?* When his eyebrows rose, she answered. "Well, it's your vacation. She finished her schoolwork so I don't see the harm in her staying up late."

"Okay." Ross gestured for the cards and began to deal.

Into the game, the phone rang. Dezarae looked at Ross briefly before answering it. It was almost midnight. "Hello?" she said into the phone. "Oh, hang on a minute." With an easy movement she handed the receiver to Ross. "Here, it's for you."

He took it. "Hello?" His eyes narrowed and his jaw clenched. "Why are you calling, Joy? I said I would see you in two days."

Moving silently, Dezarae gathered Charmane up to escort her out of the room to give Ross some privacy. Ross grabbed hold of her and shook his head, his meaning clear.

Dezarae sat back down in her chair and began to deal cards to Charmane. Ross stood behind her and played with her thick tresses. "I said two days, Joy," he ground out.

"No, you can't come here." He paused. "What the hell do you mean, you're concerned about her living situation? You are the one she runs from."

Shaking his head in disgust, Ross continued. "She is fine. Charmane has her own room here, and is happy and healthy." His tone dropped to absolute zero. "And if you or that loser boyfriend of yours *ever* lay a hand on her again, your bodies will never be found. Don't fuck with me."

Dezarae turned to look at the man who sounded so dangerous. Like the day he had taken his teammate hostage while defending her, his posture screamed warrior. Every muscle was tense and ready for whatever was thrown at him. His eyes were as sharp as a samurai sword.

Touching his arm, Dezarae waited for him to look at her before her eyes cut towards Charmane, who had a frightened expression on her own face. Immediately, his whole demeanor changed as he caressed Dezarae's cheek and then walked to his daughter and smiled at her, his hand stroking the side of her head.

Moving away, his eyes hardened at the sound of his ex-wife's voice. "What are you going to tell me, Joy? Really? Then it can wait until we meet." He hung up on her and ran his hand over his face in a frustrated motion.

Charmane waited until her father turned away from the phone before she ran into his strong embrace. The tears ran unchecked down her face as his arms closed around her, sheltering, her protecting her.

Dezarae walked, silent and alone, back to her bedroom, feeling like an intruder into their bonding. It was a very uneasy woman who undressed and crawled inside her cool sheets as she wondered what was going to happen with the drama of Joy, Charmane, and Ross.

Ross closed the door silently behind him. Charmane was finally asleep. Both of their nerves were shot as the stress of talking with her mother sank in. So now that his baby was sleeping, he just needed to unwind. He wanted to talk to someone—no not someone…Dezarae.

A bad feeling loomed over him. Joy was up to something and, whatever it was, he knew it wasn't going to be pretty. Touching the door that his daughter slept behind one more time, he walked down the hall to the large bedroom at the end.

Entering the darkened room, he immediately stripped off his clothes and slid naked into the full-size bed, the moon illuminating the slumbering body of the woman he needed to touch. The second he did, she snuggled into his body, an act that made him smile.

Brushing his lips across hers, he whispered, "I love you."

Dezarae mumbled incoherently and stirred against him. With a sigh, she asked, "How's Charmane doing? I know she was scared."

He blinked back tears. "She will be fine. Just nervous about what is going to happen to her."

"What *is* going to happen with her?" Dezarae questioned as she burrowed her face into his neck, breathing in the smell that surrounded Ross. Masculinity.

"I don't know. I can't leave her with her mother, not knowing now what I know about how they treat her." His lips caressed the top of her head.

"Are you going back to court then?" Her hand began to trail lightly up and down his arm.

His tone grew harsh. "She said she had something to tell me. So I will find out what scheme that bitch has planned out when I meet her the day after next."

"Let me know if there is anything I can do to help," Dezarae said as her eyes closed again and sleep began to overtake her.

Say you will take care of my daughter. Although he wanted to bury himself deep within her body and let pleasure take away all the bad thoughts and images in his mind, Ross knew she was exhausted. She was working so hard and now; with them around as well, it only added to her workload. So he would content himself with holding her, gathering her naked body close to him, as close as he could. Ross placed one more kiss on her head before he, too, drifted off to sleep, surrounded by the comforting presence of Dezarae.

The readout on the clock read two in the morning. Dezarae untangled herself from Ross's embrace and climbed out of bed. Slipping on her robe, she walked up the quiet hallway and outside onto the porch. Leaning against the railing, she thought about the man who had come into her life.

She had fallen in love with him and it scared her. Dezarae found herself wanting more — more time, more love, and more Ross in her life. Even Charmane had found a place in her heart.

He was an amazing man. Strength poured from every pore of his body. Determination was eminent foremost as he tried to figure out what to do about his daughter. Dezarae had to bite her tongue to stay out of it. "Just let her stay here!" was on the tip of her tongue to say.

Hell, she had even begun to hear him say he loved her in her imagination. It felt hopeless.

She released a heavy sigh as her shoulders rose and fell with each breath she took. Her dark eyes took in moon and the stars; how she loved that view of the cosmos.

"What are you doing out here?" the deep voice asked.

Turning toward the man who had spoken to her, Dezarae took in his naked torso that gleamed in the moonlight. "Just had to get some air, and think. What are you doing up?" *Dear God, he is fine.*

"You left me." He walked towards her. "I missed your body next to mine." Ross slid his arms around her waist as he turned her back toward the yard and whatever she had been looking at. "What are you thinking about?"

"Nothing, really. I'm sorry; I didn't mean to wake you." Dezarae leaned back into his chiseled chest.

"What's bothering you, Firebird?" he asked into her ear. "Tell me, please."

"I feel responsible for the problems between you and Joy." His body tensed as that name came out of her mouth. "I know how she feels about people of my skin color and I think it is only going to make the situation with her worse—"

"Don't," he interrupted her. Ross tightened the hold around her body. "It has nothing to do with you. We have never seen eye to eye on liking people for who they are as opposed to the color of their skin. When I first joined the Team, she had a problem with Hondo."

Dezarae closed her eyes and prayed for strength. "But you weren't sleeping with Hondo...I doubt it, anyway."

He chuckled as his hands sought her skin under the robe. "No, I wasn't sleeping with Hondo." His tone grew serious again as he asked, "Why are you talking about this? It seems to me that you are trying to find an excuse to stop what is growing between us."

I am too attached to you as it is, Ross Connelly. "I just think you need to concentrate fully on doing what's best for your daughter. And I am guessing that is going to mean staying away from me."

"Oh, Firebird, you aren't getting rid of me that easily. I will do what it takes to get my daughter, but *I am not* giving up on us."

He sounds so confident and sure. Dezarae couldn't respond. Short of demanding he leave, she had no other argument.

"I'm sure about that," Ross said as he kissed her cheek.

Content to just be held in his arms, Dezarae opened her eyes and looked over the life she had for herself. She loved it here in Montana — the wide open spaces, clear skies, everything. Still, she couldn't understand how he seemed to read her mind.

Ross could feel her easy acceptance of his touch. This woman was an enigma to him. He knew she had feelings for him and his daughter, but she tried to keep him at a distance, citing it was best for him and Charmane that way. "Are you scared of what is growing between us?"

"Very." Dezarae answered immediately.

"Why?"

"Because I don't want to get attached, and yet I am already very attached to both you and Charmane," she explained, stepping away from his calming touch and turning to face him.

"Why don't you want to be attached? Is it me? My tattoo? My whiteness?"

"I don't want my heart broken when you leave me," Dezarae admitted.

"What makes you think I am going to leave you?" He stroked the side of her face with his palm.

"You have to. You have a job to do and I know there isn't a SEAL base around here." She removed his hand from her face. "I don't want to fall…feel any stronger than I do now about you and Charmane."

"Tell me you don't love me," he growled out, stepping up close to her body.

"I don't love you," Dezarae said, refusing to look him in the eye.

"Look at me, Dezarae," he ordered. "Look me in the eye and tell me that."

Closing her eyes, she took a deep breath, met his gaze, and spoke. "I don't love you."

You're lying, Firebird. Regardless, hearing her say that hurt him like he had never imagined possible. "If that is what you want to convince yourself of, go ahead." Not sure she would believe it if he told her how he felt, he didn't say it, sighing. "Come back to bed." Ross reached out a hand toward her.

Blinking back threatening tears, she took his offered hand and allowed him to lead her back inside the house and to the bedroom. Once there, he gently removed her robe and helped her back into bed. Disrobing himself, he joined her under the sheet and gathered her into his arms.

Ross held her tightly as they lay in silence. He wasn't going to force her to admit her feelings, not yet. Her smooth hands moved over his naked skin, stirring his desire to life.

"Make love to me, Ross," she whispered into his neck.

Eyes closing with love for this woman, he asked, just to be positive, "Are you sure?"

Dezarae arched her body against his. "I'm sure."

Rolling her over on her back, Ross proceeded to do just that.

Twenty-Four

Dezarae awoke alone. She opened her eyes slowly against the sun that shone through her windows. How had she not woken up earlier than now? Glancing at the clock, she saw it read ten o'clock. Ten? "*Ten?* Why didn't I wake up earlier?" she asked to her empty room.

Climbing out of bed, she smiled at the bouquet of flowers that were tied with a purple ribbon lying on the pillow Ross had used. "How sweet!" She picked them up and smelled them before laying them back down and heading for the bathroom.

Showered and dressed, Dezarae made her way up to the main part of her house. The dwelling was spotlessly clean. There was a covered dish on the kitchen table that had sweet buns in it and she grabbed a pastry. Eyes rolling in pleasure as she bit into one, she walked outside into the yard.

Charmane and Ross were doing some kind of martial art which he was teaching. His eyes deepened with pleasure as he looked up and saw her watching them. "Good morning, Dez," he purred, running his gaze over her body with blatant ownership.

Struggling not to blush as his intense stare claimed her, she smiled at them both. "Morning. Sorry I slept in so long."

"I'm sure you were tired," Ross said, knowing full well that he was the one who had kept her up from two-thirty until almost six.

"Daddy made the rolls; did you like them?" Charmane asked as she delivered a kick and a *"kee-yah!"*

Polishing off the last bite, Dezarae answered, "They were amazing." She gestured at Charmane. "What are you doing?"

"Daddy's teaching me Aikido," Charmane answered proudly.

"Aikido?"

"Yes, it's not really combative. I use the assailant's energy and action against him."

"Well, way to go, Charmane. I am going to the shop to get some work done. Thanks for the rolls." Dezarae blew a kiss at Ross the second Charmane looked away from her.

"My pleasure, glad you enjoyed them."

Dezarae walked off, waving over her shoulder.

About an hour later, Charmane walked into the shop and stopped. Dezarae was under the smallest car in there. She really needed to talk but didn't want to disturb the woman or make her father mad at her.

"What do you need, Charmane?" Dezarae's voice reached her.

"I wanted to talk to you but if you are busy I can come back later," she said, scuffing her toes on the shop floor.

"I can listen right now if you want to pull up a stool. What's on your mind?"

Charmane grabbed a rolling stool and shifted it over to by the car. "I…I…I wanted to ask you why you don't want me to stay with you. I thought you liked having me around."

Dezarae put down her tools and moved her creeper out so she could look at the child who sounded so distraught. "What brought this on? What do you mean 'why don't I want you to stay with me'? I like having you around. Talk to me, Charmane, what is going on?"

"You don't know?" Charmane's eyes grew large as she realized that she made a big mistake.

Sitting up, she pushed her hat back on her head. "Don't know what?" Dezarae demanded.

"Daddy didn't say anything to you about me?"

Dezarae peered at her. "What was it you thought we had discussed already?" Charmane saw a light blink on in Dezarae's eyes. "About you staying here with me while your father was gone?"

Relief poured over her face. "So he did ask you. Are you still thinking about it? I promise I will be good, Dezarae. I will cook, clean, do whatever you want. I won't get in your way, I promise." She crossed her heart. "I just don't want to go back to my mama's house."

"We haven't worked out all the details yet," Dezarae said absently.

"Yeah!" Charmane squealed. Jumping off the stool, she crouched down beside Dezarae and kissed her on the cheek. "I love you, Dez." Then she scampered out of the shop.

After the young teen had disappeared, Dezarae rose slowly to her feet. A feeling of betrayal and treachery filled her body. *That* was the reason he'd wanted to be in her bed. He'd been softening up her attitude towards him How could he do this to her? "I knew it was too good to be true," Dezarae said as she ignored the tears that fell freely.

Not caring about her work for the moment, Dezarae walked back to her bed, removed her coveralls, and curled up on it. Her eyes closed as she allowed the tears to continue to fall.

Ross ran into the shop. Charmane had been so excited when she told him that Dezarae had said they were still working on the details about her being able to stay with her while he was gone. Panic surfaced as he knew he hadn't said a word to Dezarae about it yet. *What was she going to say?*

Skidding to a stop, his gray eyes moved to the Citroën and realized he didn't see her under or around it. He looked about the shop; not spying her anywhere, he began to fear the worst.

Suddenly his ears picked up on a sound that broke his heart. Crying. And he knew who. Remembering she had said there was a bed in the back, Ross moved in that direction.

He stopped in the doorway and looked down at the woman sobbing on the bed. She wore a pair of black jeans, gray shirt, and a pair of hiking boots. Her coveralls were in a ball on the floor. A hat was on the pillow beside her, allowing her hair to be free.

"Dezarae," he whispered.

"Go away, Mr. Connelly," her tortured words fell.

"Let me explain, Dez," he pleaded. *I never knew how much I would hurt hearing her call me Mr. Connelly.*

Sitting up, Dezarae glared at him. "There is nothing for you to explain, Mr. Connelly, I understand everything perfectly." She stood up, gathered her hair back under her hat, and shoved past him, picking up her coveralls on the way. "There is nothing left for us to say."

I am not letting it end like this between us. Ross grabbed her arm and stopped her. "I have something to explain."

Wrenching free from his grasp, she hissed, "I don't give a damn what you have to say. I get it now. Sleep with the stupid bitch and get her to feel sorry for my position, then maybe she will be kind enough to watch my kid while I am gone."

Ross closed his eyes against the unconcealed pain on her beautiful sepia face. He felt lower than a snake's belly. *No, no, no! It's not like that at all, give me a chance!* "Please," he said opening his eyes.

"I have nothing to say to you." Her face was devoid of emotion as she stared at him, totally deadpan. "I would, however, be more than happy to watch Charmane while you are gone." She moved past him, pulled on her jumpsuit, and disappeared under her car.

"Damn it!" He swore as his eyes followed her subdued motions back into the main part of her shop. Frustrated beyond belief, he ran his hand over his face and swore again. Part of him wanted to grab her and lock them both in a room until it was worked out, but he had to let her work through this on her own. Pushing her would only backfire.

So he did what he knew he could do, what he had been trained to do. Wait. Silently, he jumped up onto one of her worktables and focused his attention on her legs that were sticking out from under the car she worked on. *You are in for a big surprise, Firebird, if you think I am going to give up that easily.*

With a last wrench of her ratchet, Dezarae rolled herself out from the car and stood. She leaned into the car and started the engine, listening. Totally into her work once again, she didn't even notice the man sitting, waiting for her to finish so he could claim her attention.

Pressing buttons, she made sure the hydraulics were all working. Then she turned it off and patted the hood. "Good job, Frenchie. I will work on your body more tomorrow. I have some paperwork to attend to."

Stripping off her coveralls, she rolled them up and carried them with her as she moved through the shop. She needed to wash them. "I don't want to go back to the house," she muttered. "I will do some paperwork out here." With one strong throw, she heaved her dirty coveralls toward the door and walked back to her desk.

Grabbing a bottled water along the way, she set it down on the large platform as she rolled herself in close. She began to fill out order forms and answer letters. Her phone rang and she picked it up with a professional, "*Phoenix Restorations and Rebuilds*, this is Dezarae. Can I help you?"

She didn't hear the low, masculine growl at the joy in her voice as she continued the conversation. "Hey, Jack, what up?" Dezarae laughed a deep, husky laugh. "No, not yet. I am looking forward to that." *It would take one hell of a situation to get me to sell my Shelby.*

He had asked her out to his yacht for a weekend; and while Dezarae really enjoyed spending time with him, "I don't know if I can get away, Jack. I have to check and see if I can. I would love to visit with you on your yacht, but I have these cars to finish."

Setting her pen down on the desktop, she smiled as she shook her head. "I am not trying to avoid you. I have to keep my business going. Not all of us were born rich." She laughed again. "Okay, I have to talk to Tank and I will get back to you. Bye, Jack." Dezarae hung up the phone.

"I'll be damned if I let you go out with that man, Dez," a voice snarled, Ross materializing by her side.

Even though he'd scared the hell out of her, Dezarae was still full of feelings of betrayal. "You don't have any say whatsoever about whom I go out with, Mr. Connelly." Her words were clipped.

"The hell I don't!" he raged as he boldly lifted her out of the chair and tossed her over his shoulder.

"Put me down!" Dezarae screeched as her stomach connected with his shoulder blade.

"I don't think so. I have some explaining I want to do and you *are* going to listen to me." One strong arm latched across the backs of her thighs, holding her prisoner. Ross strode determinedly from the shop, across the yard, and up the steps to her house, ignoring all of Dezarae's protesting cries. So furious was he at the thought of her going out with Jack, he just about kicked in her door.

The front door flew open with a bang, jerking Charmane's attention up from the book she was currently reading. She stayed silent as her father marched through the house carrying a struggling Dezarae. Her brown eyes were wide as she saw her daddy ignore all the screams from the woman he held. His own eyes were narrowed with determination and unwavering purpose.

As soon as they appeared, they were gone and she heard another door slam. She felt extremely nervous. When her parents had been married, they had always fought; but Charmane had never seen that much grit on her father's face when he dealt with her mama.

Charmane had known she had messed up by speaking out of turn to Dezarae, but she had truly believed her father had already said something to her. The look of panic that had crossed his face had told her he hadn't mentioned it. "I am so stupid," she said as her hand wiped away a fearful tear that had begun to travel down her face. "I really messed things up between them."

Unsure of how to fix the situation, she put the book down on the coffee table and walked down the hall to stop before Dezarae's closed bedroom door. Sliding down the smooth wood, she sank to the floor as her ears listened in on the angry voices that filtered through it.

"You bastard!" Dezarae seethed., "Put me down!" Her throat hurt from all of her yelling. Not that it had any effect; she had been yelling at him since he'd tossed her over his shoulder and he'd totally ignored her the whole way to her room.

The bedroom door shut with a harsh slam. Ross dropped her on her bed and he stood before her, legs braced shoulder-width apart. Powerful arms crossed over his defined chest, bringing her attention to the distinct muscles everywhere on his body.

"You will listen to me, Dezarae," he vowed.

"I don't want to hear anything you have to say!" she screeched. "For all I know, it is just another lie to try and get me to feel for your situation more!"

"I wouldn't use how I feel for you for that! *Ever!*" he snapped, gray eyes darkening with rage.

"Right, so how is it that suddenly you are going to ask me about watching Charmane while you are gone? It seems pretty sudden after you got in my bed!" her accusation rang.

"I belonged in your bed a long time before I got there!" he swore. "I have been running over this in my head for a long time, ever since I got the missive that you had her with you. I trusted you then and I trust you now. Why wouldn't I want my most precious possession with the woman I trust and love?!"

Girl, he just said he loved you! "I don't believe you," she claimed, climbing off the bed and walking towards the door, only to be faced once again with an immoveable Navy SEAL.

"You aren't leaving this room, Dezarae, until we get through this," he promised in a low voice. "And what the hell don't you believe?"

"What you said. Look, I already said I would be more than happy to keep Charmane with me. I really enjoy her company. But, like I told you before, don't treat me like an idiot and think I don't know when someone is lying to me." Dezarae stomped away from him to flop down in a chair, realizing leaving the room was out of the question.

Ross moved back against the door and sank to the floor. His eyes softened as he looked at the woman who felt she had been terribly wronged. "I don't think you are an idiot, Dez, but you are wrong. I am not lying to you. I trust and love you more than I ever thought I would any woman ever again."

"No!" she yelled as she jumped up from her chair.

Brows furrowed in confusion. "No, what?"

Eyes were almost black as she clomped towards him. "You don't love me; don't lie to me like that!" A deaf man could have heard the pain in her voice.

Gray eyes darkened as thunderheads moved in. "Don't tell me how I feel. I know what love is. And I love you."

"Whatever," she scoffed, turning away before she saw the hurt move over his features. "I don't believe you, Mr. Connelly."

Ross rose in one smooth movement and was behind her before she could blink. "If I didn't give a damn about you, why am I insisting we find a way to work through this?" He spun her around to face him.

"How should I know? To make sure I don't change my mind about Charmane."

Looking into her face, Ross knew there was no way he was going to reach her right now. She was so wrapped up in her own pain from his betrayal that anything and everything he said would only be considered a lie. Still, he had to try one more time, "I love you, Firebird. I loved you before I got my memory back and I will love you until the day I die."

Ross scooped her up into his arms and carrying her over to the bed. She didn't struggle; she didn't do anything. Dezarae just sat in his arms like a stone.

He laid them both on the bed and his grip tightened around her as he refused to let her wriggle free. Over and over, he declared his love for her. The words were soft and spoken directly into her ear, but he never stopped telling her.

Eventually, her stiffly held body began to relax in his embrace. Ross knew the moment she fell asleep; and as his hand moved through her thick tresses, he closed his eyes against his own stupidity. He had almost lost her...he still might have.

"I love you, Dezarae," he pledged as her soft breath lulled him into a fitful slumber.

Twenty-Five

Ross awoke alone. Wide-eyed within seconds, he moved out of the bedroom and into the living room, searching for Dezarae. There was no one in the house; but as he made it to the front porch, he stopped in amazement.

Charmane and Dezarae were outside together, Dezarae helping the preteen to drive better. She was coaching the child as she made turns around the front yard in Dezarae's old Rover.

The sight of them together warmed his heart. Jogging down the steps, he moved towards the women who made the sun shine for him. Charmane had stopped and Dezarae was leaning in the driver's window talking to his daughter as he approached.

"So this is where you ran off to," Ross said as he stopped beside Dezarae.

"She is helping me drive better, Daddy," Charmane said.

"I can see that, baby." He turned his gray eyes to the woman beside him and found himself looking at someone who still felt betrayed. There was no forgiveness in her gaze as she met his eyes briefly before putting her attention back on his child.

"That's all, Charmane," Dezarae informed, "take her around when you are ready." Then she stepped back from Ross, as if needing to keep her distance.

Ross felt her wall going up as she moved away from him. Part of him wanted to let her have time, but most of him didn't. He was going to fight for her all the way. "Good luck, baby," he whispered to his daughter and left so she could begin driving again, walking over to where Dezarae stood watching Charmane. "We aren't done talking."

She didn't even look in his direction. "Like I said before, I don't want to hear what you have to say, Mr. Connelly."

"Don't call me that." His arms crossed over his chest as he too kept his eyes on his daughter.

"It's that or nothing."

"You're pushing me, Dezarae," Ross warned as Charmane made another turn.

"You know what? I don't give a damn. You fucking used me!" she attacked.

"I had hoped you had gotten over this. Apparently, I was wrong," he snapped.

Taking her eyes off Charmane, she pinned him with a look that should have scared him. "What did I get wrong? The fact that you wanted me to watch your daughter? The fact that you were sleeping with me before you asked me to watch your daughter? The fact that you asked me again about wanting a family when you already knew the answers from when you were here the first time, but this time your child was present? Or is it that you were hoping I would crumble under your declaration of love?" Her eyes blazed as she questioned him.

"Charmane!" Ross roared, not taking his eyes off Dezarae. "Shut off that vehicle."

Moments later, Charmane walked up to them both and said, "What's wrong, Daddy?"

"Apparently, Ms. Kerry and I have to work some more things out and I don't want you driving without one of us watching you," he said as his hand latched like a steel vise on Dezarae's arm.

"I didn't mean to cause any problems," Charmane said. "Please don't fight because of me. I will go back to Mama's."

"Let go of me," Dezarae spat.

"Don't fight!" Charmane yelled.

"This isn't about you, Charmane," Dezarae said in a remarkably calm voice. "I told your father I would love to have you stay with me. This is between us." Her eyes narrowed as she continued to glare at the man holding her hostage.

Ross refused to let her go. "I don't lie, Dez."

Dezarae tugged on her arm. "I have other things to do."

Ross shrugged. "Fine, go." He dropped her arm as if he couldn't stand to touch her anymore.

Dezarae couldn't stop the surprised look that crossed her face. Composing herself, she blinked and turned to walk off.

One step into her journey and Dezarae found herself spun back around into Ross's embrace. His lips were on hers even before she could formulate a sentence, turning her into a puddle.

The kiss was dominating as he demanded her acceptance of his mouth on hers. His tongue slid between her teeth and tasted the sweet nectar she offered. Plundering her mouth, he didn't relent until he felt her arms begin to move around his body.

As she gripped him for support and to intensify the kiss, Dezarae felt it change. It went from demanding to coaxing; he eased the pressure upon her lips. His tongue teased hers as it swept around her mouth.

Ross pulled back as he caught her moan of pleasure in his mouth. "Did you really think I would just let you go? I told you. I love you, Firebird." His lips brushed lightly against hers as he spoke.

"I just need some time to work it out in my head," Dezarae admitted, knowing she needed him in her life.

"No going out with Jack?" he asked in a half demand, half beg.

Blinking as she smiled softly at the jealousy in his voice, she promised, "Not without you at my side."

It was as if the world had been lifted off his shoulders at those words. While things weren't back to perfect between them, at least she was willing to give him the benefit of doubt. Love filled his gaze as he caressed the side of her face, "Thank you for trusting me."

"I'm trying," Dezarae said as she allowed him to tuck her under his arm before they both faced Charmane.

His hand ran idly over her shoulder. "Charmane, I'm going to talk to your mother tomorrow. You are going to stay here with Dezarae."

"Okay, Daddy." Ross stood so tall and strong while he looked at his daughter as he hugged the woman he loved to him. The happiness in his gaze was something Ross was sure Charmane had never seen when he had been with her mother or even before he'd met Dezarae. They made a great couple and Ross hoped that this would be his new family life.

Dezarae was back to work in the shop. She had finally cleared off the rest of the papers that had been waiting for her. Pushing away from the desk, she slid on a clean pair of coveralls and got back to painting the Citroën. The screens were up, separating this car from the others, and the vehicles were also covered as an extra precaution.

Her mask on, she easily and swiftly painted the French car the pale jade-green color she had chosen. Confirmation of her choice had come earlier in the day from the owner of the car. In fact, he had okayed all of her color choices for his vehicles.

Finishing and cleaning up her dirty equipment, Dezarae stopped as she felt someone watching her. Looking over her shoulder, she noticed Ross leaning against a wall, those gunmetal eyes of his on her.

"What are you doing here?" she asked as her hands shook off the extra water.

"I wanted to make sure you hadn't changed your mind," Ross said as he moved effortlessly towards her.

"About what?" Dezarae wondered, reaching for a towel on which to dry her hands.

"Trusting me." Tanned hands reached for her to bring her closer.

"I said I would try, but look at it from my point of view. How would you take it?" Dezarae asked.

"Please believe I would never do anything like that. What we have is too special to use in any other way." Ross began to unzip her coveralls.

"What are you doing?" Her hands stopped his from continuing to lower the zipper.

"Getting you out of this," he replied candidly.

"Why?"

"Because I want to make love to you. And you wearing this would make it more difficult."

"I have work to do," she said as she moved the zipper back up.

Ross pulled her closer and bucked his hips against her, showing her how hard he was. "I want you." His words flowed like liqueur over her skin.

Looking up at the man who made her burn in unimaginable ways, Dezarae answered honestly, "I want you too."

She found herself naked and being laid back on her small bed in no time as Ross settled above her. His mouth latched onto one breast and suckled it as his erection prodded at her wet entrance.

Spreading her legs wider, she gripped his back and encouraged him with mewling cries. Her back arched as he licked a path from one breast to the other. "Ross," she whimpered while he continued to tease her.

"Hummm?" he murmured against the tight nipple he had in his mouth.

"Inside," she begged.

One thrust of his hips and he was fully embedded within her molten heat. Both of them groaned in relief and pleasure. Ross moved up to kiss her mouth and his body began to move within hers.

Each stroke was deliberately slow and drawn out. He slid against every nerve inside her as he moved. In. Out. In. Out. In. Out.

Dezarae began to writhe beneath him, trying to encourage him to go faster, but he took his mouth off hers and said, "No. No fucking; no having sex. We make love this time. Slow."

"Please," she tried.

"I don't want this to end, Firebird." He continued with his purposeful strokes. "I want you to burn for me like I burn for you."

"I do, Ross, I do," she moaned.

"Not as much as you will," he promised her, closing his eyes.

Each thrust of his hips made her cries grow louder. Her fingers dug into the smooth expanse of his back as he continued his controlled strokes. Dezarae wrapped her legs around his hips, trying to keep him in deeper.

Ross began to suck on her neck as her body approached the edge of the cliff. "Faster, Ross please!" Dezarae cried, desperately wanting to reach her peak.

He began to move faster. Each plunge into her garnered a cry from her full mouth. Her eyes rolled back into her head and she pressed her pelvis up to meet his thrusts.

Faster.

Harder.

Deeper.

"Come for me, Firebird," he demanded, and his eyes watched the orgasm overtake her body. She bit her lower lip as her hands clamped down tighter into him and her internal muscles contracted around him. "You are so beautiful. I love you, Dezarae."

She was still shuddering with the waves of pleasure from her orgasm; and as she milked him, he apparently lost what little control he had and came deep within her body, screaming his release to the small room with one last thrust.

Dezarae felt his sperm cover her womb and her legs instinctively tightened around him to keep him inside her. As his body collapsed on hers, her legs remained like a vise around him.

Ross smiled into her neck. Gently disengaging her legs from around him, he rolled off her and gathered her close to his sweating body. "I love you," he said again.

I love you, too, Ross Connelly. She couldn't say it out loud to him, so she remained silent and just enjoyed his arms holding her close.

"I'd apologize for coming inside of you, but I'm not sorry," he murmured to her as his lips moved across her hairline.

I'm not, either. "What is Charmane doing right now?" Dezarae asked, not wanting to think of what ramifications could occur from their slipup.

"She is making dinner. She is still worried you think she is going to be in your way," Ross said as his hand found and played with one breast.

"I don't think she is going to be in the way. I mean it will take time for me to get used to her being here, but I think we have done fine thus far."

"She feels bad for creating trouble between us. I heard her last night praying that it works out." Dezarae tensed. "Don't even think it, Dez," he growled. "I wish you would stop looking for the worst in everything that I say. I am not trying to make it work for her. I want it to work for me, for us."

Relaxing again, she began to press little kisses along his bare chest. "How long until dinner?"

Lifting her up and settling her down on his rapidly hardening penis, he said, "Long enough."

Dinner was light-hearted. Charmane had a permanent smile on her face and the two adults were remarkably relaxed.

Ross helped Dezarae wash dishes and made more of a nuisance of himself than anything else, considering his incessant need to touch her body. Even though he never verbally said it as they worked, his eyes always told her how he felt.

After the chore was complete, Dezarae spent a bit of time on the phone setting up times for people to drop off vehicles. While she did that, Ross sat silently in a chair reading a magazine and Charmane put a puzzle together.

Once Charmane was in bed, Ross and Dezarae sat out on the porch discussing tomorrow. "What time do you have to leave to meet her?" Dezarae wondered.

He slid his arm around her as they sat on the swing. "We meet around ten in the morning."

"Okay. Are you coming home tomorrow night?" she asked, hating that he was doing this alone.

Brushing her hair back from her neck, he kissed it. "I will be home tomorrow. Will you miss me?"

"Yes." Dezarae answered immediately. "I hate that you are going to meet her. What if she decides she wants you back?"

Ross smiled in the dark. "Firebird, she can wish all she wants. There is nothing she can say that will make me take her back. Not now, especially since I have someone so much better in my life."

"You always had Charmane," Dezarae said.

"I did, but I was talking about you, my sexy firebird." Ross replied.

Dezarae smiled but remained silent. Her head easily resting against his shoulder she let the sounds of the country night flow over her.

Twenty-Six

"What the hell are you talking about?!" Ross hollered at the woman he had married right out of high school. Joy Patterson. The fact they were in a restaurant held no meaning to him.

Her brown eyes were full of hate as she looked at the father of her child. "I'm saying that if you want her, you can buy her."

Ross was incredulous. "You would sell me our child?"

"Basically. I will sign over my maternal rights if you pay me. Kind of like you buying my half of our property." Her sneer turned his gut.

Ross wanted to beat the hell out of both of them. Her scruffy-looking boyfriend Don was sitting next to her. Clenching his jaw, he asked the question he knew would send him to hell. "And how much would this cost me?"

"Two hundred fifty thousand," Joy said with a glance at her boyfriend.

"A quarter of a million dollars? And, assuming I did this, how am I to know you will go through with it?" *I don't have any way of coming up with that much money!*

"You and I will meet three days from now. Don will be at the bank waiting for confirmation of fund deposits into this account." She handed him a piece of paper across the booth table. "Then I will hand you a notarized document that says I have relinquished my parental rights to you, after he calls me and tells me the money is there."

"Three days?" Ross felt his world drop out from under him. "How do you expect me to come up with that amount in that time?"

With a careless shrug, she cooed, "Not my concern. I will see you here in three days, Rossy. Don't be late." Venom filled her voice.

"Oh, and if you don't do this, you will never see her again. I will have your rights revoked so fast it will make your head spin."

With a smile and a wave, she was gone in a cloud of cheap perfume. Ross remained seated at the table where they had eaten lunch. Dropping his head, he swore. "What the hell am I going to do about this?"

Tossing money for the bill on the table, Ross walked out of the small diner. He drove back to Dezarae and Charmane in his Explorer, not sure at all how he was going to fix this mess. "Should've left her ass back in the damn trailer park where I found her."

"What the hell am I supposed to do about this, Scott?" Ross asked as he paced around on the porch at Dezarae's house. Upon his return, he immediately called his commanding officer, Lieutenant Commander Scott Leighton, better known as "Harrier" to the SEAL team.

Scott said, "I don't know. Maybe Jayde's father can help. He's a lawyer. And you know I will lend you the money."

"No," Ross said vehemently. "I didn't call to get you to lend me the money."

"We are family. I would be more than happy to help you out. So would any of us," his superior officer stated honestly.

Slumping against the pillar, Ross swore again. "I can't believe she expects me to come up with two hundred fifty thousand in three days or she is taking Charmane away from me forever. She even gave me the account it is to be put in." Running a hand over his face, he said, only half-joking, "I could always torture them."

Scott chuckled dryly. "Let's call Tyson and have him talk to Jayde first before we go that route."

"Don't worry about it, sir," Ross said, unintentionally telling Scott he was really worried by calling him that. "I will think of something. Thanks for letting me talk to you about it. Give my best to Lex."

"I am here if you ever need to talk, you know that, Jeb. I will tell Lex you asked after her. Keep me posted." With a click, Scott was gone.

Moving silently away from the window, Dezarae was furious over what she had heard. Who ever thought about selling their child to the other parent? Two hundred fifty thousand dollars was a lot of money; she would bet anything that Ross didn't even have anything remotely close to that.

Understanding completely that he would most likely be very pissed with her for interfering, Dezarae decided it didn't matter. She could help and she would.

Ross put forth a happy face that night at dinner, but Dezarae knew how much of an effort it was for him to do so.

"What did Mama say?" Charmane finally asked as Dezarae served dessert.

"We are still working on it, sweetheart," Ross said, staring at his plate with a slight frown.

"Did you tell her that I am doing better here?" she pushed.

"I said we were working on it, Charmane," he snapped.

"Why don't you tell him what you did today, Charmane?" Dezarae broke in, seeing the flash of hurt on the child's face.

"Yes, what did you do today, baby?" Ross questioned as he sent a grateful look to Dezarae.

"I drove a truck and trailer," Charmane said proudly, shaking off her brief melancholy.

Wide gray eyes moved from the young woman to an older one. "She did what?"

"She drove the truck and trailer that was here today." Dezarae winked at Charmane. "And she did a wonderful job."

"It wasn't very far, Daddy, and only a straight line. Tank was back and he had his trailer on his big truck and they let me drive it. He said someday he will teach me how to back up with a trailer on." Charmane was totally excited.

Ross nodded and smiled. "I'm very proud of you, Charmane. That's wonderful."

"And his truck is a stick, too, just like Dez's Rover."

A few minutes later, the phone rang and Dezarae got up to answer it, allowing her hand to trail familiarly over Ross's shoulders as she passed him. "I am amazed at you, Charmane; you are doing really well here, aren't you?" he asked, even as his gaze followed the woman who had touched him.

"I'm so happy out here, Daddy. Really I am. I love all her friends and how Dez treats me like a real person."

I will do whatever it takes to keep you, baby. "Well, then, I guess we should find a way to let you out here," he said as a smile crossed his face. Briefly, he glanced at his child before his eyes moved back to Dez, who he figured out was talking to the sheriff.

Squealing with excitement, Charmane jumped out of her chair and ran around to hug her father. "Really, Daddy? Do you mean it? Really, really?"

"I will find some way of making your mother see it my way," he promised as he hugged her back.

Dezarae hung up the phone. "We are invited to Dale's house for dinner tomorrow night."

Slate eyes narrowed. "Who is 'we'?"

"All of us, my overly suspicious SEAL. He is having a barbecue and we are invited. A bunch of children will be there as well."

Ross reached one hand out for Dezarae and smiled gently at her as she put her hand in his larger one. "I am yours, aren't I?"

"Oh, gross," Charmane wailed playfully. "You aren't going to kiss, are you?"

Dezarae leaned in and placed a loud smacking kiss on her cheek. "Just you, darling, just you."

"Oh, oh! Me too!" Ross declared as he too kissed his daughter on the cheek. "But I am going to kiss my other woman as well," he said as his lips found Dezarae's.

"Yucky!" Charmane squealed as she jumped off his lap and moved away.

Ross put Dezarae on his lap and deepened the kiss while her hands gripped the back of his head, pulling him closer. Biting his lower lip, she backed off his mouth and whispered, "Yes, you are." Then she got off his lap and winked at Charmane, who was trying to look disgusted.

They played cards again that evening. Just as before, Charmane wiped the floor with them. As she put away the cards, Dezarae complained, "I don't know. I think maybe you are cheating. I don't lose that often and that badly."

"I played fair, Dez," Charmane defended herself. "I can't help it. I just played better than you."

"Better than? I don't know what I was doing but it wasn't playing cards," she grumbled even as she sent the teen a smile.

"Bedtime, Charmane," Ross said, turning off the lights.

"Night, Dez," the child said, kissing her on the cheek.

"Night, Charmane," Dezarae responded and kissed her back.

After the child had been tucked in, Ross made his way back up to where Dezarae was wiping down the kitchen counters. "Ready for bed, Firebird?" He slid his arms around her from behind.

"What happened?" Dezarae asked.

"Joy was just being Joy. A bitch. Don't worry about it." His lips teased the back of her neck.

I know the truth, Johnny Reb. "Well, if you're sure."

"I'm sure I don't want to think about her right now. I have someone more important on my mind."

Her hand reached behind her and stroked his swollen erection. "Do you now?" she teased.

"Most definitely."

Dezarae had a siren's smile on her face as she turned around, dropped to her knees, and freed him from the confines of his jeans. She slowly took him into her mouth, right there in her kitchen.

Ross groaned as her lips closed around the head of his penis. She took more and more of his length in her warm mouth. Her tongue swept up and down the rigid erection as her fingers teased the base.

When she sucked harder, he had to lean forward and brace his hands on the counter. "Jesus, Dez," Ross moaned as he began to pump his hips.

She didn't answer except to draw in more of him to her mouth until his entire length was inside. Her strong hands moved around to grip his ass, burying her nose into his pubic hair.

Looking up, she saw Ross close his eyes as he gripped the back of her head and began to piston himself in and out of her mouth harder.

"I'm about to come," he said hoarsely.

Dezarae's answer was to suck on him harder, her tongue running over the tip as he pulled back. She dug her fingers into the firm cheeks of his ass.

With a shout, his orgasm ripped through him as he poured his sperm deep in her throat. As she sucked, she let loose a contented purr from the back of her throat as she made sure she got every last drop he delivered.

Finally spent, he pulled out of her mouth and looked down at the woman who knelt on the tiled kitchen floor in front of him. Dark eyes were content as her tongue slipped out to lick her lips.

Ross reached down and pulled her to her feet. "Why?" he asked as his hand cupped her face.

"I wanted to," she admitted. Her hand closed around his exposed penis, smiling as it twitched again beneath her touch.

"I love you," Ross said as he kissed her.

And I love you. Dezarae remained silent as she stroked his rapidly hardening erection.

"I think we need to go to bed," he whispered, halting her hand motion.

"I think you are right." Reluctantly, she removed her hand from his body and left the kitchen, shutting off the lights.

Ross followed her down the hall, his erect penis still out of his pants. The second they were in her room and the door was closed, he shucked off his clothes to stand against the door, naked as the day he was born.

"Looks like you have a problem there, Ross," she purred as her body swayed closer to him.

"Think you can take care of it for me?"

"Oh, I don't know." She pulled her shirt off over her head. "It may take me all night to figure out just how to get the swelling down." Her pants were removed, leaving her in bra and panties.

"I think you may be right," he said in a guttural tone. Gray became mercury as his gaze heated up, looking over her body.

"I should probably get started then," she breathed as her remaining articles of clothing were dropped to the carpet of her room.

He took a step toward her. "Wouldn't want to waste precious time."

"Oh, no. That wouldn't be smart at all. I say this will keep me busy until about six in the morning." She closed the rest of the distance and ran her hands down his smooth chest.

A purr of pleasure left his mouth as he drew her in closer and captured her lips with his. Sweeping her up in his arms, Ross took them to the bed where he laid her down on her back.

They spent the rest of the night making love all over her room. Ross took her to the pinnacle of pleasure time and time again. She had rug burns on her body and every muscle was sore, but she slept with a smile on her face.

However, when her alarm went off, awakening her, she was surprised she was alone in her room.

Taking another shower, Dezarae got ready for her day. She snuck out of the house and went to the shop. Opening the bay door, she positioned her body to where she could keep an eye on the house and made a call on her cell phone.

Ross left the house and walked towards the woman who sat talking on her cell phone. Jealousy flared until he noticed she was looking at a sheet of paper. *You work too hard, Firebird.* With a grin, he moved toward her.

"I appreciate it," she said as he walked up. "Thanks again." Then she hung up the phone. Her eyes sparkled as she looked at him. "Morning, Ross."

"Morning, Dez," he said as he leaned down to kiss her. "Working already?"

Her shoulders shrugged easily. "Well, it isn't six-thirty in New York."

"What's on the agenda for today?" he asked.

"I finish the Citroën and begin on the Porsche. What are you and Charmane doing?" Her eyes moved over her yard.

"I have to make some calls and then I thought we would do whatever she wants to do."

"Cool. I will be in to make breakfast in a second. Just let me open up the other bay door in front of the Porsche." Turning away from him, she walked into the dim interior of her shop.

Ross waited for her outside. "Thank you," he said kissing her again when she returned, "for last night."

Dezarae blushed. "Thank *you*."

"Are you okay this morning?" He fell into step beside her.

"Fine," she admitted as another blush swept over her body.

"Good, I hoped you wouldn't be too sore." Ross held the door for her and followed her in to the kitchen.

Charmane was up soon and, as the three of them sat around the table, her gaze flickered between the two adults. Her father's affection was obvious for the woman who had welcomed them into her home.

The prospect of staying here with Dezarae was so exciting to Charmane she could hardly stay still. "What are we doing today?" she asked as she took some scrambled eggs.

Ross poured them each a glass of orange juice as he answered his child, "We are going to do whatever you want, and Dez has some things to finish."

Before she could say anything else, the sound of Dezarae's cell phone went off. "Kerry." Dezarae slid away from the table and grinned apologetically at the two sitting there. "Okay, just let me go out to the shop, hang on a sec." She was out the door in a flash.

Twenty-Seven

Ross swore as he drove to meet his ex-wife. He had pulled together as much as he could and hoped she would agree to this much as a down payment so he could pay the rest later. Meanwhile, he would see if Jayde could help him get a good lawyer who worked at her father's firm.

Pushing gloomy thoughts from his mind, a brief smile crossed his face as he thought over the barbecue at Sheriff Dale's. It seemed like a good portion of the town had come to it and by the end of the night, everyone there knew Dezarae was his woman. She had accepted his touches, kisses, and blatant possessiveness.

That smile faded as he pulled into the parking lot of the diner. He saw Joy's rental car and knew she would be pissed he was late. A sick smile appeared as he imagined her face as he said he had been making love to Dezarae before coming here. Then he sobered. He couldn't do anything that would make Joy take Charmane away from him. Had to get her happy and somehow to agree to him making payments.

So he walked into the diner with sixty-five thousand dollars on his person. His gray eyes found Joy sitting at the same table with a scowl on her face. Without a word, he slid into the booth seat and gestured for the waitress.

"You're late." Her sickly drawl reached him as she sucked down another cola.

"I'm here," he responded and looked at the woman who came to take his order. "I'll have the special, please, and coffee." The blonde waitress nodded and walked away.

"Why are you late?" the mother of his child asked.

"What difference does it make?"

She shrugged. "Tell me, don't you ever miss being in bed with me?" Her slim hand reached across the table towards him.

"No!" he snapped, moving his hand so she couldn't touch him. Ross wasn't sure what he would do if she actually did.

"Well, I miss you. You always were a good fuck." Joy's brown eyes moved hungrily over his body. "Once more for old times?" she wondered as she opened two buttons on her shirt.

She can't be serious. Raising a brow he asked, "What about Don?"

Her shoulders rose and fell in an easy motion. "Who has to tell him?" Pushing aside the material, she allowed his eyes a free preview.

It didn't attract his attention at all. "I'm not here to sleep with you. I'm here for Charmane."

She rolled her eyes in disgust and sneered. "We'll get to that. Do you even have sex, Rossy?"

His eyes narrowed; she knew he hated that name. "Yes, but I have no interest in anything you could offer."

Hatred flashed across her face as the waitress came back with his order. "You never had any problem screwing me before. In any place, either, as I recall," she said, watching the woman's reaction who set down the food. "Don't you even remember fucking like animals in places like this?"

"Times long past," Ross said emotionlessly. *Think of Charmane, think of being together. Don't let her psych you out.*

Sensing she wouldn't get a rise out of him with that, Joy dropped it. "They weren't all bad," Joy said as she picked a handful of fries off her plate and shoved them in her mouth. She had the table manners of a barn animal.

Picking up his fork, Ross began to eat. He knew Joy wanted him to lose his patience with her droning on and on about their past. She seemed to have forgotten he was trained to wait. So instead of allowing her to egg him on, he painted on a face of indifference and ate.

"Don't you think so? I mean, we did get Charmane out of it. Well, I got stretch marks and sagging breasts too," she grumbled.

Still silent, he sipped his coffee and waited for her to finish her tirade. As her mouth continued to move, Ross tried to figure out what it had been about her that attracted him in the first place. She had been one beautiful woman, petite, not more than a size six. It had been her eyes, he figured. They had been so big and he'd fallen right in.

Their marriage had been rocky at best, even before Charmane had come along. Being a new seaman recruit and desperately wanting to make it to BUDs, he hadn't been the most devoted husband. The glory of marrying a military man had quickly worn off for Joy and she'd wanted someone who earned a lot more money. *Funny, she is with a man who barely makes anything now.*

As he drank his coffee, Ross watched her mouth move. His mind pictured a woman with full, dusky lips, dark chocolaty eyes, and a figure that could make his body give a twenty-one–gun salute. Not the woman in front of him, no. Hell, no. The woman who was spending the day with his child.

"Are you listening to me, Ross?" Joy demanded.

"No," he said before he could stop himself.

"What has your attention so hard? That waitress who was here? I didn't think she was your type." Those brown eyes he used to love so much were narrowed with jealousy.

With a roll of his eyes, he answered, "I am not thinking about the waitress. I was just trying to figure out why the hell we ever got together in the first place." *I was thinking about the woman I left naked in bed to come here.*

"I don't know. And I don't care because it was a waste of my time. Now about the money…" Joy had always been like that. If the conversation wasn't going her way, she would change it.

Finally. "About that," Ross began, praying she would take the offer. "I—"

Her cell phone rang and she answered it. "Hey, baby. Is it there?"

Ross groaned. He had hoped to explain it before Don called and said there was no transaction. His eyes never moved from Joy's face as he tried to gauge her reaction to the call she had received.

"Really," she said in a low tone, her eyes flickered up to glare at Ross. "I see. Thanks, baby." Joy hung up her phone and reached for her purse.

Damn, I can't let her leave without giving me a chance to explain my position. "Joy," he began, hating the almost pleading tone in his voice.

Opening her purse, the skinny woman withdrew a paper and slid it across the table. "I must say, Rossy, I am shocked you were able to do it. But, then, you did have some rich friends. As agreed, here are the papers relinquishing my rights to *your* child."

Brows gathering in stupefaction, he picked up the papers and looked over the notarized documents. He now had full and total custody of Charmane Precious Connelly. *What the hell was going on?*

"You held up your end of the bargain and so did I." For the first time in many years, Ross saw an emotion almost tantamount to compassion fall over Joy's features as she slid out of the booth. "I hope the two of you are very happy. Goodbye, Ross." Then she was gone.

Alone in the booth, Ross couldn't let go of the papers. *It was over; Charmane was his.* Pulling out some money, he opened his cell phone and called his daughter, telling her he had to fly out to Virginia today but would be back as soon as he could and that she was free to stay with Dezarae. Then he called for a plane reservation.

Within three hours, Ross Connelly was on a flight home to get the documents filed with an attorney and to face Scott for putting the money in his account.

*
**

Ross pounded on the door of the nice beach home along the Virginia coast. "Scott!" he bellowed.

A black woman opened the door with a smile. "Ross, how nice to see you. Come on in. Scott is out running but he should be back soon."

"Hey, Lex," he answered as he heard a squeal from the front room.

"Baby's up." She rolled her eyes playfully. "He never wakes up when I am on my run, just when Scott is on his." She pulled Ross in the house closing the door behind them. "Something to drink?"

"Water's fine," Ross answered and he walked up to the crib in front of the big windows, picking up her son.

"Watch out, he's probably wet," Lex shouted as she walked to the kitchen.

"Won't kill me." Ross grabbed the diaper bag and laid Harrington Prescott Broderick Leighton IV on the floor and changed him.

"Taking over my family, are we, Jeb?" a deep voice from the patio asked.

Ross looked up from his job and saw his commanding officer and friend walking in the house. "You know how much I love Lex," he said as he finished snapping the outfit back on the baby on the floor.

"Hey, handsome," Lex purred and kissed her husband before setting the water for Ross down on an end table. Glancing at her son who was gurgling with happiness at the man who held him she said, "I didn't mean for you to change him."

"Not a problem," Ross said with an easy shrug and got to his feet. "I need to talk to you, Scott," his tone serious again.

Eyes flickering between the two men, Lex reached for her son and said, "Go talk. I will make something to eat."

As they walked out onto the porch Ross spoke. "I meant what I said. I didn't need your help to get Charmane back. I was going to give her all I had and then pay her the rest over time." He slapped a thick envelope down on the railing.

The two hundred thirty-five–pound man stepped back from the venom in his friend's voice. "Ross, what are you talking about? I offered to help and you said no. I respected that. All I did was call Tyson and get the number to his father-in-law's firm. And what is that?" He gestured to the envelope.

Gray eyes narrowed as they met and held the brilliant blue ones of his friend. "Money to repay you with. You didn't put the money into my account?"

"No, are you saying that it was there?"

"I have the papers from Joy saying Charmane is mine. I filed them yesterday and came here today."

Scott shoved the thick envelope back at him and said, "Well, take that back. I swear to you, Ross, I didn't have anything to do with it."

"Who else knows?" Ross asked.

"Tyson, Jayde, and Lex. I don't know about the rest of the Team."

Totally puzzled, the men looked at each other. "You don't think that Lex would…" Ross said.

"No, but I will ask her."

"Don't bother asking. I didn't, although I am glad someone did. You needed to get her away from that bitch," Lex said as she handed Scott his son. "Food's ready. Come get something to eat."

Ross's phone rang during the meal. "Excuse me," he said as he stood and answered it. "Connelly." A smile crossed his face, "Hey, Charmane, what's going on?"

Ross's smile faded from his face and his eyes narrowed, his body tensing as he listened to his daughter on the other end. "Let me talk to her," he ordered.

"What the hell are you going to California for, Dez?" he practically shouted into the phone. "I don't want to meet you there. I want to meet you back at your place!" Before he could say anything else, his beeper and the one strapped to Scott's waist went off. Both men glanced at them and grew somber. "I have to go, Dez, we are being summoned." Eyes blinked a few times as he realized that the voice on the other end was now his daughter. "Bye, baby. I love you. Listen to Dez, okay? Bye, bye." He hung up.

They said goodbye to Lex and the baby and then they were heading to the base to meet up with the rest of the team.

As their transportation flew them over the ocean to reach the aircraft carrier, Ross was oblivious to the smiles the men shared among themselves. He was focused on what had happened the last seventy-two hours. Charmane was his. She was safe and happy with Dezarae. Now all he had to do was convince Dezarae to marry him.

The sharp banking of the helicopter pulled his attention off the ebony woman he had left behind in Montana with his child.

**

Standing in a phone booth, Ross waited for the line to be picked up. It had been a month since he had left Montana, and this was their first chance to call home. Immediate relief filled him as he heard his daughter answer with a cheerful, "Hello?"

"Hey, baby," he said.

"Daddy!" Charmane squealed. "How are you? Are you coming home?"

"I'm doing well, baby. We are coming home soon. How are you?" *She sounds so happy.*

"I'm great. I love it here. We have been busy. Dez finished all the cars but the Miura; actually, that is where she is right now. Well, that and her Lotus."

"How was California?" Ross asked, not really sure he wanted to know.

"Good. I got to meet her friend Lateef. We went to his thirtieth birthday party. It was loads of fun."

"Oh, I see." Here he had thought she was going to see Jack. "I didn't know that was what you were going to do."

"Yep, he is one of her best friends." Charmane paused and said, "It's Daddy, Dez." Then she came back on the line. "I have gone off-roading with Shawn and Tank is teaching me to drive a tractor. Oh, and Jack says he will let me drive his yacht next time we are there."

"Jack?" His voice was dangerously low.

"Yeah. He just left yesterday."

Ross began to flex his muscles. "Why was Jack there, Charmane?"

"He came to get the Shelby. Dezarae sold it to him. Don't worry, Daddy, he didn't stay the night, just for dinner," Charmane told the man across the globe from her.

It was all as clear as the mountain stream to him now. Dezarae had sold her car to Jack and used the money to let him get his child. Dropping the crushed can in his hand, he said to his daughter, "Can I speak to her please, baby? I have to go soon."

"Sure. Dez! Daddy wants to talk to you," she yelled. "Bye, Daddy, here she is. I love you."

"Love you, too, baby," Ross said as he heard her say to Dezarae that she was going outside to play with Haley.

"Hello, Ross," Dezarae's unintentionally sultry voice reached him.

"Tell me I'm wrong," his voice cut in.

She didn't answer immediately, but when she spoke again, she sounded guilty. "About what?"

"Why did you sell your car?"

"Jack wanted it." she said.

That answer wasn't good enough for him. "Tell me you didn't stick your nose into my business."

"If you are asking if I put the money in that account, then yes, I did," she blurted out.

"What made you think I needed or wanted your help?" He swore. "Damn it, I was handling things just fine on my own. I didn't need to have your interference!"

When she answered, he heard tears in her voice. "You know what? Just shut up. I did it because I felt like Charmane should be with you instead of her mother. I don't give a damn that you didn't want my help. It was my decision to make and I did what I thought was best."

"You made it seem like I can't take care of my own child," he yelled back. "Way to make me feel like a ball-less wonder. Thanks for taking away my manhood!"

"Get over yourself, Ross. This wasn't about you or your stupid SEAL ego. It was about your daughter. *Your daughter*, who I happen to think is one hell of a kid!" Dezarae screamed into the phone. "So, fine, hate me all you want; tell me when you will be home and I will put her on the first plane there. That way you will never have to see me again and maybe you can find your *manhood* with someone else!"

"Maybe I will!" he snapped back, stupid in his anger. Opening his mouth to begin again, he was met with a dial tone. She had hung up on him.

He swore until people around him began looking at him strangely.

"What's the matter, Ross?" a voice broke into his tirade.

Ross looked over his shoulder to see the sparkling blue eyes of his teammate, Ernst "Ghost" Zimmermann. "I found out who put the money there," he mumbled as he walked out to fall into step with his teammate.

"Well, that's great, right?" the Chief Petty Officer asked.

"It was Dezarae."

Twenty-Eight

As Ross leaned against the wall, he looked over the other seven members of his SEAL Team. All of them were staring at him like he had lost his mind. "Why are you looking at me like that?" he demanded.

"We think you are insane for yelling at her like that," Merlin said. "It is obvious that she loves you, man. Look at how easily and without thought of her own life she took on your child for you."

"She interfered in something that was none of her damn business!" Ross snapped.

"She did what she thought best for your daughter," the calming lilt of Hondo noted. "A woman like that is special. Think of how important Charmane and you both must be to her. You know how much she loved that car, and without hesitation, she sold it so you, *you*, could have your daughter and Charmane could live without fear of her mother." His tone had turned admonishing.

Ross didn't want to look at it that way. He wasn't ready to deal with the logical end of things. "I thought you were supposed to be on my side!"

The men looked at each other. Maverick, who was the most confirmed bachelor of them all, spoke. "We *are* on your side. And since Dezarae is good for you, we want you to be with her. You know how I feel about getting married, but it works for you. *She* works for you. Get over yourself and crawl on your hands and knees if that is what it takes to get her back."

"I basically told her she castrated me. How do I make that up to her?" Ross asked as his body slid down the wall to sit on the floor.

"Flowers might help," Ghost offered.

"Or chocolates, women love chocolate," Osten "Baby Boy" Scoleri put in.

"What about a big ole sign that says 'I'm the world's biggest idiot, please forgive me?'" Cade said as he took a swig of his beer.

"Or 'I love you, marry me,'" Harrier suggested with an arched brow.

Ross scoffed. "I don't think she would even consider marrying me after what I said to her. She was crying."

Stretching out his long legs, Harrier shook his head. "Man, you love her. Go get her. I will give you down time when we get back. Otherwise we are all going to be miserable."

"No kidding. Look how miserable we all were before he got Alexis," Hondo teased with a wink at Harrier.

***

Ross slammed the receiver down on the recording he had gotten the last four times he called. Their return home had been delayed another three weeks and every chance he got, his fingers were dialing Dezarae's number. "Where the hell is she?" Ross asked his reflection in the mirror. They were at a hotel in Hawaii on shore leave.

"Give it some time, man," a voice said from beside him as the image of a blond, pale blue–eyed man filled the mirror. Ghost.

"Hey, I thought you had a date. What happened?"

"That blasted woman stood me up. Left a message with the bartender to give to me. Something about having an emergency." He swore. "Don't know why I asked her out, anyway."

Ross smiled. His teammate hadn't been the same since he had met Koali Cynemon Travis; she had turned the once self-assured man into a frustrated one. "Don't ask me how to deal with your woman. I have enough problems with my own," he answered, opting to stay neutral. Sort of.

"She isn't my woman," Ghost snapped.

"Right," Ross said skeptically. He had seen the way his friend watched her whenever they were around one another.

Narrowing his eyes at the dark-haired man, he arched a pale brow. "How *is* your woman?"

"Beats the hell out of me. I haven't received an answer from her. I can't get a hold of Charmane, either."

Ernst cocked his head. "Do you think there's trouble?" No longer playing with his friend's emotions, he was serious.

"No, not trouble. It is almost like she is avoiding me," Ross said, turning away from the mirror and walking towards the door. "Not that I blame her. But I was hoping to have Charmane waiting for me when we get back to Virginia."

"Did you leave her a message?"

"No," Ross admitted sheepishly. "I was upset that she didn't answer the phone."

"Man, you really need to get this straightened out," Ghost said as he slapped Ross on the back.

"No more than you do with that little spice of yours," Ross quipped. All he got in return was a low growl.

"God, it feels good to be home," Ross said as he walked into his small house. His mind was working overtime as he thought of ideas to fix up the guest room for his daughter. It would be her room permanently.

It was one in the morning but the air was thick with humidity. As he walked through the living room, he noticed his answering machine was flashing. He pushed the button as he kept moving towards his bedroom to drop off his sea bag.

Ross froze in his tracks as the smooth sultry voice of Dezarae sounded. "Hello, Ross. I just wanted to let you know that Charmane will be flying in tomorrow evening to see you. Alexis called me and said you were going to be home by then. She is flying in on…"

His mind didn't comprehend anything she was saying after that. All he could think about was how perfect Dezarae felt pressed up against his body as they made love…her smile and the feeling he got staring into those deep pools she called eyes.

Ross had to play the message two more times before he had all the information ready for Charmane's arrival. He crawled into his bed, still hearing Dezarae's voice in his mind. There had to be a way to get her back into his life, his arms, and his bed.

"Daddy!" Charmane's squeal reached him before she did.

"Baby," he said as he swept her up into his embrace. "I missed you."

"I missed you, too, Daddy. I have lots to tell you," she claimed as she hugged him back.

Ross had a grin wider than the ocean on his face as he held his child to him. "Well, do you want to go home first or eat?"

"Eat. I'm starving," she exclaimed dramatically.

"All right, then. Let's go eat; what are you in the mood for?"

Charmane moved to pick up her two bags as they appeared on the conveyor belt. "Ribs!"

His gray eyes sparkled as he watched his daughter. The change in her was amazing. Taking the bags from her he said, "Ribs it is, then." Ross led the way to his car.

The ride home didn't take long and soon he was ushering her into the house. They stuffed themselves at dinner, then opted to go for dessert and walk along the ocean. Now they were full and tired, for it was midnight. "I know it doesn't look like much now, but we can fix it up for you," Ross said as he opened the door to Charmane's new room.

Big brown eyes took in the attempts her father had made to turn it into a room for her. "I love it. It will be perfect." She set her backpack down, opened it, and pulled out a picture tri-frame that she set on the dresser and unfolded it.

Ross's breath caught in his throat as he saw them. It held pictures of Charmane and Dezarae.

In left one they were in front of her Shelby Mustang. Each of them had one hand on the first-place trophy and had huge grins. In their free hands were drink bottles. Champagne in Dezarae's hand and Coke in Charmane's.

The right one was of the women goofing off in front of the shop. Charmane was poised like a bodybuilder and Dezarae had the top half of her coveralls hanging down, showing off her tank top and strong arms. She was balancing a large power tool over one shoulder.

It was the middle photo that he loved the most. This was how he remembered Dezarae. She had a gentle smile on her face, eyes crinkling at the corners. She had one arm around Charmane and they were standing in front of her house.

"Great pics, aren't they, Daddy?" Charmane asked.

Ross stopped in mid motion while reaching for the frame. "Sure are, baby." He smiled at her, hoping she couldn't see the pain. "Have one for me?"

"I have lots more pictures with me. You can have one if you want."

"We'll go through them in the morning. You need to get some sleep," he said gently.

With a yawn, Charmane nodded. "Okay, Daddy."

Giving her a kiss, he began to walk out of the room. "Goodnight, baby. I'm glad you're here."

"Me, too, Daddy. Oh, wait." Her words stopped him.

"What?"

Reaching into her pack, she pulled out an envelope. "This is for you."

His gray eyes recognized that handwriting and his heart jumped. It was from Dezarae. "Thanks, Charmane. Goodnight."

"Night, Daddy," she said with one more kiss for his stubbled cheek.

Alone in his room, Ross lay on his bed and opened the envelope. A printed sheet fell out and on a paper clipped to it was a small square of paper in the shape of a car. Pulling the small sheet off, he read the note.

```
I don't know when you will need me to watch her
                    again.
So you don't send her there when I am gone,
             here's a list of dates
    I know I will be away from the house.
       Just call me when you need me.
                  ~Dezarae
```

Just call me when you need me. "I need you right now, Dezarae," he mumbled as he held the note to his mouth as if he could somehow be closer to her that way. The note was very impersonal and Ross knew she didn't mean that last line in the way he was taking it.

Before he could change his mind, he had picked up his cordless phone and dialed the number he knew by heart. One ring…two…three.

"*Phoenix Restorations and Rebuilds*, this is Dezarae, can I help you?" Her voice reached across the line and intertwined with the beating of his heart even more.

I love you, Firebird, please forgive me. "I-it's me." He stumbled over those simple words.

Her sigh was palpable to him. "Is Charmane okay?"

A wry smile touched his face. "She is fine. She just went to bed a bit ago. Thanks for putting her on a plane."

"She's your daughter. She belongs with you," Dezarae said simply.

You belong with me as well. "Well, I was calling to thank you and to ask you if you would like to come down for a visit. I know how much Charmane would love to have you see her new home." He held his breath as he waited.

"I don't know if I can get away right now. I have a few shows coming up that I am burning the midnight oil to get ready for," Dezarae uttered.

Crushed she didn't jump on it immediately, Ross looked down at the paper in his hands and smiled. "Well, it was just a thought. Goodbye, Firebird." His words were gentle as he pushed the button on his phone leaving her with nothing but a dial tone.

Trembling inside and out, Dezarae hung up the phone. Just hearing Ross's voice made her yearn for things long past. Wiping away a lone tear that had begun to move down her cheek, she turned her attention back to the car before her.

Car shows were where she made a lot of her money, for someone would like them and buy them. And it also spread her name around.

"You okay there, Phoenix?" The question brought her eyes up from the white 1953 Corvette.

"Fine, CJ, thanks. And thanks for coming out to help," Dezarae said with a smile.

"Not a problem. I love these cars, especially since I have one of yours. I can't tell you how many compliments I get on that baby."

Dezarae had restored a 1958 Corvette for CJ as a gift. Her friend loved it and the attention it got her. "I bet. I loved that car."

"I know you did. And I think it was amazing what you did to help that guy out, selling your Shelby to Jack. I know how much you loved that car. You had been waiting a long time for it to come to you."

"I can get another one," Dezarae said with a sad smile as her brain replayed the harsh words Ross had said to her.

Seeing how sad Dezarae was becoming, CJ asked, "What do you want me to do next? I finished detailing the Nash. That baby is shining like a ruby, inside and out."

"It doesn't matter. All the cars need to be detailed." Dezarae stood and stretched as her dark eyes moved around the shop. There were five vehicles inside. "You could begin to load them in the semi trailer. We have three done since I am finished with this one." She closed the door of the car. "Then we could see about getting something to eat."

"Oh, food, my favorite word! I will have these cars loaded up in few," CJ said.

Dezarae watched her friend carefully drive the cars up the ramp and into the semi. She had three shows to go to. Her goal was to sell these vehicles.

In her trailer she was taking a cherry-red 1954 Nash Convertible, one of two hundred twelve made. Next was a polo-white 1953 Corvette convertible with a sportsmen-red interior. She then had a 1955 Bel Air Chevrolet that was two-toned pale yellow and white and a black 1954 Buick Skylark convertible that was one of eight hundred thirty-six made. Finally, she had a 1954 Kaiser Darrin, a fiberglass-bodied roadster with unique sliding doors.

Already loaded in the oversized trailer was a blue-gray 1961 Jaguar E-type Roadster and a 1962 Bedouin beige MGB Roadster. She had potential buyers for both cars.

"I feel good about this," Dezarae said as she moved towards the Chevy to begin detailing. She worked until CJ yelled for her attention. "What?"

"Come help me secure these and then let's grab some food and some shuteye. Tank will be here early to help us finish the rest so we can get going."

"Good point." Cracking her neck, Dezarae joined CJ on the upper tier in the trailer and secured the vehicles. The last two would be put on the bottom. Her trailer could fit eight cars in it.

"I see we are only taking seven. Keeping a spot open to buy?" CJ teased as they made their way inside the house and to the kitchen.

"I like to keep my options open," Dezarae answered with a wink, reaching in and pulling out a lemon supreme pie from the fridge.

"*Ohhh*, pie. I love you, Phoenix!" CJ said.

"Well, I need to have someone eat it. Charmane didn't finish it before she left..." Dezarae trailed off, not wanting to talk about that.

"Don't worry. I will make short work of this," CJ teased, trying to lighten the mood.

Twenty-Nine

"Jesus," Dezarae swore as she pulled into her parking area. "It is frickin' hot here." She wiped away the sweat from her brow as she shut down her rig. Even with a black tank top, white Capri's, and sandals on her feet, Dezarae was still sweltering.

"What did you expect in the South?" CJ teased, also sweating.

"I don't know, anything but this."

"Welcome to my life, darlin'." CJ winked at her as they both opened the doors and jumped down.

"Feel free to keep it. Damn," Dezarae quipped as they moved towards the main building where she would get her numbers for the remaining three cars she had. The other four had sold at the previous two shows.

The overanxious teen pulled on her father. "Come on. Why are you moving so slow? Don't you want to see her?"

Full of mixed emotions, Ross let go of Charmane. "I am looking at the rest of the vehicles." *I am scared shitless she will tell me to leave her alone for the rest of our lives.*

"Can I go ahead?" Charmane asked.

"I don't want you wandering off alone," Ross said, shaking his head.

"I will go with her if that's okay by you," Hondo offered.

"Are you sure you want to?" Ross asked, giving his teammate a chance to back out. His whole Team had decided to come with them, including the two wives in the group.

"I like her enthusiasm. Besides, I am still looking for that car you have to buy me."

Latching onto Hondo like he was her surrogate father, Charmane began to drag the ensign away. "Bye, Daddy," she yelled over her shoulder, leaving Ross with the remaining men who were looking at cars and women.

"She seems delighted to get to see Dezarae again," a soft voice said beside him.

Ross looked down into the eyes of Alexis. "She loves her," he answered with a sad smile.

"So do you," she observed.

"She hates me. When I called her the day Charmane arrived, she couldn't get off the phone with me fast enough." Ross sighed and ran his hand over his head.

"I thought she was getting cars ready for the shows?" Scott asked as he and his sleeping son joined the conversation.

"She did answer like she was in the shop," Ross admitted. His hand strayed to the front pocket of his khakis. "I just don't know; it sounded like there was someone else there."

"Stop looking for the worst in everything, man. Go get your woman," Scott said.

"No kidding; we need more wives here. Jayde and I are feeling a bit outnumbered." Alexis grinned. "Besides, I like her."

"You've met her?" Ross asked.

"No," she responded. "From when I called her. And because of what she did for the two of you."

And look what I did to her to thank her for it. Nevertheless, Ross smiled as they continued to walk at a slow, leisurely pace.

"That is a gorgeous car," Hondo breathed as he stopped beside the Jaguar, keeping the preteen from walking on by tightening his hold on her. "Wait just a minute, Charmane, I wanna look."

Upset because she hadn't found her friend yet, Charmane huffed but waited.

"Beautiful, isn't it?" a feminine voice broke into his musings.

Hondo looked up into the pale brown eyes of a stunning woman. "Yes," he said. "It sure is."

"Phoenix sure does amazing work."

That got Charmane's attention. "Dezarae is here?" her question came as her brown eyes moved to the large sign that read Phoenix Restorations And Rebuilds. "Where is she?"

The slim woman smiled. "I believe she is right behind you."

Charmane turned and yelled as her young body launched itself into Dezarae's waiting arms. "Dez! I missed you."

"Missed you, too, squirt. I missed you too," Dezarae responded affectionately as she hugged the child back. Setting her back on the ground, Dezarae looked at the large black man standing there. "Aidrian, right?" she asked.

"Aye," he said with a grin. "That's me. And you are?" his question was directed at the other woman.

"I'm CJ," she answered with an easy smile. "Nice to meet you."

"Likewise," Aidrian responded.

"Charmane, what are you doing here?" Dezarae asked the girl.

"Daddy asked me if I wanted to come to this show. We came with the whole Team. Plus Alexis and Jayde."

Ross was here? *What will I say to him?*

"How about hello," Ross murmured into her ear as he slid his arms around her waist. CJ arched a brow as she watched the scene before her. The remaining members of his team also watched avidly.

Immobilized by his touch alone, Dezarae mumbled, "Hello, Ross." *How does he know what I am thinking?*

"Hello, Firebird," he drawled, turning her so they could be face to face.

Dezarae was lost in the swirling heat of his eyes. In the gunmetal depths, she read his cry for forgiveness. And his love. "Didn't expect to see you here."

"Well, you wouldn't come to where I was." He shrugged. "Besides, you asked me a question that I need to answer."

Her eyes moved over his chiseled features that were highlighted by the setting sun. "What question did I ask?"

Two knuckles stroked the top of her cheek. "You don't remember."

I can't think straight. "No, I don't."

"You asked me if being a SEAL was like it was in the movies. If he got the woman of his dreams and carried her off into the sunset." Ross spoke in a strong voice; it carried to the people around them who had begun to fall silent and watch as well. "Do you remember, now?"

Dezarae nodded. "I remember. And you said it wasn't exactly like that. As for the sunset bit, you said you would let me know."

"Right." Ross took the pins out of her hair so it fell about her shoulders. "Scott did, Tyson did, and—God willing—I will too." He dropped to one knee before her. The audience around them gave a collective gasp. "Dezarae, I know I said some harsh things to you, but I didn't mean any of them. You mean so much to both me and my daughter. You know she loves you."

Ross ran a sweaty hand over his face and caught the eye of one teammate who nodded his encouragement. "God, I never realized how nerve-racking this would be. I don't know what I have to offer you. I don't make much money and I'm gone most of the time, but I promise I will love you for the rest of our days." He reached for her left hand. "You reignited the flame within me. In more ways than one, you have saved my life. I don't want to live without you. I love you. Dezarae Phoenix Kerry, will you marry me?"

Reaching into his pocket, he pulled out the small black box, opening it to show her the diamond ring that sat inside.

Unable to form a word, all she could do was cry. After a few moments, Ross looked up at her and prompted, "Say something, Firebird, I'm getting nervous down here."

"Yes!" she gasped.

Slate eyes closed in relief for a second before he slid the ring on her finger and rose to kiss her. "I love you, Firebird."

"I love you, too, Johnny Reb. Does this mean you will carry me off into the sunset?" Dezarae muttered against his firm lips.

To the thunderous applause of those around them, Ross laughed. "Excuse me, y'all. I am going to carry her off into the sunset." Strong arms swept her up into his embrace.

"CJ?" Dezarae asked.

The woman nodded, her own eyes teary. "Got it covered, Phoenix."

"Scott?" Ross asked, already leaving the premises.

"Charmane will be fine with us." Scott assured his friend. "It's about time. Welcome to the family, Dezarae!" he yelled as they walked off through the crowd into the setting sun.

Six months later

"A bit higher on your end, Ross," Dezarae instructed. "There, perfect."

Her husband joined her, his arms sliding around her waist to settle on her growing belly. "I think we had it before you said so," Ross said as he kissed her neck.

"Possibly. But I wanted to keep looking at that ass of yours," she teased.

"Looks great, Mom!" Charmane yelled as she ran by with her new puppy.

"It still makes me tear up to hear her call me that," Dezarae whispered to Ross as they looked at the newly hung sign, Phoenix Restorations And Rebuilds.

"She has loved you from the beginning. Well, after you threatened her with jail."

Dezarae smiled as she recalled that first meeting with Charmane. "I love her so much."

"Ready for the grand opening?" Ross asked.

"I think so. It is going to be weird not doing as much," Dezarae said.

"No working on cars for you until after the baby is born," he ordered.

"I know." Her eyes took in the new shop and track.

"Thank you for coming down here," he mumbled into her ear.

Dezarae had sold her home and shop to Tank, who was going to convert it for more construction-oriented uses. It had been hard to sell, but she knew her father would still be pleased she was continuing the family business. The child she carried would learn it, as would Charmane. "My place is with my husband. I want to be with you."

"I know it had to be hard for you."

"Being with you and Charmane makes it easier. I can make a name for myself here."

"You already have a name for yourself. Haven't even opened yet and we are fielding calls." His lips nibbled on her neck.

"Have I told you today that I love you?" she asked.

Shaking his head, he muttered, "Don't think so."

Rolling her eyes because she knew she had, Dezarae said, "I love you, Ross Murdock Connelly of Virginia."

"And I love you, Dezarae Phoenix Kerry Connelly of Virginia."

Later that night while Charmane was in bed, the couple sat out on the porch swing and took in the night sounds. Dark chocolate eyes were closed while gunmetal ones were open, watching over and guarding his family.

Tucking his wife closer, Ross smiled as he realized she was truly a legendary creature with the ability to carry him from death back into the folds of life. She was CONNELLY'S FLAME.

About the Author

Aliyah Burke loves to read and write. Her debut novel, *A Knight's Vow*, was released in 2004. She loves to hear from her readers and can be reached at aliyah@aliyah-burke.com or aliyah_burke@hotmail.com, and feel free to join her yahoo group at http://groups.yahoo.com/group/aliyah_burke or friend her at http://www.myspace.com/aliyahburke.

Please stop by her Web site, http://www.aliyah-burke.com for more available titles—just don't forget to sign the guestbook!

Aliyah is married to a career military man. They have a German Shepherd, a Borzoi, and a DSH cat. Her days are spent splitting her time between work, writing, and dog training.

Made in the USA